THE OMEGA DECEPTION

THE OMEGA deception

T 18011

a novel

JOHN F. BAYER

BROADMAN
& HOLMAN
PUBLISHERS

Nashville, Tennessee

0-8054-1966-7

Published by Broadman & Holman Publishers, Nashville, Tennessee

Dewey Decimal Classification: 813
Subject Heading: WORLD WAR, 1939–1945—SECRET SERVICE—
UNITED STATES—FICTION
Library of Congress Card Catalog Number: 99-046480

Library of Congress Cataloging-in-Publication Data
Bayer, John.
The Omega Deception : a novel / John F. Bayer.
    p.   cm.
ISBN 0-8054-1966-7 (pbk.)
    1. World War, 1939–1945—Secret service—United States—
Fiction. I. Title.
PS3552.A85868 O44 2000
813'.54—dc21

99-046480
CIP

1 2 3 4 5   04 03 02 01 00

DEDICATION

This book is dedicated to the men and
Women who gave of themselves
So a world
Might be free of tyranny.

It is especially dedicated to two men
Who fought and lived through the
Horrors of WW II:
My father, James E. Bayer, and
My father-in-law, W. E. Wynn.

Thank you both.

GLOSSARY

Angermünde—city in northern Germany

ASDIC—British-developed form of sonar

BdU—abbreviation of Befehlshaber der Unterseeboote

B-Dienst—radio intelligence service of the Kriegsmarine

Befehlshaber der Unterseeboote—Commander in chief, U-Boats

Bombe—coded text transmitted by B-Dienst

Budapesterstrasse—Berlin street leading into the Zoologischer Garten

Das Boot—German-made film about U-Boat operations

Eberswald—city in northern Germany

Führerprotokoll—official document issued by Hitler

Geheime Kommandosache—German designation for top secret

Geheime Staatspolizei—Gestapo

Grossadmiral der Kriegsmarine—Grand Admiral of German Navy

Hauptmann—Luftwaffe captain

Hauptsturmführer—SS captain

I. G. Farbenindustire—chemical factory on the Rhine River

Kaleu—diminutive of Kapitänleutnant

Kapitänleutnant—Captain of a U-boat

Kapitän zur See—Senior Captain in German Navy

Kiel—port city in northern Germany

Kriegsmarine—German Navy

Leitender Ingenieur—U-Boat engineer

Leverkusen—German industrial city on the Rhine River, where sarin was invented in 1938

Luftwaffe—German air force

Oberleutnant—1st lieutenant in Wehrmacht

Oberleutnant zur See—lieutenant senior grade

Operation Paukenschlag—Operation Drumbeat

OSS—Office of Strategic Services (forerunner of the CIA)

Paulstrasse—Berlin street

Peenemünde—German rocket research center in the Baltic

Prenzlau—city in northern Germany

Prinz Albrechtstrasse—street address of SS in Berlin

Putsch—German uprising attempted by Hitler

Reich Chancellery—Hitler's Berlin headquarters

Rue de Rennes—fictitious street in Lorient, France

Schlüssel M—German Navy's Enigma code machine

Schutzstaffel—German SS

SOE—Special Operations Executive. England's Commando unit

Store Baelt—straits off east coast of Denmark

SS-Oberstgruppenführer—SS general

SS-Reichsführer—Commander of the SS, Heinrich Himmler

SS-Standartenführer—SS colonel

SS-Sturmbannführer—SS major

SS-Unterscharführer—SS 2nd lieutenant

Totenkopf—SS death's head insignia

Vergeltungswaffen—weapon of retaliation

Wehrmacht—German army

Wewelsburg—17th-century headquarters of SS in Westphalia

Wolgast—city in northern Germany near Peenemünde

Zoologischer Garten—zoological garden in Berlin

PROLOGUE

october 9, 1942
siasconset, nantucket island

The promise of winter rode on the building breeze blowing in from Long Island Sound. Already the leaves on Nantucket trees were changing, displaying the vivid oranges, yellows, and reds of autumn. The colorful scene belied the danger that lay beneath the waves of the Atlantic.

In the distance, a dark squall line raced across the sound as Jon McDowell leaned against the communications panel on the bridge of the 3000-ton cargo steamer *Mary Glen.* McDowell craned his neck out the open window of the bridge, watching the low clouds scud across the rapidly rising sea. Whitecaps were beginning to froth against the side of the hull. "Rain in ten minutes," he murmured to himself. McDowell was anxious to get under way. The sooner he began the 160-mile trip back to lower Manhattan, the sooner he'd be back in the snug Cape Cod rental he shared with his wife.

In the five months that McDowell had been captain of the *Mary Glen,* he'd not had an opportunity to take his wife house hunting. She'd been patient, but McDowell knew his even-tempered wife had her limits. After seven years of marriage, she wanted a house to call her own. After all, he had promised as much when they had moved to Brooklyn Heights. McDowell knew he'd have to make good on that promise, and soon. They had found a small community church, and McDowell knew his wife's involvement with the congregation was the only thing keeping her from badgering him. Given the relative merits of house and church, he was happy they'd found the church first.

McDowell peered about through the gathering gloom where four crewmen wrestled with a hawser as they struggled to release the stern line. Glancing at the instrument panel, he noticed that the barometer was falling through 28.78 inches of mercury and showed no sign of stopping anytime soon. Slate black clouds gathered rapidly in the darkening sky. He knew his engineers were watching the steam pressure gauges with particular intensity. The old coal-fired boilers were temperamental under the best of conditions, and these were not the best of conditions.

The deckhands had the stern lines loose as McDowell walked out onto the flying bridge. The first raindrop reached the *Mary Glen*. McDowell raised his megaphone to his mouth and yelled to the forward deckhands. "Take-up on the bow line!"

The sailors wrapped the two-inch rope around the deck pulley and took in the slack created when the stern line was cut loose. The fantail slowly rotated away from the wharf as the bowline tightened.

McDowell reached for the microphone hanging just over his head. "*Mary Glen* to navy escort seven-three-two," he radioed. "I'll be backing out in thirty seconds."

"Roger, *Mary Glen*," came the immediate response. "Your maneuvering area has been swept, and we are proceeding with normal search patterns commencing now."

Seven-three-two was an American subchaser, an old WW I converted minesweeper. It seemed strange to require an escort for the trip from Nantucket to *Mary Glen's* berth at the foot of Fletcher Street in lower Manhattan, but those were the fortunes of war, McDowell mused. German U-boats operated in the waters off New York, almost with impunity, and the danger was real.

McDowell ordered "dead astern," listening as his quartermaster repeated the order and rang it up on the ship's telegraph. He watched the acknowledgment as it registered on the telegraph, and in seconds foam surged beneath the stern as the *Mary Glen's* twin screws roiled the harbor waters. A shudder went through the old ship as it began to back away from the wooden wharf.

"Release bow line!" McDowell ordered.

The line fell into the frigid Atlantic waters.

"Starboard back one-third, port ahead one-third," McDowell barked.

"Aye aye, captain," the quartermaster responded, ringing the order on the telegraph.

The ship pirouetted, pulling to the right into deep water off the southern coast of Nantucket.

"Starboard ahead one-third."

"Starboard ahead one-third," the quartermaster repeated.

"*Mary Glen* clear," McDowell radioed as the ship took up its position astern the converted minesweeper, now only two points off his rusting port bow.

Jon McDowell had never become accustomed to the escort. The threat of German U-boats was real enough, but he'd refused to accept the U.S. Navy's claims that the battered old supply ferry was in danger from U-boat torpedoes. What was gained by sinking a ship like the *Mary Glen*? It would cost time, torpedoes, and fuel, none of which the German Navy had in great supply.

McDowell ordered "half ahead" as the steamer cleared the breakwater. The Edgartown light on Martha's Vineyard should have been barely visible to the north. With the squall line moving in, even that comforting landmark had disappeared. The wind was building and the chop was getting worse as McDowell guided the ship into the channel behind the navy escort. He wasn't looking forward to the crossing.

The thermometer attached to the center window post showed thirty-one degrees and dropping rapidly. It was cold for October, even for Nantucket. He'd have freezing rain to contend with before long. They'd been lucky on the passage from Manhattan to Nantucket. A warm front had drifted north and the temperature had remained above freezing. It appeared their luck was fading as the falling rain began to freeze, coating the ship's exposed metal surfaces.

Already the waves were running well over ten feet. McDowell estimated that the severe weather would double their transit time. He didn't know how the navy sailors manning the old minesweeper ever relaxed, given that the effects of such weather were multiplied many times over on their smaller ship.

On the other hand, from McDowell's perspective, the weather was a good omen where German U-boats were concerned. The bad weather would hamper their effectiveness—assuming they were even out there—far more than it would affect the *Mary Glen*.

Barometer at 28.50. McDowell made a mental note to correlate the reading with the height of the waves for future reference as the ship pounded through the whitecapped seas.

"Seven-three-two to *Mary Glen*," the radio crackled.

McDowell reached for the microphone and thumbed the talk button. "*Mary Glen,* go ahead seven-three-two. How's the weather?"

"*Mary Glen,* we're going to have to back off a little. This sea is running a little more than we thought. We're getting beat to death up here. Besides, there's not a U-boat in the German Navy that can hear us the way this wind is kicking up. Provided they even wanted to, that is."

McDowell grinned at the gentle potshot the escort captain had taken at the *Mary Glen*. "Backing off, seven-three-two. Making turns for seven knots. Hope that'll let you boys sleep up there," McDowell taunted. He knew there was no way that any of those sailors could rest under these conditions. In their ninety-seven-foot wooden craft, the ride was akin to tackling a Coney Island roller coaster on skates. The *Mary Glen* was almost thirty times larger than the converted minesweeper, and even the *Glen* crew would not rest on this crossing.

The freezing rain changed to sleet mixed with snow. October was too early for such conditions, but here they were. McDowell knew he was in danger of losing sight of his escort vessel if the weather got much worse.

"*Mary Glen,*" the radio barked. "Making turns for six knots." The tiny escort was barely making headway against the intensifying wind.

"Turns for six knots," McDowell ordered. "This is going to be tricky," he muttered to himself.

"Six knots, aye aye, sir," the quartermaster echoed as he stole a glance at his captain. In the worsening weather, six knots was nibbling at the *Glen's* minimum controllable steerage speed.

The steamer rose on a wave and slammed down into a deep trough, sending a reverberating shudder throughout the ship. McDowell grabbed for a handhold. He lost sight of the escort as the *Mary Glen* rose on the next crest. Just before slamming into the next trough, McDowell caught a glimpse of the tiny craft making its way up the face of a monster groundswell. "Those boys are living a nightmare," McDowell said under his breath. He would never denigrate the sailors of the tiny ship again.

"*Mary Glen,* we're losing sight of you. Close it up," the captain of the escort radioed.

"Closing to seven hundred yards," McDowell responded, beginning to wonder if there might be more danger in closing too closely with the escort than fighting the degenerating weather. "You guys must have weak eyes," McDowell radioed, trying to lighten the feeling on his own bridge.

The *Mary Glen* rose once again on a giant swell. This time, McDowell could plainly see the escort less than a half-mile off his bow. He raised his binoculars, examining the subchaser through the slanting rain. There were no sailors topside. He could clearly see the ice building up on all the exposed surfaces of the ship, just as it was on his.

All at once, his heart was in his throat!

Man overboard, port side of the tiny escort! Where did he come from, and what was he doing?

McDowell adjusted the binoculars, thinking his eyes were playing tricks on him. No! There he was, not more than fifty yards off the port beam of the escort!

McDowell reached for the microphone. "Seven-three-two, you have a man overboard!" he radioed urgently, knowing the man had little chance in the freezing water.

"Negative, *Mary Glen.* We don't know what you see, but we don't have a man in the water. Repeat. We do not have a man in the water. We're coming about on your directions. Where is your man?"

McDowell felt the deck fall out from under him as the *Mary Glen* dove down another wave. As she rose on the next swell, McDowell desperately searched the rolling water for the body. *There he is.* The man was wearing an orange kapok life vest. There was no way the *Mary Glen* could reach the man in this weather. It was left to the escort.

McDowell began directing the smaller escort using his radio. He watched with rapt attention as the small ship battered its way through the turbulent seas.

McDowell lost sight of the bobbing orange body and the escort. He waited until the *Mary Glen* came atop the next swell and scanned the horizon. Nothing.

It would take a miracle to find *anything* in the raging waters. It seemed like an eternity before the escort radioed.

"*Mary Glen,* we have the man aboard. He is not, I repeat, *not* from either of our vessels."

McDowell could hear the bewilderment in the man's voice. It was amazing that they had been able to reach the man, much less get him aboard. But if he was not from one of these ships, where had he come from? Was he even alive? The last question was answered with the next transmission.

"The man is dead. Repeat, the man is dead. And *Mary Glen,* you won't believe what we've got here."

The sailors on the escort gazed at the frozen body before them; a silver skull—the death's head insignia of the German SS—shone on the corpse's black wool field cap. The skull was as lifeless as the man's eyes below it.

CHAPTER

1

october 12, 1942
germany's rocket development center
peenemünde, baltic sea

Rear Admiral Karl Dönitz, grim faced, examined the plans spread before him. His hawk-like appearance, cold blue eyes, and economic mannerisms conveyed a sense of urgency, an urgency which was not lost on the two other men in the room. Dönitz shuffled through the technical papers, reading each notation, studying the data. His mind raced, absorbing the details, assimilating the technical difficulties along with the political implications and the military consequences. What he saw was a new beginning, or—at the very least—*time.*

"Is such a thing possible?" he asked, a slight tinge of awe in his voice.

Wernher von Braun, the Germans' preeminent rocket scientist, reached across the desk to pick up the plans. "May I?" he asked Dönitz.

"By all means," the admiral replied, sliding the papers across the polished wood surface.

Von Braun scanned the blueprints with a practiced eye, unconsciously fingering the top button on his suit coat as he weighed the possibilities. Before he spoke, he shot a quick, wary glance at the third man in the room, who stood leaning against the far wall, but Heinrich Himmler's impassive eyes were obscured by the glare of the lights on the lenses of his pince-nez.

Von Braun laid the blueprints on the desk, ran his hand over his high forehead and through his combed-back hair, and said, "Yes, Admiral. It's possible."

"Then do it," Dönitz ordered. "Immediately. I must have this before next year. The outcome of the war may well depend on this single weapon." Dönitz went back to the blueprints, knowing that what lay before him could mean life or death. His mind was already developing the logistics necessary for deploying the new device as a supply-interdiction weapon against Russian supply lines in the Baltic states. But there was another foe even more dangerous. Dönitz envisioned the possibilities. He could do it with this weapon. He could actually attack the mainland of the United States.

"Admiral Dönitz, . . ." Wernher von Braun began, hesitating as he eyed Himmler once again.

Dönitz noticed von Braun's nervous glance and his reticence. He turned and faced the scientist. "Please, Herr von Braun," Dönitz encouraged, "speak your mind. This is the time for truth."

Von Braun cleared his throat. "Admiral, forgive me, but I do not believe this can be completed in such a limited time," he began. "The plans are good ones. The theory is sound. It *can* be done, of that I am confident. But there are other considerations. Metallurgical, chemical, and mechanical problems must be overcome. Most important are the proposed guidance systems. We do not have any systems with the necessary accuracy. We are close, it is true, but we are not yet there. And then tests must be conducted. The blueprint calls for a completely new and radical rocket motor unlike any we have been working on. That motor has not yet been invented. There will be problems we cannot possibly anticipate at this point. We are talking about the unknown, Admiral. It will take a long time," von Braun concluded.

Dönitz turned and walked to the tiny window overlooking a small balcony outside von Braun's office. "We may not have the time you speak of, Herr von Braun," Dönitz said quietly.

A light rain, blowing in from the North Sea down the Kattegat Strait, began to pelt the balcony, pooling beneath the window. The air was clean here in the Baltic, Dönitz reflected, much like it was in Kiel, where his U-boat command had begun.

Back in 1937, he'd had only thirteen U-boats with which to provide naval support for Adolf Hitler's widespread, ambitious war plans. And those had been the older, type II models, whose limited range made them suitable only for coastal patrol. Now, five years later, 346 U-boats stalked the Atlantic in deadly wolf packs. Most were the advanced VII and prefab IX models, with more under construction. The shipyards in Bremen and Hamburg, and the Germania yard in Kiel were turning out class VIID and F models, along with the longer-range IXC, at a staggering pace. New U-boats were deployed every day from the western bases along the coast of France.

The new U-boats, with their larger pressure hulls and expanded ranges, could operate anywhere in the Atlantic Ocean, from the tip of South America to the southern coast of Newfoundland. The wolf packs were wreaking havoc from the western approaches of the British Isles to Freetown on the coast of Africa. With the addition of the XIV supply boats, dubbed *milk cows*, whose refueling capabilities provided extended coverage, Dönitz's U-boats had forged an almost impenetrable barrier in the Atlantic.

Operation Drumbeat, in January and February, had been an overwhelming success. Drumbeat U-boats had ranged from Cape Hatteras to just south of Newfoundland, sinking U.S. ships within sight of the east coast. The few WW I destroyers and lightly armed, undersized subchasers assigned the task of protecting the vulnerable cargo ships had proved ineffective. Most had gone to the bottom of the ocean along with their charges.

But lately, the war in the Atlantic had begun to change. Weather in the North Atlantic was always a factor, and the U.S. Navy, learning the hard lessons of experience, was turning out to be a formidable foe. Surface radar added a new dimension to the war in the Atlantic, forcing U-boats to remain submerged for longer periods. No longer could a U-boat commander disable a ship with one torpedo, then surface to finish the job with its deck gun, saving valuable torpedoes for the next ship.

The power of the United States lay as much in the spirit of its people as in its industrial might. And Dönitz could see the inevitable consequences. It would be impossible to destroy or diminish the Americans' awesome industrial strength, but perhaps this new weapon could sap the fighting spirit of the American people.

Dönitz turned from the rain-streaked window. "We must have that weapon, Herr von Braun, and the Kriegsmarine is prepared to pay for it."

Wernher von Braun sighed. "Admiral, it is not just a question of money, although that is a factor. I will need to assign a special team to the production center and one to the ordnance testing area. I do not have the manpower, Admiral," von Braun argued. "As it is, we are stretched nearly to the breaking point. I do not think you grasp the reality of the situation."

"Nor do I think you grasp the realities of the situation, Herr von Braun," Heinrich Himmler interjected, speaking for the first time.

Von Braun felt a chill run down his neck, a chill that had no connection to the cold Baltic rain. He turned to face Himmler.

"Herr Reichsführer, there are some things the SS can control, but this is not one of them. It will take hard work and manpower. The results will be directly proportional to the number of hours invested in the project. That is the way it has always been and that is the way it will be, even for this project."

Himmler's lips turned up in a thin smile. "You will have your manpower, Herr von Braun. This will be a combined project of the SS and the Kriegsmarine. We will expect expedient results."

Von Braun knew he'd lost the argument. That was the problem with nonscientific minds; they thought genius was a commodity to be bought and sold like wheat.

"And the financing?"

"Joint funding from the SS and the navy," Dönitz said. "Both have an interest in the enterprise. When the plan becomes a reality, it will provide the navy with interdiction and psychological possibilities we've never dreamed of."

"And the SS has its own use for the weapon, Herr von Braun, in conjunction with the Kriegsmarine, of course," he added, nodding toward Dönitz and smiling.

Wernher von Braun shifted his attention to the blueprints on his desk. There was no dream, only a nightmare. The project was possible, he knew. After all, he had the best scientific minds in the world on the island fortress of Peenemünde, where he had constructed the most advanced rocket-development center in the world. But even German genius had its limitations.

"I will need men, Herr Reichsführer," von Braun said.

"You shall have men, and money," Himmler replied. "SS-Oberstgruppenführer von Liebeman will have overall command and coordination responsibility during the project. You will report directly to him, and he will keep Admiral Dönitz and me informed. Von Liebeman will have total control of manpower, matériel, and funding. How the funds are routed in and out of Peenemünde will not be your concern. You will be free to devote your entire time and effort to the development of this weapon," Himmler said.

"I have other duties, Herr Reichsführer," von Braun stated flatly. "I cannot be expected to devote every minute of my time to the development of a single weapon system when we have many such systems under development."

"You *will* devote your time to this weapon system, Herr von Braun. Not only does the future of the Third Reich depend on its development, but so do the lives of every man assigned to the project, including yours," Himmler said without emotion.

Von Braun felt an involuntary muscle spasm deep in his abdomen.

"What the Reichsführer is saying," Dönitz explained, "is that this particular weapon system will take precedence over anything presently under development. The Third Reich needs time—you need time, Herr von Braun, to develop your other systems. But time is something we may not have without this particular system. I'm sure you understand the urgency."

"I understand, sir. We will do everything within our power to provide the navy—and the SS—with the system."

"That is commendable, Herr von Braun," Himmler smiled wanly. "I have already taken the liberty of reassigning living quarters in the residential community to segregate those working on this project from the rest of the workers. During the development and testing, your people will be completely separated from the others here. I have also cordoned off an area in the rocket development and research center to be used exclusively for this system. The SS will see to it that strict security measures are enforced at all times. There are, of course, more adjustments to be implemented, but that is the progress to date." Himmler nodded with self-satisfaction.

"Herr Reichsführer, Peenemünde is *my* responsibility, not yours. We will construct your weapon, but it will be done my way," von Braun emphasized, not caring to disguise his resentment of Himmler's interference.

Himmler's smile disappeared. "Of course, Herr von Braun. The SS will yield to your wishes, when possible. For the moment, however, you will have to trust my precautions. It is for the good of the Reich."

Von Braun shrugged and began to gather the papers on the desktop. "We will build your weapon, Herr Reichsführer. And may God have mercy on our souls."

Heinrich Himmler's face contorted as if in pain; his eyes bulged and his complexion darkened. A tight, thin line replaced the benign smile he'd worn until now. "There is no God but the Third Reich, Herr von Braun," Himmler hissed. "And the SS is the soul. You will do well to remember that." Himmler clicked his heels and strode imperiously out the door, followed shortly by Admiral Dönitz.

A flash of terror gripped von Braun as he watched the two men leave his office.

CHAPTER

2

"British? *British?*" Mark Daniels repeated as he fumbled incredulously through a stack of 8 x 10 photographs. "I think it's probably expecting too much to think we would have deduced that from these photographs."

Harlon Spencer took the photographs and perused them once again. "Yeah, well, that's not the way Donovan sees it. He thinks OSS should be up to speed with their British counterparts. He has a special affinity for the SOE. The fact that this is one of theirs won't have any bearing on it, either."

Daniels positioned the photos on the desktop. They showed a man in a black SS uniform. The man's handsome features and blond hair were offset by his unseeing eyes, opaque in death. Daniels secretly wished someone had closed the dead man's eyes before the photographs had been taken. The man's uniform collar carried the two lightning runes of the SS, and the single square insignia of his rank of second lieutenant. "Give me the story again," Daniels demanded, reaching for the photos.

Spencer tossed the pictures to Daniels before resuming. "Not much to tell. A week ago, an American escort retrieved the body off Nantucket. At first, they thought the man had fallen overboard, either from a supply ship or another escort. When they got the man aboard, you can imagine the shock when they saw this uniform. The question remains, where did he come from? Certainly not from any of the ships involved."

"How long had he been in the water?" Daniels asked.

"Doctors can't be certain. The water's so cold, he could have been in there anywhere from a few hours to a few days. And that's not all. Which," Spencer paused for emphasis, "is why you're here. They found this wrapped around his body. He'd hidden it in some oilcloth and wrapped it around his torso, almost as if he expected to die and wanted to make sure someone found it." Spencer tossed a piece of paper to Daniels.

Mark Daniels, for all of his twenty-seven years, was one of the best code breakers working on Nebraska Avenue in Washington. Spencer hoped the young man could decode the message that had been found on the body of the SS-Unterscharführer, who he now knew had been a British agent.

Daniels examined the paper once again. "To begin with, it's a cipher, not a code. The number sequence tells us that much. And it's not a long message. That'll make it more difficult to break."

"I would have thought a short message would be easier to break," Spencer said, mystified.

"Nope. A longer message contains more sequences of repetitions. More known combinations. The greater the number of combinations, the greater the chance of finding duplicate letters. Thus the easier to break the cipher." Daniels muttered to himself and continued examining the message. From all indications, it consisted of only three words. Of course, that could be a false lead in itself, but chances were it was just a short message. It could even be a British cipher. He made a mental note to contact Bletchley Park, just to be on the safe side. "How did the OSS end up with the body?"

"The escort accompanying the supply ferry was navy. When they finally made it to Fletcher Street wharf, they turned the body over to the Coast Guard. When they found the message, they passed everything along to the OSS. I think they were glad to get rid of it."

"And the British claim him?"

"They do, but that's all we have so far. Donovan hasn't told them about the message."

"They'll know soon enough," Daniels said. "I'll have to tell them I suspect it's a British cipher, and they can probably tell me what it says over the phone."

"Probably, but Donovan won't allow it. There's an airplane waiting for you this very minute. Donovan wants you in England by tomorrow."

"Wait a minute," Daniels protested. "If Donovan arranged for a plane, he must have suspected that this is a British cipher. How long has he known?"

"Not long. We just got word today that this guy was a member of MI-6. Donovan's a lot of things, but dumb isn't one of them."

"Obviously. When do I leave?"

Harlon Spencer consulted his watch. "Technically, fifteen minutes ago, but what Donovan doesn't know won't kill us. I have orders to put you on the plane personally, although without the briefing you just received. Orders are to bundle you, the photos, and the message off to England, pronto. But I thought you might like to know what's going on."

"Thanks for the courtesy. It's something your boss could learn."

"Wild Bill Donovan's not the head of OSS because he follows correct etiquette," Spencer smiled.

"So I've heard. Well, let's go. The sooner I get to London, the sooner I'll be back. To tell you the truth, I'm a little curious about this myself."

Spencer smiled again. "That's what makes you a good cryptoana-
lyst; you're curious."

"It's feline-fatal."

"Curiosity killed the cat, don't forget."

"Huh uh. *Fatal* better describes it. Keeps us on our toes."

"Plane's waiting," Spencer said. "If you crack the cipher, call it in
to Nebraska Avenue using one of your own codes. They'll pass it along
to us. Donovan says he wants to know what it says within thirty-six
hours."

"What makes him think it's that important when he doesn't even
know what it says?"

"He has a feeling about this one, and his feelings are seldom
wrong," Spencer answered. "A bad feeling," he concluded.

october 16, 1942
12:01 a.m.
over the north atlantic

Mark Daniels shifted his weight in the most uncomfortable seat
he'd ever sat in. The C-47 he traveled in droned over the black North
Atlantic between St. Johns, Newfoundland, and Julianehaab,
Greenland, some fourteen hundred miles away. The last hours had
been nothing short of wretched, and the remaining hours of the flight
to England held no promise of any improvement.

Daniels twisted again, trying to get comfortable, knowing all the
while it was impossible. The trip was something to be endured, and
survived. He repositioned the leather attaché case in his lap. The small
chain rattled, reminding him of the importance of the three-word message contained in the case. *Tomorrow,* he thought. *Tomorrow, I'll
know what it says.* The thought comforted him some, and he drifted
off into a fitful sleep.

october 16, 1942
nebraska avenue, washington D.C.

It was late afternoon when the call finally arrived in the decoding section at Nebraska Avenue. The message was simple.

To:	Donovan, OSS Headquarters
From:	Daniels, Bletchley Park
Subject:	Message, translation
Text:	*Der Betrug Omega*
Translation:	The Omega Deception
End message	

William Donovan handed the succinct transcript to Harlon Spencer. Spencer read the message twice before looking at his boss.

"What is it?" Spencer asked.

"No idea," Donovan responded. "Nebraska Avenue says there's another message from the Brits being decoded as we speak. It came with Daniels's translation, but they sent this one on ahead. Maybe the second message will tell us what their agent was up to and why he ended up floating in the North Atlantic. Until we get that, we're stumped. We might as well get some coffee while we're waiting."

An hour later, a messenger delivered a two-page document that had been received from British Intelligence.

William Donovan read the message in silence before handing it to Spencer. Spencer glanced at the flimsy sheet of paper and looked up at Donovan. "Something tells me our friends in British Intelligence know more than they're saying."

Donovan sat thoughtfully for a moment, then smiled. He had always been an optimist, and there was no reason to change now. "I think our British counterparts will willingly contribute what information they have about this."

"Not for free. What are you going to offer them to make it worth their while?" Spencer asked. He'd seen the same expression before on the face of the irrepressible Donovan.

Wild Bill Donovan sat back in his chair, his hands behind his head, and smiled. "I'm going to offer to replace their lost agent with one of our best men," he answered.

"And who is that?"

"Michael Shaw," Donovan replied.

Spencer thought for a moment, trying to recall the name. There were thousands of OSS agents roaming the earth—far too many for him to know everyone. Still, the name Michael Shaw did not ring even the tiniest bell. And if Shaw was their best agent, as Donovan was suggesting, it seemed logical to Spencer that, as the OSS Director of Field Operations, he would at least know the name.

"I don't recognize the name, Bill," said Spencer.

Donovan smiled broadly, looking younger than his almost sixty years. "That's because he doesn't know he's an agent."

Spencer smiled and shook his head. That was the way Wild Bill Donovan operated—off the cuff, and on the fly. Still, the question remained: Who was Michael Shaw?

CHAPTER

3

october 23, 1942
missisquoi bay, ontario

The silent killer came out of nowhere. No warning. No telltale bubbles or phosphorescent wake. One minute he was walking back to his cabin on the British-registered Athenia, *bound for Montreal; the next thing he knew he was flailing in the frigid waters of the Atlantic, watching as the last shadows of the ship slipped beneath the dark surface of the ocean. Barbara—the only woman he had ever loved— was gone. When the German torpedo ripped the* Athenia *in two, there had been no time, no chance to reach her. As the ship sank, Shaw felt the life go out of him. The water around him was filled with people and flaming debris, the vestiges of destroyed lives and decimated memories floating on the smoky waters of the Atlantic. The eerie glow of burning fuel lent an otherworldly aura to the nightmarish scene. It was the closest thing to hell he'd ever seen.*

Shaw came awake, sweat pouring from his body. He sat up in bed, remembering where he was. It had been more than three years now, but the vivid horror of the nightmare had not diminished. It was the only thing that kept Barbara alive in his memory, and he was not prepared to give it up. At least not yet.

A full moon lit the interior of the cabin as Shaw made his way to the spartan kitchen. It was cold in the cabin; winter was not far off. He retrieved two sticks of split wood and tossed them into the cast iron stove that dominated the small kitchen area. Embers from the banked fire ignited the dried wood. The warmth began to fill the small cabin. Shaw shivered once, his mind racing back to the night he'd lost Barbara. He shivered again, trying to shrug off the feeling of complete despondency. He expected the nightmares, but the intrusion of the memories in the middle of the day chipped at the edge of his sanity, and he tried to ignore them. Usually, like now, it did not work.

Shaw walked to the window. The morning would be clear, he could tell, but a building westerly wind would blow moisture in from the Great Lakes, and cold would follow closely. Shaw quickly reviewed his supplies. Potatoes, dried beans, a little flour, and the remains of a side of bacon constituted his total stash. That, and a full tin of coffee. He never let the coffee supply get too low. He would have to head into Phillipsburg as soon as the sun was up. If the westerly winds continued, as expected, he would need more than what he saw in his cupboards.

Shaw poured water into a dented coffeepot and added the grounds. He placed the pot on the stove top and trudged back into the bedroom.

With the white brightness of the reflected moon filling the small cabin, Shaw pulled on his pants and rummaged in the dresser drawers for a sweater. Inevitably, his thoughts drifted back to September 3, 1939, the night Barbara had died, murdered by a German torpedo. Part of him had died that night as well. In the deepest reaches of his mind, Shaw knew he was just going through the motions of living, waiting for his time to come. He'd lost everything that ever mattered to him in the cold depths of the Atlantic: his precious wife, his joy, his faith.

All because of the Nazis.

Shaw had been happy living in post-war Germany. The Treaty of Versailles had secured the peace—at least for a while. But the treaty had been an attempt to punish, and punish it had, to the detriment of a sleeping Europe. The stringent terms of the treaty had stripped the Germans of their dignity, and they had retaliated. The Nationalist Party had emerged with its fanatical leader, Adolf Hitler.

Despite the building horror, Shaw had been happy.

But Shaw's happiness had had nothing to do with his job as a newspaper correspondent and everything to do with Barbara. She'd been with him every step of the way, supportive and loving. The two of them had been a strong team. The stories that had distinguished him back home were every bit as much a product of her creativity and insight as they were a testimony to his ability as a writer. Barbara had been his sounding board, editor, researcher, wife, and friend. She had been the one who had seen the rising Nazi menace and suggested that they take a vacation back in the United States. If only he had listened sooner, maybe they would have been out of harm's way before the outbreak of war. Instead, his beloved Barbara had become one of the early victims of the Nazis' murderous rampage.

Deep in his soul, Shaw knew that was the only reason he still lived. Revenge was as strong a motive as love. He knew that someday he would have his chance. Just how that chance would come about, he had no idea, but it would come, he was certain. He was counting on it.

Shaw pulled the bulky knit wool sweater over his head, ran his hand through his hair to settle its tousled mess, and slipped his feet into the boots next to the bed.

The smell of coffee filled the cabin. Shaw removed the pot from the stove top, poured the coffee into a deep mug without the preamble of settling the grounds, which swirled in the coffee's darkness. As he sipped the steaming liquid, he thought about cooking breakfast but discarded the idea in favor of starting for Phillipsburg. The round trip from his island refuge would take five hours, counting the time he'd spend catching up on the war news out of Germany and England. News from the Pacific held no interest for him. He had a private war to occupy his waking thoughts, and retribution to plan.

He'd have to get started with the sun. In these northern latitudes there was little enough sun, and Shaw didn't want to get caught by the setting sun and the cold temperatures that would ride in on the darkness. Despite the emptiness in his soul, he still had an instinct for survival. It might be a perverted instinct, but it was still there.

Shaw carried his cup of coffee to the window where the sun was just beginning to peek through the thick pines and leafless hardwoods populating the small island. Time to go.

Retrieving three more split oak logs from his woodpile next to the far wall, he loaded them into the stove and shoveled ashes from last night's fire over the mound of dried wood. With the fire banked in such a manner, there would still be embers when he returned. Those embers, Shaw had long ago concluded, were not unlike the spark of revenge that burned deep within him, banked against the day when he would have the opportunity to kindle it into a blazing inferno directed at the Third Reich and its black soul, represented by the *Schutzstaffel,* the barbarous SS. Shaw shivered again, this time not because of the cold. The very thought of the SS sent ripples of anger coursing through his veins.

Shaw stepped out of the cabin and began the trek to Phillipsburg. He relished his weekly visits to the Canadian town. The grizzled owner of the dilapidated general store was as worn and friendly as the weathered boards of the store itself.

The sky was clear and cold rays of sunshine poured down on the changing leaves, highlighting their color. It was a beautiful morning, despite his depressed state of mind, and the glowing leaves served to lift his spirits. Then he thought of how much Barbara would have enjoyed the beauty, and a melancholy spirit settled over him.

Shaw made it to the dock, launched his small sailboat, and watched as the building wind filled the sail, propelling the craft at a satisfactory rate. Running with the wind, he calculated he would make Phillipsburg in less than two hours. The return trip would be against the wind, and would not be nearly as enjoyable.

An hour and twenty minutes later, the weathered gray boards of the general store showed through the trees and Shaw heaved a sigh of relief. He'd lost track of the time. At one point, he'd not been certain that he had maintained the correct course. One section of the Canadian shore looked pretty much like any other. He had begun to think that dying in the Canadian wilderness would not be such a bad idea. But Phillipsburg was just off his bow now, showing through the trees.

The town was a collection of low-ceilinged log cabins scattered about the edge of a clearing that had been formed by infrequent foot traffic. The single road through the area lay beneath snowpack most of the winter. Before long, the snow would come, and travel by automobile and truck would cease. Not that traffic was a common occurrence in the village. Motorized traffic was rare, and Shaw was surprised to see a green sedan parked near the store. Winter supplies, when they were needed, were usually flown in by one of the bush pilots up in Montreal. Cars were a strange sight in Phillipsburg.

The worn patina of the old store was a welcome sight for Shaw, looking for all the world like a friend waiting. The store, owing to its central location, served as church, town meeting place, post office, makeshift hotel, and store. If there was a stranger in town, as the sedan suggested, he would be in the store.

Shaw mounted the wooden plank steps leading to the covered porch and pushed through the door, stamping the clinging mud from his boots. He removed his sunglasses and looked around.

The store hadn't changed in the three years he'd lived on Mississquoi Bay. Among its other functions, it was a place of refuge. Jean-Claude Richelieu, the short, rotund owner, was the only man on the face of the earth Shaw counted as a friend. There had been others, but they had, one by one, fallen by the wayside during his long trek into the dark depression that possessed him like a black demon.

Richelieu stood behind the counter as Shaw entered. "Ah, my friend. I knew you would come," the portly owner greeted. "It is good you come today. After tonight, it will be very cold, and your small boat would not be safe I think. Very cold, indeed. Too cold to trample the woods of Quebec."

"I just need a few things, Jean-Claude. Enough to get me through the next few weeks. I'll be back next week to get winter supplies. Be sure you have what I will need, my friend. I will not be back until the sun shines after the snow."

"And you do not feel like playing the pack mule either. Am I right?" the gray-haired man joked.

"You are always right, Jean-Claude. Just the basics for now, please. I'm going to warm by your ridiculously small fire."

Jean-Claude took the list Shaw handed him and worked at pulling the supplies from the sagging wooden shelves as Shaw went to the potbellied stove that glowed in the middle of the store. Chairs of various types and sizes were sprinkled around the stove, and Shaw had failed to see two men who were seated there, their presence shielded by the stove's bulk. Shaw moved near the heat, feeling instant animosity for the invasion by the two strangers.

One of the interlopers, Shaw noticed, was an older, heavyset man with intelligent, inquisitive eyes. *The eyes of a lawyer,* Shaw thought. The other was a younger version of the older man. Each wore identical heavy woolen coats. Both looked up as Shaw warmed himself near the stove.

"Michael Shaw?" the older man asked.

Shaw was surprised. He looked at the man and nodded, not wanting to be drawn into an unwanted conversation.

"I'm Bill Donovan," the man said, rising from his seat. "This is Mark Daniels," Donovan continued, indicating his partner. Donovan held out his hand and Shaw ignored it. "I heard you were not the sociable type. I didn't hear that you were rude."

"I prefer to pick my own friends, Mr. Donovan," Shaw said.

"Like you've already picked your enemies?"

Shaw glared at the squat man. "What's that supposed to mean?"

"I heard you had certain enemies is all." Donovan removed a black and white photograph and handed it to Shaw. "Enemies who wear that particular uniform, I believe. The U-boat that sank the *Athenia* was under direct command of the SS to strike targets of opportunity. Civilian targets."

Shaw accepted the photo and stared at the image, the black SS uniform burning into his mind. The portrait of a sinking *Athenia* flashed through his memory. He closed his eyes against the horrific sight. After the scene evaporated, he returned the photo to Donovan.

"I'm sorry," Donovan said with genuine concern. "I wouldn't have done that if I'd known how it would affect you."

Shaw looked at Donovan. "I thought that was the idea," he said, not bothering to disguise his contempt.

Donovan shook his head. "That's not the way I operate."

Shaw watched the man with a grudging respect. "Donovan, you said. Wild Bill Donovan?"

Donovan smiled. "I've been called that. I don't necessarily agree with the assessment, but that's me."

Mike Shaw felt his heart rate increase; his senses came alive.

"I know your story, Shaw. About your time in Germany, about your wife's death, and about your feelings for the German Navy and the SS. I'm offering you a job. I can promise you that you will be dealing directly with both those entities, and one more you may never have heard of."

"I don't know what you think you know, Mr. Donovan—"

"I know you speak perfect German," Donovan interrupted, "albeit with an Austrian accent. You could pass as a native. Your grandfather and father are both from Austria. They got out, along with you. You were a syndicated correspondent after World War I, and you left when it became apparent that Hitler was not the savior he professed to be. You were on the British ship *Athenia* when she was torpedoed and sunk by a German U-boat September 3, 1939. Your wife died that night, and you disappeared from the face of the earth. I got your location from your syndicate. Friday is your resupply day. I also know you hate the SS and the Nazis with equal fervor, and I'm about to give you the opportunity to strike back. But it's up to you. Technically, I could have you drafted into the army and then have you assigned to OSS from there, but that would not work. You and I both know why."

"I don't believe you, Mister Donovan," Shaw said.

Bill Donovan glared at Shaw.

"In the first place, my syndicate does not know where I am. I send my work, what work I still do, via courier, with no return address. So you see, that's out."

Donovan smiled. "Seems I've been caught," he said.

"So it would seem. What do you want?" Shaw asked.

"I suppose I owe you an explanation," the head of the OSS said.

"This I want to hear," Mark Daniels spoke up, his statement seeming like an intrusion. Donovan had remained tight-lipped about Michael Shaw, but Daniels had bided his time, knowing an explanation would eventually be offered. Now was the time.

"An explanation would be nice," Shaw conceded, looking away from Daniels and back to Donovan.

Donovan cleared his throat. He glanced in the direction of Jean-Claude Richelieu. The store owner was going about the business of filling the order Shaw had given him. Donovan turned back to Shaw and Daniels.

"It's simple, and complicated," Donovan said.

"I thought you looked like a lawyer," Shaw quipped.

Donovan roared in mirth. "A lawyer? No. Deceitful? Most definitely. It comes with the territory."

"And that territory would be?" Shaw continued.

"Development of the most important organization in the world, at least to my way of thinking, Mr. Shaw. The Office of Strategic Services. The OSS."

Shaw nodded. "I've heard of the OSS," he smiled. "You can't force a man to be a good agent, can you, Mr. Donovan? Provided, of course, that's what you had in mind."

"No, Mr. Shaw, I can't. But I can give a man the opportunity to serve his country and himself. Especially to a man who has served so expertly already."

"That's an interesting statement, Mr. Donovan," Shaw said. A noise to his right drew his attention. Mark Daniels had almost fallen over a chair trying to move closer to the conversation.

Donovan turned to Daniels. "Don't worry, Mark. I'll not leave you out of this conversation, provided Mr. Shaw gives me permission to continue." Donovan looked back at Michael Shaw.

Shaw sat in one of the chairs surrounding the stove and waved his hands expansively, the signal to continue.

"So be it, Mr. Shaw," Donovan said, taking a seat, then waiting until Daniels had seated himself. "As you probably have guessed, we have mutual friends."

"Apparently. Otherwise you would never have found me. As I said, my syndicate has no idea where I am."

"But our mutual friend does. A friend, I might add, whose name is known around the world, but perhaps we should save that for later."

"It's your story," Shaw said.

"Our friend told me where to find you. He said to explain that he would have never violated a confidence if the situation had not called for it. He fully expects you to be angry but hopes my explanation will suffice to quell your temper."

"We'll have to see, won't we?"

"So," Donovan began, "finding you would have of course done nothing to further our victory in the war effort had you not been worth finding. I made a rather ambitious statement to my director of field services, Mr. Daniels here. I think it was something to the effect that you were the best agent we had in the OSS. Of course, he was somewhat dismayed. Mr. Daniels has never heard of you.

That's not the case, of course, with our other friends across the Atlantic."

Mark Daniels moved forward in his chair. Donovan's story, or at least his rendition of it, was fascinating.

Shaw waited for Donovan to continue. He crossed his legs, the heat from the stove soaking into him. The warmth was welcome. He was not sure what he was about to hear from Bill Donovan.

Donovan glanced from Daniels to Shaw, adjusted his chair, and began. "My information, as I understand it—and here, Mr. Shaw, feel free to dispute anything I might say—is that although you were, and are, a legitimate correspondent for an American newspaper syndicate, you are much more. While your professional life may seemingly be controlled by the newspaper syndicate, there is another side to your personality, and your interest. Here I think it is wise to use the nomenclature of the business. That is to say, your de facto control for your time on the European continent came from the central London offices of MI-6." Donovan paused, waiting for Shaw to respond, to refute the claim. Shaw said nothing.

Mark Daniels was completely absorbed by the tale.

"Admiral Sir Hugh Sinclair, before his death, was your direct control. A bit unusual, I must say. The chief of MI-6 does not customarily control field agents. At least that was my understanding."

Shaw smiled thinly. "Normally that is true."

"But 'normal' does not apply to you, does it Mr. Shaw?"

"This is your story," Shaw replied.

"So it is. To continue. It was your father who actually began the somewhat informal relationship between the Shaw family and MI-6. Your father and Mansfield Smith-Cummings, the first director of MI-6, were friends. 'A long-time British Navy connection,' I believe, is the way it was put. Living in Europe, and in Germany in particular, gave your father access to information, and he judiciously used it. It was a natural progression for you to join your father in his endeavors with MI-6. But you went a step further. You actually were trained in all the nasty little nuances so necessary to a British agent. You are familiar with British code devices, field craft, and such. In short, you are an agent in waiting. I'm here to end that waiting, Michael Shaw. The rest is up to you."

"I'll have to think about it," Shaw said after a pause. "There are some other commitments I have here. I doubt I can do what it is you want of me."

Jean-Claude Richelieu approached the small group carrying a wooden box of supplies. "I don't mean to interrupt, my friend," he began, directing his attention toward Shaw, "but you must do what this man wants. Forgive me, gentlemen, for listening to your conversation, but, as you see, it is a small store. I could not help myself."

"Quite all right," Donovan answered.

Richelieu turned his attention back to Shaw. "Michael, you yourself have told me what is in your heart. Of your desire to strike back at the evil that has taken over in Europe. I have told you of God and how he hates the evil. You have no interest in God, but I know of the desire to strike at the heart of evil in Germany. It is possible to do God's bidding and rid yourself of the torment within you at the same time. The two are not mutually exclusive." Jean-Claude paused. "You must go," he whispered.

Michael Shaw buried his face in his hands. Donovan and Daniels at first thought the man was crying, but when he raised his face to meet theirs, he was dry-eyed.

"When will I need to leave?" Shaw asked.

Donovan looked to Daniels and the younger man spoke for the first time. "Immediately, Mr. Shaw. We have a deadline which is fast approaching. Events are happening quickly. We want you in Berlin by November 9. Your journey begins there."

Shaw's face twisted in hatred. "I'll be there," he said simply.

CHAPTER

The cold rays of winter sunlight breaking through the gray over-cast did nothing to warm Wernher von Braun's mood. He gazed at the barren yard outside his window. There had been an early winter surge, and the weather was verging on the unbearable. Von Braun couldn't help but compare his mood to the grayness of the day. Despite the chilling cold that painted his office windows with geometric patterns of ice, von Braun was sweating. He glanced once again out the window, wanting for all the world to be free of the nightmare that had invaded his life. He leafed through the papers littering his desk and glanced at his colleague, Kurt Daluege, who was across from him.

"These calculations are correct, my friend?" von Braun asked. His concern was evident despite his attempt to control his voice.

"Yes, Herr von Braun. I have gone over them repeatedly. I can find no errors. Perhaps you can detect any error I might have overlooked. I have become too familiar with the data."

Von Braun sighed as he reviewed the calculations, searching for an obvious mistake. It was not there. He glanced again out the window, watching the beginning of a new snowfall, a prelude, he knew, to another severe night. He shifted uneasily in his chair, wishing that this thing he knew as the Omega Project, along with the SS, would disappear. He knew neither was possible. Von Braun forced his attention back to the man across the desk.

"According to this," he began, "what is wanted—no, *demanded*— for this project will not be possible within the assigned time frame. I will have to report this to Oberstgrüpenführer von Liebman. Dönitz will also have to be informed."

"Forgive me, Herr von Braun, but this . . . this . . . project does not *feel* right. I have never before seen a request for such a motor. If I were to speculate. . . ."

Von Braun held up his hand. "Do not speculate, Kurt. It will not be good for either of us. We do what we are told and hope that someday our efforts will be utilized in other directions. Until then, we work for Germany."

Kurt Daluege nodded his understanding, but it was his fears he voiced. "I hope that that will be a defense should it become necessary," he said, regret evident in his voice. "I will, of course, continue my efforts. But you should know that the atmosphere in the rocket engine research and development center does not go well with the black uniforms so much in evidence."

Von Braun understood. It was the same throughout the Peenemünde complex. The black uniforms of the SS dominated the rocket engine center as well as the test sites to the west, the housing units to the south, and the military camp. The Wehrmacht, itself, was having its own problems with the SS.

What von Braun—as technical head of the German research facility—had feared had become reality. Peenemünde was falling into the capricious hands of the Schutzstaffel.

They had gained a foothold with the installation of General von Liebman, the de facto head of Omega. In the beginning it was to have been nothing more than a supervisory position, but that had quickly changed when Heinrich Himmler moved greater numbers of SS troops into the Baltic complex. Now, as von Braun reflected, he realized how completely Himmler, through von Liebman, controlled the development of what he called the Omega System.

The Omega System was not simply a new weapons system, but a completely new concept in waging war, involving not only the use of tactical weapons in a strategic role, but the introduction of psychological warfare. But, as he pondered it, the concept was not so new. It had been tried during the last great war. To a degree, it had worked then, but eventually the tactics had failed, which had forced Germany back to conventional warfare. Von Braun wondered what would happen this time.

Von Braun, as a theoretical scientist, was not interested in or restricted by the possible targets for the new weapon system. But he, like Kurt Daluege, could and had speculated. Several possibilities existed, but the only one that encompassed all the ramifications being built into the system always came up the same: the United States.

"Leave the SS to me, Kurt," von Braun finally said, addressing Daluege's concern. "I will speak to Oberstgrüpenführer von Liebman myself. When I point out the detrimental effect the presence of his men is having on this project, he will listen."

"Be careful, Wernher," Daluege replied, using von Braun's first name to demonstrate his concern. "I believe the SS is more committed to the Reichsführer–SS than to the good of Germany."

Von Braun smiled ruefully. Daluege had just said what he had known in his heart: The goals of the SS and Germany did not always coincide. It was something that had become apparent but was, nevertheless, dangerous to voice. But what still bothered von Braun the most was the coalition between the SS and the Kriegsmarine. *That* made as little sense as anything else that was going on.

"Be careful yourself. Such words, if spoken outside this office, could see you gone from here in short order. It is extremely dangerous to speak so. And I need you in the motor shop."

Kurt Daluege grinned. "If I did not know better, I would think you are interested only in getting this rocket off the ground."

"I'm a scientist, Kurt. Nothing more. I am interested only in perfecting my ideas and designs."

"Even science for science's sake will be no defense when used against humanity, Wernher. Then it is nothing more than a tool of the leaders, the politically powerful. Politics and science create a dangerous mix. And justice will be only a function of the powerful. Power is the only standard by which this war will be judged. The winner will have the power, the loser will be powerless. Under these circumstances, we must win. There will be no defense for what we do here should we lose. This . . . this . . . holocaust will bury us in that case."

Von Braun listened intently to his friend and fellow scientist. Such thoughts had also intruded his mind—disturbing, malignant ruminations that offered no answer. As he listened to Daluege, something about what his friend said made sense. There was another aspect, however, that left him cold. The word his friend had chosen, he feared, would turn out to be apocalyptic: holocaust.

Daluege stood to leave. He had seen the look in von Braun's gentle eyes, the look that sought justification where there was none. He gathered his notes and diagrams, bundling them under his arm as he moved toward the door.

"Don't underestimate von Liebman or Himmler. Befehlshaber Dönitz does not yet have the political prowess necessary to compete with the likes of the Reichsführer-SS. He can be no solace in this situation."

Von Braun watched Daluege exit the office, the door closing as he left. Von Braun felt the weight of the silence as it closed in on him in the solitude. Outside the window an early snow began falling. The Baltic would be cold this year, colder than normal. Before too many more weeks, winter would strike with full fury. Peenemünde would be as isolated by the torturous German winter as von Braun now felt.

CHAPTER
5

Michael Shaw's mind reeled from the events of the past week. When he thought about it, the meeting with Wild Bill Donovan had not only been expected, it had been inevitable. Donovan's recitation of Shaw's exploits with MI-6 had been almost comical. The reaction of Mark Daniels had been extremely amusing. What had not been such a flight of fantasy had been the intervening seven days since the meeting.

Shaw had accepted the assignment Donovan had offered, demanding only sketchy information up front. The details would be filled in later. In a whirlwind of activity, Shaw had accompanied Donovan and Daniels back to Washington. That trip alone had taken the better part of three days. It had been somewhat of a surprise, but a British Lancaster bomber had been waiting to ferry him across the North Atlantic to London. He'd been assigned berthing on arrival and had been immediately thrust into the harrowing world he had left behind three years earlier.

Station X, known officially as the Government Code and Cipher School, the British decoding section of British Intelligence, was not as Michael Shaw remembered. He had, of course, known the station was located at Bletchley Park, but until now, he'd not had the opportunity to visit. All his previous contacts had been made via radio or courier.

The main building was a stone and timber mansion northwest of London that seemed rather ostentatious for its purpose. Adding to the incongruity was the motley collection of white clapboard buildings located behind the mansion, which reminded Shaw of pictures he'd seen of the Oklahoma dust bowl during the Depression years. Temporary wooden steps led into the elongated buildings. Inside, a seriousness permeated the air like an uneasy cloud.

When Shaw had been briefed at OSS headquarters in Washington, he'd come away with the feeling that the men and women sequestered within the brick walls on Nebraska Avenue were playing an engrossing game. But here at Bletchley Park, perhaps because it was that much closer to the actual war, every face in the narrow hallway reflected a deadly earnestness. Following the directions he'd been given, Shaw soon came to a sparsely furnished reception area at the end of the hall.

"Captain Shaw?" said the young man seated behind a scarred wooden desk.

The title *captain* caught Shaw off guard, and he didn't respond right away. He'd been assigned the rank of captain in the U.S. Army to satisfy some perverse regulation within the OSS, but this was the first time he'd been addressed as such. "Captain Shaw?" the young man repeated.

"I'm Shaw," he answered.

"The major is waiting for you, Captain. He said to show you in as soon as you arrived. Follow me, please."

Shaw fell into step behind the dark-haired clerk. He wondered whether the young man could tell that he, Michael Jason Shaw, was merely a civilian dressed up in the uniform of an army captain. By Shaw's reasoning, his uneasiness had to be apparent. The clerk stopped in front of an unmarked door and knocked. Without waiting for a reply, he entered, holding the door for Shaw.

"This is Captain Shaw," the clerk informed the secretary seated behind another battered wooden desk. The secretary nodded, and the clerk proceeded to a door behind the desk.

Shaw noticed that the outer office was devoid of any type of personal paraphernalia. No pictures on the walls, no photographs on the desk. Aside from the straight-backed chair occupied by the secretary and the desk, the only other article of furniture in the room was a wooden bench along the side wall. It was a room for work, functionally sterile. A room where pleasure knew no presence.

The clerk tapped lightly at the second door, this time waiting for a response before entering. Shaw heard the muffled reply, and the clerk opened the door.

As Shaw followed the young man into the room, he was surprised to see an elegant contrast to the outer office. The walls were painted a muted blue, accented in a darker, richer tone. Polished oak flooring gleamed between the vibrant colors of an assortment of oriental area rugs. English watercolors, mostly landscapes in shades of gray and muted blues, hung on the walls. The furniture was leather, worn to a nice patina by the many visitors who had passed through the office during the last four years. The smell of rich tobacco filled the office, reminding Shaw of his father. It suddenly occurred to Shaw that everyone who had ever meant anything to him was dead.

His father had died while Shaw was covering the political climate in prewar Germany. The message from his mother had come too late for a return trip to the States to attend the funeral. A few months later, his mother, who had suffered a series of respiratory ailments throughout her adult life, simply gave up on living. The doctor's report said she had died of unknown causes, but Shaw now understood the debilitating emptiness that followed the death of a spouse, and her death was no longer a mystery to him; he understood more than he cared to. Still he wondered whether his presence would have made a difference.

Again he'd been unable to attend the funeral, because the note from the coroner had not arrived until weeks after his mother's burial. Before his mind could wander to the events of September 3, 1939, Shaw forced his attention away from his brooding and back to the balding man who sat behind the large desk in front of him. The major pulled on a well-worn meerschaum pipe as a blue cloud of smoke rose above his balding pate. Shaw noticed the emblems on the major's uniform, indicating his rank and membership in a British commando regiment. Shaw was familiar with the regiment.

"Please sit down, Captain," the major said, motioning to the chair directly across from the desk.

Shaw eased into the chair as the major continued to peruse the papers in front of him. The leather was cool and soft. The weariness that Shaw had battled since leaving home swept over him.

"Your folder," the major requested, not bothering to look up.

Shaw felt himself blush when he realized that his eyes were closed and his chin was resting on his chest. He had almost gone to sleep. He shook his head and handed the thick, brown file to the major.

"Thank you, Captain," the major replied with typical British decorum as he took the envelope with his left hand. His right hand moved instinctively to adjust the old meerschaum between his teeth. He deftly slit the sealed envelope with a burnished brass letter opener and removed the contents. As he methodically worked his way through each of the forms contained in the file, he puffed absently on his pipe.

Shaw waited, amused that his life could be as interesting as the British officer seemed to find it.

"Good," the major muttered. "Very good, indeed," he repeated and looked at Shaw. "You speak perfect German, Captain?"

"With an Austrian accent, yes, but fluently," Shaw answered in proper Austrian German.

"Very good. Where you are going, your German will be put to the test. But that won't be new to you," the major said, looking up. "You've been there before and done an excellent job."

"And where will that be, Major?" Shaw asked, ignoring the commendation.

The major smiled. "At this moment, Captain, I'm not at liberty to say."

"When *will* you be at liberty to say?"

The major met Shaw's gaze with a determined stare. "All in good time, Captain," he answered with no warmth. "Now," the major began again, pushing the file to the side, "what do you know of a place called Wewelsburg?"

"Only that it's a castle of some sort, in the mountains of Westphalia. Near Paderborn. It was rumored to be the . . ." Shaw thought for a moment, "for lack of a better description, the spiritual headquarters of the Schutzstaffel."

The major laughed, a cold, bone-chilling chortle that shocked Shaw. "Yes. You would say that, I expect. I noted your tendency toward the religious, shall we say, in your file."

Shaw instantly wondered what was contained in the forms that reflected his religious tendencies. Whatever they were, he'd considered them dead since that September night in 1939.

"You would be well-advised, Major, to forget any *religious tendencies,* as you call them, on my part. That was a long time ago."

The major read Shaw's reaction perfectly. "Oh, it's only a passing comment, I assure you, Captain; but enough. And your description of Wewelsburg is probably closer to the truth than what most of us in British Intelligence care to ascribe to the hellish place. It *is,* as you say, the spiritual headquarters of the SS. We've yet to penetrate the place. And . . . ," the major noticed that Shaw was shifting uncomfortably in his chair. "Don't worry, Captain, infiltrating Wewelsburg is not your assigned mission. I asked simply to determine your knowledge of the SS."

"It's not, I'm sure, what it will be after you are through with me."

"You are quite correct, Captain," the major replied. "Your religious background may be an asset in this situation, though."

Shaw knew what the man was talking about. He *had* been religious, he realized. But it had been part of his being, not the tacked-on
encumbrance he'd seen in so many people considered to be religious.
It had been a natural result of the home in which he'd been raised. His
father had been old-line German Protestant. "Strictness tempered with
compassion" was the way his father had termed it. And Shaw, until
that September night, had had no reason to stray from the truth he'd
learned as a child. Now, as he thought about it, he envisaged how the
Holy Trinity had died within him as surely as the three people he loved
most had died. At times he still felt deep in his soul, with a pang of certainty, the workings of a spirit. But he could not attribute the feeling to
the Holy Spirit he'd once known so well. But how this would apply to
the German SS was beyond him.

"Collins," the major said, addressing the clerk who had escorted
him to the office. "Would you fetch the captain and me some tea,
please. Would you like anything else, Captain?" he asked Shaw.

"Tea will be fine, Major," Shaw replied. He would have preferred a
cup of coffee, but he knew that such a luxury was impossible.

"Tea, then, Collins, for two. Now, Captain, let us begin."

The bald major rearranged the forms and papers on the desktop
and then, with more formality than Shaw deemed necessary, began.

"Does the date November 9 mean anything to you, Captain?" the
major asked, his tone changing from congenial to formal. "In relation
to Germany?"

"It's eight days from today and the date of the Munich putsch, 1923,"
Shaw answered, reciting facts he recalled from some of his research.

"That is correct, Captain. For all practical purposes, it was the
beginning of Hitler's power. By most standards, the putsch was a failure, at least if one considers its original objective."

"To create disarray within the German political parties of that day.
A bluff that shouldn't have worked," Shaw added.

"And, as far as it goes, it didn't work. What it did do was to bring
the National Socialist Party into the limelight of German politics. Until

the November debacle, Hitler's party was nothing more than a local gathering of Bavarians. But from the debris of the putsch was born the Frontbann."

"The emergency formation," Shaw translated.

"I am impressed, Captain. You are indeed well-informed. Yes, the emergency formation. Men from the SA, the Free Corps, and the North German National-Socialists joined the new organization, providing Hitler with an even larger base from which to work."

"Forgive me, Major, but we're talking ancient history here. What has this to do with me?"

The major smiled again just as the door opened and Collins delivered a silver tea service with two cups and saucers. Both men waited until the tea was served and the clerk had gone.

"Bear with me, Captain," the major continued. "You may find a note of logic in my madness."

Shaw nodded.

"The now defunct SA, renamed the Frontbann, which never had more than two thousand men, suddenly jumped to over thirty thousand."

"But the Frontbann never had anything to do with the SS. Not directly, anyway."

"That is true, Captain. But the beginning of the end is dated from that November 9 date. Hitler and his cronies finally marched on the War Ministry, where some of Hitler's men were occupying the building. The German police overreacted, resulting in the death of sixteen National Socialists and three German policemen. All the leaders of the Nazi party were arrested. It would have been a devastating blow to most organizations. For Adolf Hitler, it was the perfect springboard."

"Forgive me, Major—" Shaw started to interrupt, but the major held up his hand.

"The point, Captain, is that November 9 is more than just a date on the calendar for the Nazis. And we want you in Germany, Berlin to be specific, before that date."

"Why?"

It was a simple question with a complex answer. The British major knew deep in his soul that Michael Shaw might never see the free world again if he accepted the assignment he was about to be offered. The major also knew that withholding certain information was essential to the success of the mission. Consequently, he felt a certain amount of apprehension as he prepared to send Shaw into the lion's den.

With a measured calmness, the major began, "The Nazis have an initiation rite scheduled for the ninth at 10 p.m."

Shaw sat forward in his chair, his tea forgotten. He felt the hair on the back of his neck stand up at the word *initiation.*

"What kind of initiation?" Shaw asked.

"An initiation into the Order of Nordic Men of the Third Reich," the major answered.

Shaw felt his breath catch in his throat. The name had an ominous ring to it. "And we're talking about . . . ?" he asked.

"The Schutzstaffel. The SS. You will be present at the SS initiation next Monday, Captain."

Shaw felt his pulse accelerate; his heart thumped against his chest cavity with alarming intensity. For the first time since entering the office, Shaw was unable to speak.

"One of the reasons I'm interested in your religious background is because of what you will find inside the SS. Heinrich Himmler has created a mirror image of most religious orientations. You will find an organization dedicated to the evils of the Nazi party, and the only chance you have of understanding this abomination is to relate it to a religious experience. For those in the SS, the organization is the savior. Himmler has touched every facet of an SS man's existence. It is imperative that you understand this because understanding may be the only edge you'll have."

Shaw sat back, expelling breath he did not realize he was holding. This was not what he'd expected. It was far more diabolical than he'd envisioned, and this major had yet to tell him why he was becoming a part of the most fiendish organization ever created.

"You will have a couple of days here at Bletchley. We will familiarize you with certain codes and procedures you will use when and if you contact us. Your previous training and experience will put you in good stead. I see you can use a key."

Shaw nodded affirmation. "I send about seventeen words and receive twenty-five. I'm out of practice, though."

The British major made a notation on a piece of paper in front of him, and smiled. "Not what I'd hoped for, of course, but better than nothing at all. And you will have the opportunity to practice in the coming days."

Shaw stared into his half-empty teacup.

"You will enter France by way of the northern coast and make your way to Berlin by train. You are expected."

Shaw's head jerked up at the statement, surprise showing on his face.

"I know you've been told about the man found off Nantucket. Prior to his death, our agent made arrangements for a second man to join him in Berlin. That man will be you, only you will be alone."

Shaw shook his head in amazement. "Has it occurred to you that this 'second man' might also be facing certain death? Given the circumstances of your agent's death, compromise is almost certain," Shaw argued.

"We don't think so. The information was passed along only for our consumption. Our man was not actually working in the section where he obtained the information."

"I don't buy that," Shaw snapped. "Sounds like you're sending me to almost certain death. Imprisonment as a spy, at the very least. What's so important that such a risk must be taken?"

The major cleared his throat. "What I'm about to tell you, Captain, is classified, your eyes only. Three copies exist. I have one copy here in this office; one is at 10 Downing Street, and the third is at 1600 Pennsylvania Avenue. The limited distribution should tell you something."

Shaw nodded slightly and waited for the major to continue.

"We have a name—Omega, one dead agent, and numerous reports out of Germany, none of which is conclusive in and of itself. Our best intelligence people, here and across the pond, all come up with the same conclusion. The Germans are about to produce a weapon that we must never allow to be used. As I said, there is no definitive material in any of the reports, just allusions and conjectures. But those conjectures come from some of our best people. Unfortunately, none of those people has the necessary requisites to penetrate to the heart of the project, to where we believe the main systems will be developed."

"Where is that?" Shaw asked wearily.

"A fishing village named Peenemünde, in the Baltic, believed to be the main development area for particular classes of weapons."

"What classes, Major?"

"We don't know, Captain Shaw. We have been doing our best to obtain information on the place. So far, we have only scattered reports and troop movement information in the Baltic."

"None conclusive, right?"

"Exactly," the major answered. "According to our information, the Sturmbannführer you are to replace is to be assigned to the defense detachment at Peenemünde. About this we are certain. It's the one chance we've been waiting on. This has been in the works for almost a year. We cannot let the death of one agent, an unrelated agent at that, disrupt the plans that have been laid."

"If this has been in the works for almost a year, then you must have had someone else in mind to take the Sturmbannführer's place. Someone other than me. I was recruited just over a week ago."

"Quite true, Captain. Our man was prepared to carry through on the assignment. Unfortunately, we discovered, quite accidentally I might add, that he will be unable to continue due to a chronic health problem. He was willing, but the prime minister put the bash on it. You were considered for replacement as long ago as midsummer. You might say you are the first alternate."

"And the original man. Where is he?"

"Here in England, where he will remain until this operation is concluded. You can see, from your vantage point, the inadvisability of having even the possibility of compromise."

"Since it's my life that would be compromised, I would have to agree with you."

"Good. Then let us move on. You will be landing in the north of France and travel by rail to Berlin, where you will be met by members of the SS Totenkopf division, your new unit. We have another agent in the same division, in records and personnel. You must understand that the men with whom you will be dealing are true SS members. Our agent was able only to verify your existence to them. They will think they are meeting another true SS man. With our agent in place, we've been able to have you assigned to Peenemünde, replacing the original Sturmbannführer. You will never know who that agent is, for security reasons. After the ceremony on November 9, which you will be privileged to attend as an SS-Sturmbannführer, you will transfer to Peenemünde, where you will be a field officer in the garrison there, assigned to base security."

"And from there?"

"From there, it's up to you. We need to know whether the rumors concerning a special weapon have any validity. That will be your assignment. Find out about that weapon."

"The problem as I see it, then," Shaw began, moving once again to the front of his chair, "is to distinguish between what is being produced there as a normal course of development and what, if anything, is being produced as a specific weapon with a specific target in mind."

"I know it sounds nebulous, but that's about it, Captain. Now," the major said, getting up, "you have a lot to learn in your few days here. I suggest you get to it. Should you have any problems, please, do not hesitate to let me know. I'm sure we can iron out any rough spots that may—how do you Yanks say—pop up."

"Thank you, Major," Shaw answered, following the major's example and rising. "But I don't even know your name. That would make it rather difficult to let you know, wouldn't it?"

"Yes, it would, Captain. Good luck," the major said, escorting Shaw from the room.

The same clerk, Collins, was waiting on the bench when Shaw emerged from the office. "Strange man," Shaw said, pointing toward the major's office.

"Follow me, Captain. The encoding offices are in another building."

Shaw fell into step behind Collins, finding the clerk's reticence as irritating as the major's. Somewhere, deep in his soul, he felt the first stirring of a long forgotten emotion coming to life. No, not emotion, he told himself, realization. The realization that a spirit lived deep within him. It would be interesting to learn the nature of that spirit.

After Shaw was gone, the major moved back behind the desk, gathering the papers as he made ready to leave. The door opened without preamble and the major looked up.

"How did it go?" the new man asked.

"As well as could be expected, sir," the major answered.

"How much did you have to tell him?"

"Not as much as we thought, sir. I have the feeling that Captain Shaw would have liked to have asked more questions but is content, for the moment, to play the game."

The new man sat in the chair Shaw had just vacated and lit a noxious smelling cigar, much to the displeasure of the major. The man, noticing the discord he was about to produce said, "Excuse me, Major. I forget you do not like cigars."

"Quite all right, sir."

"Is that the file?"

"Yes, sir," the major answered, handing the thick manila folder across the desk.

The man took the file, noting with satisfaction that the original seal was the one broken, and not a duplicate.

"I told him there were three such files, rather than only two."

"Good. Telling him that this file is restricted to the president of the United States and the prime minister of England might have had an adverse effect on our Captain Shaw."

"Like it has on me, sir," the major quipped.

"Like it has on all of us, Major," the man said, rising to leave. "Major, let me clarify this situation, if I may. I am to understand that you did not have to tell him about the black section of this file. *That* information remains restricted? Is that correct?"

"Quite, sir. You will notice that the inner seal on that section remains intact. Not even I know its contents."

"Very well, Major. Thank you for your cooperation in this matter. Someday, maybe sooner than any of us realize, I might be able to enlighten you as to that particular information."

"Yes, sir. Perhaps."

"Good day, Major," the man said, leaving the office.

"Sir," the major saluted.

The man walked out into the cold rain pelting down. The drive back would be bothersome, bothersome and cold. It was little enough hardship, he knew. Others, perhaps this very night, were dying for their island fortress, their England. The least he could do was endure the ride back to 10 Downing Street in the cold.

Winston Churchill tucked the file into his briefcase and climbed into the waiting car. Where do they come from, these men like Michael Shaw, he pondered for a moment before the stone fortress of Bletchley Park disappeared in the growing gloom.

CHAPTER

6

The 1,621-ton U-3009 lolled gently in the rising tide of the Second Flotilla U-boat base in Lorient, France, on the Bay of Biscay. From his vantage point in sub bay B3, Guy La Forche eyed the dark, cylindrical shape with a mixture of awe and disgust. U-3009 had arrived, along with an exact duplicate, U-3021, more than two months ago. Modifications on the type XXI U-boats had begun immediately.

La Forche's task was to weld reinforcement seams along the large, external ballast tanks of U-3021. The tanks were situated outside the pressure hull, straddling the center portion of the boat like a saddle on a horse. These tanks were not an integral part of the pressurized system of the U-boat but were used to crash dive the boat. When necessary, the submarine's commander could fill the tanks with seawater, producing massive negative buoyancy in seconds. The U-boat would quickly sink due to the weight of the water ingested by the ballast tanks. Once at the required depth, the tanks would be blown empty by air pressure, and the boat maintained in a state of negative buoyancy using a combination of diving planes and forward motion, much like an airplane flying level at altitude.

La Forche had recognized immediately that both U-3009 and U-3021 had been modified in such a way that the main ballast tanks were isolated from the series of pipes and valves that would normally allow them to be used for crash diving the boat.

La Forche checked an annotated blueprint before inserting a thick welding rod into its handle. With a practiced movement of his head, he flipped his protective face mask down and touched the rod to the smooth metal of U-3021. He instantly picked up the white-hot bead through the dark glass of his welding mask. Even with the main ballast tanks isolated from the other systems, the welding was critical. Whatever these tanks were intended to carry, it would not be seawater. Consequently, a pressure differential would likely exist between the surrounding ocean and the interior of the tanks. The deeper the U-boat dove, the greater that differential would be. Unless every seam was flawlessly welded, the tanks could rupture at depth.

La Forche slapped a fresh rod into his holder with confident ease. He'd been welding steel hulls on seagoing vessels for more than thirty years. His fellow welders would say he could weld the nipple back on a baby's bottle. But not only was he the best welder in the Lorient shipyards, he was also one of the staunchest resistance fighters in all of occupied France.

La Forche hated the Germans with a passion hot enough to weld steel. And he'd killed his fair share. So many, in fact, that he'd lost count. With his welding prowess, he knew exactly where to weld and where not to weld, and he could cover his trail so well that no inspector would ever detect the one, possibly fatal, flaw he'd left along a critical seam.

The Frenchman changed rods again and continued his work. He saw movement out of the corner of his eye, around the edge of the welding helmet, and smiled to himself. Karl Schneider was coming.

Schneider wore the oblong identification badge of the *Geheime Staatspolizei* with pride. He reveled in the power afforded him by his affiliation with the Gestapo, the Nazis' secret state police. And he despised the French.

La Forche felt the vibrations through the steel hull as Schneider approached. He smiled again. He was one of the few who enjoyed the game that Schneider played with every worker in the yard. He loved to exploit the Gestapo agent's arrogance. "After all," he liked to tell his friends, "arrogance is nothing more than ignorance matured." Schneider had taken ignorance to a new level of perfection.

"Herr La Forche," Schneider called from a distance, not wanting to get too close to the sparks flying from La Forche's welding rod.

La Forche ignored the Gestapo agent, smiling into the darkness of his mask all the while.

"Herr La Forche," Schneider repeated, louder this time, with obvious indignation.

"*Herr* Schneider," La Forche acknowledged, speaking into his welding helmet and continuing to weld. "What can the French do for the Gestapo today?"

"Inspection," Schneider said.

"Indeed," La Forche replied. "And who will conduct this inspection?"

Schneider flushed at the obvious insult to his abilities. "*I* will conduct the inspection, Herr La Forche," he said angrily.

"Oh, of course, Herr Schneider, how silly of me. Please," La Forche motioned to Schneider, "inspect to your heart's desire. If I can be of assistance, please let me know," La Forche added in a sweet, solicitous tone that further angered the Gestapo agent. La Forche removed his welding visor and stepped away from the bead on which he'd been working.

The Gestapo agent moved in for a closer look. The weld had cooled to a natural color, but it was still blazing hot. Schneider put out his hand.

La Forche's first instinct was to stop the German from touching the hot metal, but he kept silent and watched with amusement as

Schneider ran his hand over the weld. The German immediately jerked his hand away, but not before the acrid smell of burned flesh reached his nostrils and a howl of pain came from the agent.

Master race indeed, he chuckled to himself.

Schneider rubbed his damaged hand. Already blisters were beginning to form. He was furious, an anger which he now directed in La Forche's direction.

"Why did you not tell me that weld was hot?" he almost screamed.

"Forgive me, Herr Schneider, but I was not watching which weld you were inspecting. A natural mistake, was it not?"

Schneider fumed. "Not natural at all, La Forche. As a matter of fact, it was probably a deliberate attempt to discredit and injure a member of the Gestapo."

"Not at all, Herr Schneider," La Forche denied. "Forgive me for my oversight. Next time I will be more observant."

"See that you are," Schneider said as he walked down the long hull of U-3021 and onto the quay.

"And the inspection, Herr Schneider. It was satisfactory?"

Schneider turned as he set foot on the wharf. "Commendable, as always, Herr La Forche. Keep it that way."

La Forche almost laughed out loud. He'd intentionally left a bubble in the weld, a defect so obvious, so potentially destructive to a submarine hull, that anyone remotely familiar with the requirements for a pressure hull would notice the defect at once. *Schneider knows less about welding than my five-year-old daughter,* La Forche thought disgustedly, as he went back to his welding. But then, that was good. In his arrogance, Schneider had probably cost more German sailors their lives than all the Allies' antisubmarine warfare ships.

"Another inspection?"

La Forche looked up into the face of his foreman, Charles Rousseau, and grinned. "Right. I thought Schneider was going to burn his hand through to the bone. I've never seen a man so absolutely ignorant and happy to be so."

"He is a dangerous man, Guy. More so because of his ignorance. Always remember that. Not all Gestapo are like Schneider. Most are ex-policemen. They are professional and thorough. You would do well not to antagonize them. Tread lightly, my friend."

"I will, Charles."

"And," Rousseau added, "that bubble in your last weld will not fool the real inspectors of the security forces, should they choose to examine it."

La Forche laughed deeply. "Then I shall do better this time," he said, picking up another rod and donning his welding helmet.

La Forche began again with the seam he'd ruined intentionally to teach Schneider a lesson. Unfortunately, this particular Gestapo agent never seemed to learn his lesson very well. La Forche glanced again at the U-3009 along the far quay. The modification of U-3009 had been a simple operation. It had required nothing more than sealing off the plumbing that afforded interconnection with the rest of the submarine's internal systems. The ballast tanks had simply been isolated from the rest of the boat. Whatever would fill the now independent ballast tanks was not exotic, but it was, for all its calculated commonness, nonetheless a mystery.

The work on U-3021, on the other hand, could best be described as a transformation. As soon as the submarine had entered the dry docks two months ago, large pyramids of wood had been erected to support the outer hull while the water was pumped from the dock. Then an army of yard workers had attacked the boat in a frenzy, removing everything that gave the submarine its familiar, sinister profile. The conning tower cover, periscopes, and radio antennas had yielded to cutting torches and large wrenches. Meanwhile, another crew of workers had secured the necessary systems to allow the outer hull to be removed, exposing the pressure hull underneath to the master planer's knife.

The work had gone quickly, taking little more than two weeks to complete. Then the work had turned strange. The carbon steel ballast assembly—the same tanks that had been isolated on U-3009—were completely removed from U-3021. Most of the interior plumbing had had to be rerouted, which had taken almost a month. The procedure was akin to relocating and rerouting every blood vessel in the human body.

After the pipe work had been completed, a type of insulation had been installed directly onto the pressure hull where the ballast tanks had been removed. The entire process had been a secret operation, or as secret as it could be in an open dry dock, which meant that every worker in the yard knew what was happening.

After the new pipes and insulation were installed, new ballast tanks had arrived in the train yard. They had been painted to look more or less like the original carbon steel ones, but La Forche's curiosity had been piqued.

One night at quitting time, La Forche's inquisitive nature had overridden his instincts for self-preservation. On his way to the gate, he had walked past the new ballast tanks, his knife held low, out of sight from all but the most astute observer. He'd scratched the paint away as he passed and been rewarded with the bright shine of the underlying metal. At first he had thought the tanks were nothing more than standard issue, but with a layer of chrome applied, possibly as an experiment. But later, as he and the other shift workers talked it over, he'd concluded that the tanks must be made of stainless steel, a rare commodity in the Third Reich.

La Forche decided that anything the Nazis had gone to such trouble to conceal must be important enough to report to the resistance leaders. That night, he had risked a radio transmission on his hidden unit and had sent the information along.

Since that night, he'd logged no less than a dozen reports on the progress of the U-3021. He'd reported the stainless steel connections, the additional insulation, the special, noncorrosive valves, and the unusual pressure gauges that directly monitored the internal pressure of the new tanks.

Clearly, these new tanks were never meant to be flooded with mundane seawater. He still had no idea what the tanks would carry, but he was certain he had the attention of his friends across the English Channel.

La Forche raised his visor and examined his latest weld in the cold light of day. He'd removed and rewelded the bubble that had been so obvious to Rousseau and invisible to Schneider. For a fleeting moment, he considered allowing another bubble in the seam, but deduced, correctly, that the U-3021 would be inspected as no other submarine had been before. The U-3021 would put to sea with the tightest seams that had ever sailed from the Lorient yard.

La Forche dropped the last bit of used welding rod from his holder and began packing up his equipment to move to another job.

Maybe, he hoped, the information he'd supplied would shed some light on the mysterious, stainless steel ballast of the U-boat.

Guy La Forche had no idea the maelstrom his reports had generated in his English cousins across the Channel.

CHAPTER

7

A series of waves broke over the bow of the fishing vessel, slowing her progress and drenching the decks as it plowed through the rough waters of the English Channel. As the worn vessel, its paint long ago stripped away by the battering seas, worked its way toward the French coast at eight knots, every man on board, except for one, seemed impervious to the numbing cold and bone-chilling spray.

Michael Shaw, his clothing dry beneath layers of stained oilskins, scanned the far horizon for a glimpse of his destination, the French port city of Le Havre. He'd been told that he would be transported to France on a fishing boat to begin his trek to Berlin via French and German rail, but no one had mentioned that he would be delivered into France's largest seaport in broad daylight. Whoever had planned this operation was crazy. And he was even crazier for agreeing to go through with it. It had sounded reasonable, even logical, when he was sitting in a warm office reviewing options. But now, amid the angry waves and gray skies, all he could think was that fools rush in where angels fear to tread.

The British agents who had briefed him for his mission had assured him that these fishermen were known from Bremerhaven to Brest. In fact, the Germans had even stopped searching their boat. Of course, they had never used the vessel to smuggle commodities into Germany—only people. Shaw hoped that the old saying was true that the best hiding place is out in the open.

He had to admit that the plan was elegant in its simplicity. The boat he was on was a real working trawler, and the crew were actual fishermen. They had a full load of fish to sell when they reached Le Havre. Once the boat was in port, Shaw would simply slip away from the docks, remove his oilskins, and head for the nearest train station. His papers were all in order, and he was, after all, an *SS-Sturmbannführer.* He should have no problems.

The forty-foot wooden craft slammed down into a shallow trough, rattling Shaw and causing him to spill the last of his coffee. The shattered wave flew over the gunwales in a fine spray that clung to every exposed surface. Shaw noticed that some of the spray was beginning to freeze on the small cabin and the tackle that littered every open space on deck. He thought about Canada and the coming winter there. It would have been a fine season. It was hard to believe that barely two weeks ago he had been comfortably secluded in his cabin on Missisquoi Bay. Now his entire world had changed.

Shaw had begun the crossing in the boat's tiny galley, protected from the elements. But an unidentifiable feeling had overwhelmed him, and he had fled onto the open deck, preferring the icy winds and freezing rain to the claustrophobic confines of the galley. After check-ing his outer clothing to make sure the oilskins were secure, he moved forward, toward the rise in the deck that began about fifteen feet aft of the bow. After almost slipping overboard twice, he reached the forward hatch in the center of the forward deck.

The wind was whipping the tops of the higher waves into a froth that blew over the freeboard, combining with the snow that was beginning to fall, and coating men and gear alike with an ever increasing layer of ice. Shaw moved back from the bow. The ice crackling from his clothing and falling to the deck in a spray of glittering light reminded him of the cut glass of an expensive chandelier.

He could hear the drone and feel the heavy vibrations of the diesel engine below deck as it strained against the current and the prevailing winds. A man clad in oilskins emerged from the galley and started toward him. When he was within five feet, Shaw recognized the vessel's skipper, Gregor Strasser. Shaw waited for the short, muscular captain to reach him. A thin layer of ice clung to Strasser's outer garments and filled his ragged beard with crystals.

"Maybe an hour," Strasser shouted above the wind, cupping his hands so Shaw could hear him.

Shaw nodded his understanding.

"You can warm yourself in the cabin, Herr Sturmbannführer," Strasser said in German, addressing Shaw by his SS rank.

Shaw was temporarily taken aback by the greeting, though he had been instructed to speak only German on the crossing and to become accustomed to his rank.

"I'll stay out here, if you don't mind, Kapitän," Shaw answered in flawless German.

"It's below freezing, my friend."

"Thank you for providing adequate clothing," Shaw shouted, not wanting to discuss his real reason for not remaining in the boat's galley.

"As you wish, Sturmbannführer."

"Thank you," Shaw replied.

"Sturmbannführer. A word of advice."

Shaw cocked his head to show that he was listening to the skipper.

"An SS-Sturmbannführer would never thank me. It's part of their feeling of superiority over their conquered foes."

"I shall remember," Shaw replied more curtly than he'd intended.

The captain smiled. "That is better," he said as he turned and headed back to the warmth and protection of the small cabin.

Shaw retraced his steps back toward the bow, taking care not to slip on the icy deck now coated with more than half an inch of solid ice. It was a good thing, Shaw reflected, that the channel crossing would terminate in an hour or less. Any longer and the small boat might capsize from the sheer weight of ice accumulating on the superstructures and the mast, he thought.

Moving further forward, Shaw strained to catch a glimpse of light from the shore. Despite the assurances of British Intelligence and the captain of the fishing vessel, he was nervous.

He was just about to give up when a pinpoint of light appeared as the bow rose, then plunged forward and down, the fishing boat falling back into a trough.

"That is it, Sturmbannführer," the captain said.

Shaw whirled in surprise. He hadn't noticed that the captain had returned to his side. He took a deep breath to compose himself, hoping the sailor hadn't noticed how jumpy he was.

"France."

"Yes, Sturmbannführer, France," the captain said.

"It's hard to believe we will be able to sail into Le Havre without being challenged," Shaw remarked.

"A German patrol boat has been shadowing us for the past two hours. We have been in radio contact with them. They know us well. We sell fish up and down the coast. The Germans are some of our best customers. We have become a fixture to be ignored, and the Germans have become complacent."

"'Woe to them that are at ease in Zion,'" Shaw said out loud without realizing it.

"I beg your pardon?"

Shaw raised his voice over the crashing ocean waters and the background noise of the boat's diesel. "'Woe to them that are at ease in Zion,'" Shaw repeated loudly enough to be heard, shocked by his words, and the context.

The captain stared at Shaw. "Are you a religious man, Sturmbannführer?"

"I don't know, Captain. No. Not now. Once, yes, I suppose I was. But that died a long time ago."

The captain nodded his understanding. "It is the same with the ocean, I think. Many times I left her. I was a farmer, a mechanic, once I even taught school. But I always returned to the sea. And each time I returned, she was here for me. I was the one who always abandoned her, not the other way around."

Shaw nodded at the captain but didn't reply. He wasn't sure why he'd quoted the verse from the Book of Amos, or even how he had remembered it.

"We are a strange lot, we humans, Sturmbannführer," the captain continued. "We're content most of the time to forget about God until we have need of him."

Shaw continued to stare at the approaching coast. "Are you a religious man, Captain?"

Strasser smiled. "Every fisherman is religious, Sturmbannführer. In one way or another."

"You may be right, Captain."

"We are coming up on the first light, the entrance to the harbor. It will not be long now. Please join me at the helm for the rest of the trip."

The shipping traffic increased dramatically as they approached the mouth of the harbor—mostly German naval vessels. Shaw felt a tap on his shoulder and turned as Strasser pointed off the starboard beam of the fishing boat. A one-hundred-foot German patrol boat passed within two hundred feet and Shaw realized that it was the boat that had been monitoring them. Strasser was right. The patrol continued past them into the harbor. Shaw made a mental note to be more observant. Such oversight in enemy territory could get him killed. The verse from Amos came to mind once again: *"Woe to them that are at ease in Zion."* For some inexplicable reason, Shaw felt better.

Strasser maneuvered the fishing boat among the larger, deadlier craft of the German navy and the other commercial vessels that were arriving and departing the French port. Within twenty minutes, he had expertly steered the fishing boat alongside a civilian dock connected to a military dock on the seaward side. To Shaw's way of thinking, it would have been preferable to dock further down, along the civilian quay on the other side of the harbor, far away from the German navy. But once again, Captain Strasser was two steps ahead of him.

"No one coming out of the military side in uniform gets checked very closely," Strasser said, as if reading Shaw's mind. "The civilian checkpoints are more thorough. The Germans are so arrogant as to think they cannot be infiltrated through the military establishment here in port. We have landed dozens of agents because of this."

Shaw felt the deep-throated thump as the boat's hull contacted the heavy pilings of the wharf. Crew members rushed to secure the bow and stern lines of the fishing vessel.

"Come with me," Strasser said to Shaw.

Shaw followed the bearded captain as they climbed onto the dock. Already a ragged line of sailors, soldiers, and some civilians had formed to purchase the fish carried in the hold of the boat. Uniformed military personnel pushed their way to the front of the line. Here, away from the open sea, the temperature was more moderate. The snow had ceased, and a gentle rain fell.

The crew members were beginning to off-load the fish with shovels and baskets as Shaw and Strasser stepped onto the docks.

"Strasser!" a voice called.

Strasser and Shaw turned to see a German naval officer approaching, wearing the uniform of a sublieutenant. Shaw felt his stomach tense as the bearded young officer drew near.

"Zapp," Strasser greeted the officer. "How are things in the Reich?"

"Strasser, shut up, will you?" Zapp ordered benignly as he

approached. "The French are hard enough to get along with without you stirring things up."

Strasser laughed, and Shaw was amazed at the ease with which the man fell into his role.

"I need something for tonight," said Zapp. "My wife is on my back about the food here. Maybe a good fish will take her mind off this place long enough for me to have a nap."

"Zapp, only a German would complain about French cooking and food," Strasser said, shaking his head in mock disgust.

"A fish, Strasser," the German insisted.

Strasser reached into one of the baskets of fish that now lined the dock. "I think this will satisfy your wife. Please take it with my compliments," Strasser added.

"Thank you, Strasser. I shall," Zapp replied as he turned to walk away.

Shaw stood in wonder at the exchange. Not once, in all the time the German officer was near, had he so much as glanced at Shaw.

"You see, my friend. Complacent. Now that a crowd has gathered to buy these fish, you can blend in and be on your way. Good luck to you. I will pray for your success."

"So you *are* a religious man," Shaw said.

"I am," said Strasser.

CHAPTER

8

Heinrich Himmler breathed slowly, deliberately, trying to regain his composure. His hands were working at his sides, alternately flexing and relaxing. He reached up and removed the pince-nez from the bridge of his nose and cleaned them with a handkerchief before turning to face the man occupying the chair opposite the Reichsführer's desk.

Reinhard Gluecks, Himmler's deputy assistant for internal affairs, sat calmly, the ends of his long fingers touching, waiting for Himmler to control himself.

Himmler turned to Gluecks, replacing the pince-nez before speaking. "I can see your point, Reinhard," Himmler said. "But this course of action would not be wise at this particular time. There are too many contingencies to account for in this latest effort. I can assure you that we would meet great resistance from Admirals Raeder and Dönitz. No," Himmler continued, "I do not think it wise at this time."

"Herr Reichsführer," Gluecks began, "we have a great opportunity here to eliminate many Jews. The Americans are the ones we fight, but we both know who the real enemy is." He knew that his controlled manner and high-pitched voice irritated Himmler. Not to mention that he always referred to Himmler as *Herr* Reichsführer, and not simply *Reichsführer,* as Himmler had ordered.

Himmler turned back to Gluecks. The assistant was a mixed blessing. Gluecks was everything the perfect SS man should be. Tall, blond, Nordic, his bright blue eyes possessed a piercing quality about them that unnerved Himmler. In addition, Gluecks's brother, Richard Gluecks, was head of the concentration camp inspectorate, and even though both brothers reported directly to him, Himmler didn't trust either one.

And both Glueckses were intelligent. Perhaps dangerously so.

It was almost more than Himmler could tolerate. Himmler's short stature, coupled with his unathletic build and rounded features, presented a less than desirable image of the head of the SS. But Himmler had realized early on that he needed a man like Reinhard Gluecks. Whereas Himmler was politically astute, with the ability to manipulate the infrastructure of the German empire and the National Socialist Party to best advantage, Gluecks was the consummate organizer, a perfectionist down to the smallest detail. Gluecks reminded Himmler of another Reinhard: Reinhard Heydrich, the assassinated ex-head of the Gestapo. Himmler had felt equally uncomfortable around Heydrich, for many of the same reasons he disliked Gluecks. He did not like to be reminded of his own fallibility.

Reinhard Gluecks, like Heydrich before him, hated the Kriegsmarine, though not for the same reasons Heydrich had. Whereas Heydrich's hatred had stemmed from his broken naval career, Gluecks's disdain was directed at the rising star of the Kriegsmarine, Admiral Karl Dönitz. Or to be more specific, the family of the admiral. Gluecks had never revealed to anyone just how deeply his loathing ran, but to that end, he had proposed developing the operational change to the Omega system at Peenemünde.

"Yes, yes, Reinhard. I agree that you have a valid point concerning the Jews, but the agreements have been made, the process begun. We will retain the earlier proposals as they are and possibly talk again after we have seen the results."

Gluecks smiled. Himmler, he knew, was always the same. The man could not make a decision if it were necessary to save his own life. On the other hand, he, Reinhard Gluecks, had the ability to cut to the heart of most situations, properly identify the problem, and instigate corrective measures. He grudgingly admitted that he would never have had the opportunities he'd had were it not for Himmler's continued confidence. Each man, Gluecks admitted, needed the other. He would have another chance to express his wishes concerning Omega at a later date. In the meantime, it would be interesting to see the interplay he had initiated between the SS and the Kriegsmarine. It would, he knew, be a test of wills.

"As to another matter, Reichsführer, our agents in Lorient at the Second Flotilla U-Boat base tell me that the refitting of the U-3009 and U-3021 has neared completion. That is ahead of schedule."

Himmler, satisfied to change the topic and pleased that Gluecks had dropped the *Herr,* located an operational report he'd read earlier that morning. He quickly reviewed the short document and handed it to Gluecks. "Read this, Gluecks," he ordered as he handed the paper to his assistant.

Gluecks took the paper, quickly consuming the contents. When he was finished, he casually flipped the report on the desktop. "They don't suspect anything?"

"No. Not if you can believe the reports," Himmler said.

"They're true. I can feel it. This strike will be of a magnitude that even Dönitz will not expect."

"It is a matter which must remain within the confines of the SS," Himmler warned. "After we have achieved our objective, we will describe to the Führer how the SS came to the aid of the Reich in its days of greatest need."

Gluecks controlled his response to Himmler's words. Himmler lived in the past as much as in the present. Likely as not, Himmler saw himself as an avenging medieval knight coming to the rescue of a damsel in distress. Gluecks, on the other hand, saw the ploy for exactly what it was. If successful, it would mean power and influence within an invincible Reich. If they failed, it could well mean they would see the inside of the concentration camps that Himmler was so proud to oversee. In any case, the unfolding events would prove interesting.

"What about the U-135?" Gluecks asked.

Himmler fidgeted in his chair. He'd hoped Gluecks would not ask about the third submarine. But, characteristic of Gluecks, he never left anything to chance.

"There have been some problems with the refit. It is difficult to coordinate the activity of so varied an assortment of units. The engineers sent a set of blueprints to the shipyard which proved untenable. The shipyard personnel told the engineers to redraw the specifications. Somewhere in the process of sending the blueprints back and forth, the engineers failed to receive a set, and, not knowing that the shipyard had requested certain changes, continued to work based on an incorrect set of blueprints. It cost time and tempers. The shipyard has the correct set now and tells us that they will meet their time constraints." After explaining the situation to Gluecks, Himmler felt a flush of embarrassment. He'd been explaining a situation to a subordinate in much the same manner of a new lieutenant to a commanding general. That Gluecks had accepted the explanation in much the manner of a general receiving a report from a lieutenant did not serve to mitigate Himmler's embarrassment.

"It is good, Reichsführer," Gluecks said, leaving the *Herr* off yet again in an attempt to placate his boss.

"Yes," Himmler responded. "I wish I could be there to see the destruction in person."

"*That* would not be advisable. There are too many variables, too much chance for something to go wrong. No, Reichsführer. Germany is the place to be when this weapon is unleashed."

Himmler felt an immediate sense of dread grip him. Gluecks had voiced the possibility of failure, which Himmler, himself, had refused to allow his mind to consider. Nothing must go wrong with the operation. But hearing Gluecks's matter-of-fact concern was rather unsettling.

Gluecks rose to leave. *"Herr Reichsführer,"* he saluted sharply.

Himmler watched his blond assistant leave the office. For the first time since the inception of Omega, Hienrich Himmler felt fear. Was failure a possibility? And should it fail, what would his response be? He needed time to think, to rationally and calmly analyze this new information. It might have been an error of judgment to link the fortunes of the SS, along with the Kriegsmarine, to the success of Omega. But it was too late to worry about that. He would now need a plan to extricate himself from Omega should failure become a reality.

Himmler rose and walked to the window, wondering at that moment what Befehlshaber Dönitz was thinking. Rumor had it that Dönitz, currently the Commander in Chief of U-boat operations, was to be named Grand Admiral of the German Navy, perhaps as early as January. Himmler wondered what effect, if any, that promotion would have on Omega.

CHAPTER

For the second time in thirty minutes, Admiral Karl Dönitz found himself counting the small sailboats riding at anchor in the northern waters of the Bay of Biscay. Behind him, his staff continued to pore over the large grid map that covered the far wall. Each grid defined an operating area from the Arctic Ocean in the north to the south Atlantic and around the tips of South America and Africa. Each grid block contained a two-letter designator, and Dönitz could hear the discussion as it turned to the block designated "CA." Dönitz knew without looking that CA was the sector covering the area north of New York City down to Cape Hatteras on the east coast of the United States.

The five-story stone château in which his office as commander in chief of U-boat operations was located provided Dönitz with a clear view of the mouth of the harbor at Lorient. From his vantage point, Dönitz could see the U-boat pens down the coast at Pointe de Keroman near the harbor entrance.

Again Dönitz caught himself counting the small harbor sailboats outside his window. He turned to the assembled staff clustered around the map.

Captain Emil Kurtz, Dönitz's chief of staff, was explaining the finer points of wolf-pack operations in block CA to Captain Ulrich Folkers, operations officer; Captain Karl Latislaus, intelligence; Senior Captain Paul Hoffman, navigation; and SS Colonel Franz Loosen, Gestapo.

"Each block, in this case CA, is divided into nine additional blocks numbered from one to nine," Kurtz explained for the benefit of Loosen, the senior Gestapo agent at Kernével and newest member of the senior staff. "Each block, one through nine, is divided once again into nine more, giving us a two-letter and two-number designator for any single patrol area."

Kurtz waited until he was convinced that Loosen understood the concept. Kurtz had opposed divulging such information to anyone not directly affiliated with U-boat operations, but Dönitz had ordered him to brief the new Gestapo officer.

"Given this designating scheme," Kurtz continued, "New York City lies in the area designated CA-24."

Franz Loosen moved closer to the plastic-covered map, visualizing with the aid of the lines on the map what Kurtz had just explained. If he was aware that the other officers in the room were staring at him with impatience, he didn't show it. After several minutes, Loosen backed away from the map and nodded. "I understand, *Kapitän*."

Kurtz sighed impatiently. The chief of staff was not sure he agreed with the assessment of the other staff members, that Loosen was an imbecile. While it was true that the Gestapo agent could be exasperating, Kurtz suspected the show of incompetence was more a cover than a natural fact. He did not trust Loosen.

Loosen knew he was not held in high regard by the other men in the room. After all, he wasn't navy, and "navy" was a very exclusive club at this level. But Loosen was far from stupid. He'd earned the rank of Standartenführer on the basis of his brains and wit, not with his

money, like so many other senior SS men. His ploy of lulling others
around him into a false sense of superiority was one of the operational
tools that had served him well. It apparently worked, even in the rar-
efied atmosphere of the Kriegsmarine high command, although he suspected that Kurtz knew more about him than he would have wished.

"Gentlemen," Admiral Dönitz interrupted as he rejoined the group.
"We have another operation we should talk about."

The group turned their attention to the admiral, grateful to be done
with the tedious briefing of Franz Loosen.

Dönitz moved to the huge map on the wall, staring at it as if he
were trying to decide what he wanted to do with it. He turned to the
staff and began, "Operation *Paukenschlag* was a success, gentlemen,
far beyond what we here at BdU had expected."

Kurtz and the others nodded their understanding. Only Loosen had
not been a part of the planning and implementation of the U-boat campaign, known to the English and Americans as Operation Drumbeat.

"Pardon me, Admiral. I have heard of Operation *Paukenschlag,* of
course, but I am not sure what it encompassed. Perhaps your staff
could provide me with the pertinent details after the briefing."

Dönitz stared at Loosen. He'd never heard an SS man operate like
this. *Keep an eye on this one,* Dönitz warned himself. "Kapitän Kurtz
will provide you with that information, Standartenführer. But for now
it is only important that you know that Drumbeat was the first U-boat
operation into American waters off the east coast of the United States.
The exact figures will be supplied in the material from Kapitän Kurtz,
but suffice it to say that American losses to our U-boats were in the
millions of tons."

Dönitz stopped for a moment, letting the significance of his words
sink in. Even he had been shocked to learn the ease with which his
U-boats could strike American and British shipping literally within
sight of the Empire State Building. At first, the Americans' apparent
complacency within their own waters had both infuriated and pleased
Dönitz. It was as if they were saying that their shores were

invulnerable to the might of the Third Reich. As a consequence, millions of tons of shipping now lay on the shallow shelf off the east coast of the United States, from Boston to Miami.

When the U-boats began to sink shipping in massive quantities, the British Admiralty offered the Americans the use of British sub-chasers and destroyers for antisubmarine service. The Americans had refused, but mounting losses eventually forced them to adopt different strategies.

Now Dönitz was facing properly escorted convoys, huge movements of ships screened by warships, whose only purpose was to protect the valuable cargo aboard the Liberty ships. And it was working. Matériel began arriving in England with maddening regularity, and Dönitz knew he would have to change his tactics to meet the new threat of the convoys.

Even after the Americans responded to the threat on the open seas, they continued to allow single warships and unescorted freighters to operate within sight of land.

Dönitz needed desperately to reduce the number of screening vessels available for convoy duty. That would be the only way to sink more freighters. Omega would be the operation to demonstrate to the Americans the necessity of protecting their own shores. He was about to reveal the details of Omega to his senior staff.

"Gentlemen, we will discuss Operation Omega now."

A subdued murmur went through the room. As senior staff members, they understood the purpose of Omega, but they had never before heard the details. Indeed, some staff members questioned whether the operation would ever be developed.

Dönitz pulled a thick file from his valise—the words, *Geheime Kommandosache* (Top Secret) emblazoned on the outside—and began the briefing, hoping his feeling of reticence did not show on his face.

If Franz Loosen noticed anything unusual in Admiral Dönitz's demeanor, he did not show it. He listened intently as Dönitz began, his

ears perked for any indication, any clue, any scrap of information suggesting that Dönitz had somehow discovered the enhanced capabilities
that Heinrich Himmler had ordered.

It quickly became evident that the office of BdU had no knowledge
of Omega's true capabilities. Loosen relaxed, feeling smug in his
knowledge.

CHAPTER

10

As the military troop train rumbled to a halt, Michael Shaw jerked awake, surprised that he'd been able to sleep on the overheated, over-crowded train. He was amazed that the trip to this point had been so effortless.

True to Strasser's word, there had been no check on the military side of Le Havre harbor. Shaw had disembarked with the rest of the crew and simply walked away from the crowd that had gathered to pick over the fresh catch of Atlantic fish. Feeling almost ridiculous, he'd strode down the long quay, found a warehouse filled with military wares destined for Belgium and the Netherlands, surreptitiously used the chaos within the place to shuck his diesel-stained oilskins, and walked from the building in the pale gray tunic of an SS-Sturmbannführer. For a moment, as he made the outward transition from seaman to SS major, a feeling of fore-boding—almost terror—had seized him. For a split second, Shaw felt as if his body and soul had been confiscated by some powerful, unseen, malevolent force, with an appetite only for evil. As he'd assembled his uniform, the aluminum Totenkopf (skull and crossed bones) insignia had caught his eye, the death's head grin on the skull a chilling reminder of what he was fighting.

But that almost spiritual confrontation had been the only one so far, and Shaw had boarded the train with his bag and had headed for Paris. Out of Paris, he'd had no trouble booking passage on a troop train headed for Strasbourg, by way of Nancy. It had been decided that this was the safest route to take, if it could be done. The route would require only one border crossing, as opposed to multiple crossings for other routes through Belgium, and therefore offered a reduced risk of exposure.

Shaw was beginning to wonder about the famous German reputation for efficiency. He'd been traveling now for more than twelve hours and had yet to be challenged by so much as a train conductor.

Raising up in his seat, he kneaded the stiffness from his back as best he could with his balled fist. Although he'd slept, it felt more like he'd been hibernating for three months. His mouth was dry, he needed a shave, and the gray SS uniform was rumpled.

A few hours back, the train had crossed the Meusse River south of Châtons-sur-Marne. Shaw had marveled at the beauty of the countryside, even in the midst of war. He wondered, as the train rumbled on deeper into the German-occupied lands, what it would be like should the Allied forces ever bomb this deeply into France. He found, much to his surprise, that the possibility bothered him. The sudden surge of emotion had come as a surprise. Nothing had so affected him since that night in 1939. He'd been in France and Germany many times, and there was something of a homecoming flavor to this return. What was different was the absence of Barbara. Shaw quickly subdued the pain produced by the thought of his dead wife.

Snow began to fall outside the coach window. Here in the deeper valley where the train was waiting for a troop transport headed for Paris to pass, the temperature was just above freezing, and the snow was melting as quickly as it fell. Shaw could see the distant mountains and the snow line that traced around and through the higher valleys.

The car in which Shaw was riding was crowded. Although every seat on the train was occupied—some with as many as four men crammed into a space for two—the seat next to Shaw was occupied by a single Luftwaffe officer. The aviator had been seated when Shaw had boarded. The train had just begun to fill when Shaw took the window seat next to the man. After that, despite the overflow conditions, no one attempted to force their way into the seat next to him. On one level, that had suited him just fine, but when he realized that it was the SS uniform that kept everyone away, he'd felt a strange detachment. While it served him well as he traveled, it inexplicably bothered him too.

"You are headed for Munich, Herr Sturmbannführer?" the Luftwaffe Hauptmann asked.

Shaw was temporarily shaken by the question. He'd been riding the train for hours and no one had said a word to him. The control officers, French police, and Gestapo agents checking travel papers and orders had each time passed him by. Only the Gestapo agents had nodded a passing acknowledgment. The Luftwaffe Hauptmann had occupied the seat next to him for more than twelve hours but until now had said nothing.

Shaw recovered and turned to the aviator. "Berlin, Herr Hauptmann," Shaw answered, wishing immediately that he'd dropped the sign of respect and simply called the man Hauptmann.

The Luftwaffe pilot nodded once, then turned again to Shaw. "Why this direction, Herr Sturmbannführer? Would it not have been quicker to travel through Belgium?"

"Quicker perhaps, if I could have boarded a train, but none was available for a soldier going on leave."

"Yes, I see," the pilot remarked and returned to his silence.

Shaw mentally chastised himself for breaking SS protocol. Even a minor slip like referring to the Luftwaffe Hauptmann as *Herr* could prove fatal. He would have to be more careful.

Shaw began to notice an almost sinister feeling as the train moved deeper into the German empire. He'd been watching the people—the soldiers, the workmen, the ordinary citizen of France—who were traveling this day. They were, for the most part, ordinary human beings like himself, forced into circumstances beyond their comprehension and control.

Shaw scanned the faces in the coach. Resignation was the overwhelming emotion present, he decided. Some, from the spiritless gaze registering in their eyes, were past resignation.

The feeling of a malicious spirit strengthened with each mile traveled. The physical world outside the window was a thing of beauty and order. The snow continued in the mountains. As the train passed through the picture-perfect villages of western France, Shaw could almost believe it was another place and time.

The shrill whistle of the engine shattered his meditation. He looked out the window, out into the darkening evening with its purple-tinted long shadows. The clickety-clack of the wheels over track joints changed, and Shaw found himself staring into the Rhine River valley. In minutes, the train would cross the border from France into Germany.

Woe to them that are at ease in Zion.

Shaw watched the darkness settle over the land as the train rumbled into the heart of the Third Reich. He could not be certain whether the darkness was more physical or spiritual.

After the train cleared the checkpoint at the border, the journey became a series of stops, ID checks, and tedium-producing delays. The train was repeatedly shunted onto sidetracks to allow higher priority troop carriers to pass. Shaw's ID, orders, and travel papers were checked and rechecked. Had he for one moment entertained the idea that Germany was not a police state, the thought soon vanished in the endless questions and examinations by control officers. By the time he reached Berlin in the early morning hours of November 8, Shaw had become short-tempered and curt to the point of rudeness. To his surprise, he discovered that such abrupt behavior was expected of an SS-Sturmbannführer.

The orders he carried with his other travel permits and identification papers directed him to number 23 Wilhemstrasse, a renovated hotel being used for transiting SS officers. When Shaw entered the building, his stomach was churning and his mind racing. He was back in Germany, but it was as if disparate elements of his being, long sequestered, had suddenly merged here in this hotel, in this place. It was not a mental state he would have wished for anyone. He was one person, and he knew he was alone.

After situating himself in a third-story room, Shaw was walking out the door when he was hailed from the desk.

"You are *Sturmbannführer* Schmidt?" the clerk inquired.

"Yes, I am Sturmbannführer Schmidt."

"A message for you, Sturmbannführer. Forgive me for not mentioning it earlier."

"No matter," Shaw replied. Opening the message, he read the contents carefully. He was instructed to meet a certain Hauptsturmführer Höss in front of the hotel on the morning of the eleventh. Upon receiving Shaw's orders, Höss would direct him to the correct mode of transportation for his trip to Peenemünde. Until then, Shaw was free to roam Berlin. Of course, he already had orders to attend the SS initiation ceremony on the following night.

Shaw still marveled at the efficiency shown in getting him into Germany. Someone had gone to a lot of trouble to make sure he made it to Berlin. Now all he had to do was remain alive to do what he'd been sent to do. Shaw had a feeling that would be more difficult than he had anticipated.

CHAPTER
11

The scene outside the Reich Chancellery building provoked a sense of dread and awe. Ten thousand Hitler youth, resplendent in their black-shirted SS uniforms, filled the square in the darkness. The only light came from the flickering flames of a thousand torches. Small glints of light reflected from the polished black helmets worn by the youth, ten thousand pinpricks of light in a sea of darkness. Red banners adorned with black swastikas ringed the assembly. The massive columns of the Chancellery building were backlit by the same torches, each standing twenty feet high and measuring five feet across. To Michael Shaw, they appeared as a thousand Olympic flames reaching into the night sky.

As he scanned the sea of young faces lit by the lurid sacramental flames, Shaw felt the increasing weight of responsibility settle onto his shoulders. He'd agreed to fight the SS, not out of some boyhood notion of good against evil, nor even a sense of duty, but from a motive of simple revenge. The SS, along with the German navy, had killed Barbara. He would kill them. It was that simple. It was not a grand motive, not even a complicated one, but it *was* a motive, and that was all he needed. He had to admit it had taken that visit from William Donovan to rekindle his hatred, but from that morning on, he had been more than willing, even eager, to enter Germany.

But as Shaw witnessed the surreal baptism of German youth into the Nazi cause, he suddenly knew he was out of his league. He'd overstepped his bounds; he'd entered a world of evil and darkness beyond anything he'd ever imagined. Shaw felt an involuntary shudder pass through him like an arctic wind blowing through his soul. Then, just as quickly, the chill was replaced by a strange warmth in the depths of his heart. He suddenly realized that he'd been wrong to turn his back on God when Barbara died. *In the face of such unspeakable evil, God is our only true refuge,* he said to himself.

Lord, he prayed, *forgive me for walking away from you in anger. Help me to do what must be done and to keep you in sight at all times.* Hot tears flowed freely down his cheeks. At first he was embarrassed, but when he looked around, he saw that others also had tears in their eyes. But those tears spilled out of a deep darkness—a depth of depravity Shaw could see and feel.

Loudspeakers perched high above the crowd boomed out the words of Heinrich Himmler as he commenced the surreal ceremony. Shaw felt the press of evil settle on the gathering like a great cloud of darkness rising from the earth to envelop all who drew near.

At the microphone, Himmler recited memorized questions. Ten thousand voices responded in unison, creating an eerie, unearthly rhythm.

Shaw knew that the questions and answers were a brainwashing technique designed by Himmler to eliminate the need for the novice Nazis to think on their own. Shaw felt the hair on his neck rise as he listened to the mesmerizing cadence of question and response.

The tone of Himmler's voice suddenly changed from cheerleading questioner to serious teacher as he began to speak of honor, fidelity, and German national pride.

Shaw felt an ever-increasing weight of horror settle over the black-thronged crowd. The flickering torch flames were having their intended hypnotic effect, coupled with the carefully orchestrated droning of the Reichsführer's voice. Shaw found himself reviewing the words of the oath of allegiance that each of these young men would recite on April 20, Hitler's birthday, when they became full-fledged members of the SS.

Ichs schwöre Dir, Adolf Hitler,
Als Führer und Kanzler des
Deutschen Reiches
Treue und Tapferkeit.
Ich gelobe Dir und den von
Dir bestimmten Vorgesetzten
Gehorsam bis in den Tod,
So wahr mir Gott helfe.

I swear to thee Adolf Hitler, as Leader and Chancellor of the German Reich, loyalty and bravery. I vow to thee, and to the superiors whom thou shalt appoint, obedience unto death, so help me God.
The phrases tumbled through Shaw's brain, a whirlwind of words and perceptions, spawned in hell and nurtured by evil. He'd memorized the words as part of his training, but they'd left a foul taste in his mouth even as he'd rehearsed them.

Out of the corner of his eye, Shaw noticed that the SS officer next to him was looking at him curiously. With a start he realized that he had been shaking his head with disgust at the words of the SS oath. Gathering his wits about him, Shaw turned to the officer and said, "Reichsführer Himmler is such a powerful speaker; he always moves my heart." The officer nodded, said something that Shaw couldn't hear, and turned his attention back to the ceremony.

Shaw breathed a sigh of relief and reminded himself that—however distasteful it might be—he must play the role of Sturmbannführer Schmidt without any further mistakes. Just then, the noise in the plaza rose to a thunderous crescendo as the ceremony came to its climax. Without hesitation, Shaw threw his right arm into the air and joined the chorus of roaring voices. *"Heil Hitler! Heil Hitler!"*

CHAPTER
12

november 10, 1942
kiel, germany

Harsh blue-white light lit the damp concrete walls of the cavernous submarine bays in the Deutsche Werke yard. Massive cranes loomed like gigantic birds of prey over the ships at the edges of the dry docks. Giant butyl rubber hoses, some more than six inches in diameter, carried compressed air, fuel, and water for the various shipyard operations. So many black rubber lines snaked across the docks that they presented a hazard to walking. Explosions of white light flashed as welders worked on the many ships and submarines. The noise was deafening. Air-powered hammers, saws, rivet guns, grinders, and paint rigs joined in a deafening chorus.

Submarine captain Günther Mohr stepped from the Number 8 streetcar from Kiel, grateful to be free of the strident, raucous chatter of the shipyard workers who rode the trolley. He had counted at least seven different languages in the short ride from his house to the Deutsche Werke yard, and he much preferred the metallic cacophony of the shipyard to the discordant clash of human voices.

As he strode purposefully through the gates, Mohr saw his U-boat engineer, lieutenant senior grade Otto Reinertsen, standing off to the side waiting for him. Reinertsen had overseen the work on U-135 for the past three months, and his vigilance had largely accounted for the progress to date. Captain Mohr, who had assumed command of U-135 in early October, had spent the bulk of his time since on the Balkan island of Usedom, at the German research center known as Peenemünde. What he had seen there had chilled his bones to the marrow.

Reinertsen saluted as Mohr approached, and Mohr self-consciously responded. Saluting was something that was not done on patrol, and submarine crew members, including the captains, sometimes overlooked the standard military protocol.

"LI," Mohr began, "How is the boat?"

"A fine boat, Herr Kaleu," Reinertsen answered, using the shortened form of Mohr's rank, "but some strange modifications. I'm curious about our next patrol."

Mohr nodded. He had been authorized to share information at his own discretion, and he had pondered how much to tell his trusted friend. He knew that the master engineer would sooner or later figure out the purpose of the framing and hydraulics being installed on their submarine.

"It is stranger than you can know, Otto," Mohr remarked as the two men walked across the shipyard. "How goes the work?"

"If you mean, how are we coming with the installation of the specified equipment, then all is well. If, on the other hand, you're asking what I think about the equipment being attached to our boat, then I have to say it is a particularly egregious task we perform."

Mohr laughed at his LI's astute assessment of the project. "Monstrous might be a better description, I think. That would encompass both the equipment and your sentiments."

Reinertsen covered his mouth and whispered in a conspiratorial tone behind his hand. "I think, Herr Kaleu, that this refit has something to do with the rumors we have been hearing lately. The crew has been listening to the shipyard gossip. Some of it is very interesting. And, as you no doubt are aware, we have a special crew of five men directing the work. They don't do any of the work, but they have their noses in every phase, as if we were building a delicate watch, not a frame for a submarine."

As they neared sub bay A-7, Mohr could see the tent-like covering used to maintain secrecy during the refit, as if secrecy were possible amid five thousand workers.

The U-135 was completely hidden beneath the dark fabric. Electric lights shone from beneath the pavilion, lending an air of secrecy and excitement to the proceedings. Arc welders flashed blue and white as the framing was attached to U-135.

Mohr and Reinertsen showed their identification badges and entered the highly restricted area near the submarine. To Mohr, it looked as if some gigantic hand had taken an oil derrick, miniaturized it, split it lengthwise, and affixed it to the aft portion of the sub.

The U-135 was a 1,120-ton type IXC boat. At emergency flank speed, she had a surface speed of slightly above eighteen knots, and a submerged speed of 7.3 knots. With all the scrap iron attached to the deck of the boat, however, Mohr calculated that he'd be lucky to get four knots submerged out of the boat.

Of course, Mohr reminded himself, submerged speed was not the most important factor. The boat would go down only in response to a clearly defined threat. He'd always thought that the U-boat should be called a submersible, rather than a submarine. The term *submarine* suggested a craft that could operate indefinitely underwater. A submersible, on the other hand, was simply a boat that could go down temporarily as needed—which Mohr believed better described what a U-boat did. Most skippers submerged only to fire torpedoes, then surfaced and used the deck gun to finish the job. Virtually all transit was accomplished on the surface. With a submerged endurance of about one hour at maximum speed, it made no sense to travel under the water when travel on the surface was possible.

Mohr and Reinertsen skirted the welding platforms rigged to the side of the sub, walked along the fringe of the dry dock, and tried to evaluate the contraption that was growing from the deck.

"It's something new, yes, Herr Kaleu?" Reinertsen asked.

"It is new, LI. New and deadly, if our leaders are to be believed."

Reinertsen glanced at his captain from the corner of his eye. Only a man of Mohr's reputation and ability would dare to question the logic or veracity of the German leadership. Mohr was one of the best U-boat captains in a group of perhaps a dozen or so superior officers. Even so, such talk was dangerous.

Born in the Baltic port of Danzig in 1910, Mohr had first commanded type II boats on coastal patrols, graduated to type VII boats during Operation Drumbeat, and had finally been assigned to U-135. He wore the Knight's Cross with Oak Leaves for his valiant efforts during the campaign in the Caribbean.

Reinertsen had sailed with Mohr since the early days, and he appreciated the captain's ability to retreat as well as attack. Mohr didn't take unnecessary chances, but when he moved in for the kill, he usually scored.

"How much longer do you think, LI?" Mohr asked as he circumnavigated the steel vessel.

"One, maybe two months, Herr Kaleu. Add two weeks for sea trials and you have maybe three months total. Three and a half if we run into problems."

Mohr stopped, rubbed his chin, and turned to Reinertsen. "Make that two months, LI. There will be no sea trials. In two months, we sail for Usedom Island."

Reinertsen's eyes were wide with disbelief. "Kapitänleutnant, that is impossible," he said in astonishment. "Without sea trials, we cannot be certain what will happen with the boat in this configuration. It would be foolhardy and possibly deadly to sail without trials."

"We can test the stability of the boat on the way to Usedom. Sea trials with only the framework aboard will be of little value, Otto," Mohr replied, using Reinertsen's first name in an effort to reassure the engineer. "There will be an addition to this spiderweb of steel we have here. It will be of more value to know the handling properties after we have taken on our cargo." Mohr crossed the wooden walkway leading to the deck of the U-boat, climbed the conning tower, and slipped down the open hatch.

Reinertsen watched his commander disappear into the bowels of the steel monster. His mind was reeling with what he'd just heard. Was it possible that the shipyard rumors were true? *God,* he thought, *let it not be so.*

CHAPTER

13

november, 1942
peenemünde, germany

The Polish work crew struggled with the crosscut saws and heavy, double-bladed axes. The pine trees that covered the eastern portion of Usedom Island offered little protection from the elements as the men cleared a corridor for the final approach of the road connecting Ahlbeck with Swinemünde, the easternmost village on the island. Though they were sturdy men—fishermen and laborers accustomed to the biting cold and blowing wind—and dressed in heavy clothing, with shirts and trousers of dense peasant fabric and tattered jackets in various stages of deterioration, the brutal, chilling wind limited their effectiveness.

The fishing village of Peenemünde lay almost thirty miles to the northwest, but not even the distance, the terrible weather, and the thick pine forest could muffle the strange noises that filtered down from the German research center. Today was no exception.

The first indication that something odd was again happening at Peenemünde were the vibrations that reached the Polish work party.

Walter Kolinsky had heard the sound before, but he stopped chopping nevertheless, leaving his axe in the tree, and listened to the bizarre sounds that floated out over the Baltic. The sound had an ethereal quality about it, like a group of angels descending on a beating of wings. The sound came and went, an alternating beat of intense, harsh sound followed by an exquisite quiet. The pulsing sound swept over the work party, causing some of the men to stop their tasks and look out to sea; but most had heard the sound before and didn't even slow their work pace.

Kolinsky had heard the sound many times before. At forty-six, he was the youngest member of the work party but the senior member of this particular group. He had managed to remain when others, many older, had been conscripted into the German Army or had forsaken the rugged island work to join the Polish Resistance. Kolinsky had been retained as the foreman of the work party because he had a reputation for getting the job done. The Pole knew he had a knack for getting the most out of the old men who made up the work crew, while watching over them carefully. He was not a man to sacrifice his own countrymen in the name of the Third Reich. There were no more young men to work the manual labor jobs of Usedom Island, and the Germans needed him.

Walter Kolinsky was also a member of the Polish Resistance, and if what he suspected was true, he knew he could do more to expel the Nazis from his native Poland by working on the island rather than on the mainland.

The sound suddenly ceased altogether, and Kolinsky checked his watch. Almost sixty seconds this time, he noted. Longer than the last time. It might be information worth setting up his tiny radio for. After work, he would transmit what he'd heard to a contact in German-occupied Denmark. The contact would see to it that the information made its way across the English Channel to a radio operator some-where northwest of London. Kolinsky had no idea who had the responsibility for collating the information he sent, but he hoped it was not all in vain.

He'd just returned to his chopping when another sound penetrated his thoughts. This was a new sound, a constant, piercing thunder that was not only audible to the work team, but palpable—almost like standing on the train tracks and waiting as a huge steam engine bore down on you. To Kolinsky, it meant that whatever was producing the noise was closer than the earlier, pulsating sound.

Kolinsky surveyed his work crew, noting that the new sound had drawn every man from his work and produced a look of bewilderment on most of their faces. For Kolinsky, it sounded as if the entire world was coming to a blundering, crashing, climactic end. He'd forgotten to look at his watch as was his custom whenever he heard a new sound emanating from the northeastern portion of the island. He did so now, estimating that he'd been thirty seconds tardy in noting the time. He'd add that thirty seconds to the duration of the sound he was now monitoring and transmit the information about the new sound along with that of the first.

The sound ceased, leaving in its wake a deathly stillness. Kolinsky checked the time. Almost five minutes. In those five minutes, the sound had climbed over the Baltic and almost disappeared. Certainly whatever was making the constant sound he'd just heard was not the same thing as what had produced the pulsating sound that had lasted only a minute.

Then, just as the men were going back to their chopping and sawing, a flash streaked into the sky in the east. Each man turned toward the sound yet again. The same thunderous wave of noise swept over them. This time they knew the origin, for it was rising from Usedom Island, just to the east of where they worked.

Walter Kolinsky would later recount his first impression of the object as it rose, slowly at first, then, after no more than five or six seconds, with the speed of a bullet. It looked like a white and black fence post from where the men stood. Kolinsky knew that they were perhaps ten, maybe fifteen miles from the object. That meant it was probably as large as some of the thirty- or forty-foot pine trees they were cutting.

Its black-and-white pattern—alternating boxes of black and white—made it clearly visible against the dark gray of the winter sky. After six seconds, it accelerated at an unbelievable rate, riding a tail of white-hot fire into the high clouds before disappearing into the Baltic.

The noise had been frightening, soul-wrenching. The twenty men of the work team stood as if paying homage to some great, mythological god, their eyes turned skyward, awed expressions plastered across unbelieving faces.

There was no doubt now, Kolinsky knew, that he'd identified one source of sound. It had just flown into the heavens, destination unknown. This evening's transmission would cause a stir, wherever it was received.

Walter Kolinsky, his eyes still glued to the trail taken by the rocket, wondered for the first time if the Germans had finally developed the ultimate weapon.

CHAPTER
14

There was little for Michael Shaw to do as the train droned steadily toward Wolgast, pushing its way through the forested countryside in northern Germany toward its destination near the Baltic Sea.

The 125-mile trek from Berlin to Wolgast, the terminal village before crossing the narrow strait to Usedom Island, had been accomplished with typical German efficiency. The towns of Eberswald, Angermünde, and Prenzlau, normally scheduled stops along the line, had been bypassed by the military-only train. And the journey had been both physical and spiritual. Shaw had no doubt now of the evil he was being sent to battle. The evidence was everywhere around him. Uniforms of the Wehrmacht, the Luftwaffe, the Kriegsmarine, and, perhaps the most diabolical of all, the Schutzstaffel—the SS—surrounded him. He had become more aware of his own vulnerability as he moved north, toward Peenemünde and the mystery that had presented itself through British Intelligence and the floating body of the

SS-clad British agent. He was less confident than he had been when he'd accepted the assignment. He had been—was—a journalist, a writer, and in the manner of many an MI-6 agent, a warrior. But his battle had been a war of intelligence and knowledge. This was different. But it was too late to think about it now.

Of the troops on the train, fewer than a dozen were SS. Except for an SS-Standartenführer occupying the next seat, Shaw was the senior SS man on the train. The colonel had been arrogantly extolling the virtues of the SS as compared to the rest of the German uniformed services. Shaw had been cordial in his agreement with the man.

The colonel was headed for Kiel and the submarine base there, and Shaw had feigned disinterest as the man talked about his assignment. It was, the colonel admitted surreptitiously, a secret assignment worthy only of the SS. His orders had come directly from Reichsführer Himmler himself with the admonition of silence.

"Yes," Shaw acknowledged. "The *Reichsführer* is correct in his pursuit of security. Silence is a weapon as surely as bombs, airplanes, and tanks," Shaw continued, making reference to the troops surrounding them. "It is up to those of us in the SS to be vigilant in carrying out his orders."

"I agree," the colonel answered. "That is why I cannot speak of the submarine which is, at this moment, being prepared for a special assignment as directed by Himmler himself."

Shaw felt a prickle along his spine. The SS colonel leaned closer; Shaw followed suit, moving toward the man, one superior human being to another.

"There is only one," the SS colonel whispered. "One U-boat with the capability of changing the war in the Atlantic. Dönitz has requested such a boat, such a weapon, and Kiel is to provide it, but with certain refinements, certain alterations, if you will. Alterations ordered by Himmler."

Shaw wondered if the colonel would be so brazen as to refer to Admiral Dönitz simply as Dönitz were the admiral himself present.

He doubted it. But the man was speaking of things better left unsaid, better relegated to the lips of others. A U-boat with a special capability.

Fascinating!

Frightening!

The colonel was proud, arrogant, and stupid. To speak of such things to another person, even another SS member, would not be acceptable in the corridors of SS power. On the contrary, it could mean sudden death. But Shaw needed to know certain things. Things the colonel had said that made no sense.

"Colonel. What you say is interesting. But you say you are headed for Kiel. Why on this train? This direction? Would it not be easier and quicker to go by way of Hamburg and then north?"

The colonel leaned closer, maintaining his posture of secrecy. "It would," he agreed. "But I have an assignment on the island of Usedom too." The Colonel's eyes darted around him quickly, scanning the faces of the other soldiers in the crowded coach. Satisfied, he continued. "There is a fishing village on the northern tip of the island. Peenemünde. It is no longer a fishing village, Sturmbannführer," the man said, obviously pleased with himself and his knowledge.

Shaw felt his stomach tighten, his mouth go dry.

"There is a connection between Peenemünde and Kiel. More than that," he said quietly, "there are two submarines in the pens at Lorient that have been prepared for an important mission. A mission that complements the mission of the U-boat at Kiel."

Shaw tried to control his racing pulse, his thoughts, his conjectures. This man knew much, perhaps even what Shaw had come to learn. How, Shaw marveled, had this colonel come by such information? Why had so obvious a fool been entrusted with such information? A thought intruded. Perhaps, Shaw realized, he knew why such a man was in such a position.

"Colonel," Shaw began, continuing the clandestine nature of the conversation, "you are very well-informed. You must have the ear of the Reichsführer himself." Shaw hoped the flattery would open up another avenue of information.

"I was a banker before the SS," the colonel said, confirming what Shaw thought. "One of only a handful of non-Jewish bankers. Our—the German people's—economic condition is due to the policies and practices of Jewish bankers. But you know that, of course."

"Of course," Shaw agreed, detesting the lie, realizing at the same time that he had correctly assessed the colonel's stature.

"After I was fired by my bosses, I joined the SS. I can truthfully say that the SS has been my salvation. I had enough money, money stolen from my Jewish bankers, to purchase a commission in the SS. Himmler was overjoyed to have the money and me," the colonel said proudly.

That was it! He should have known. The ignorant man had literally bought his way into the ranks of the SS. No matter that the man admitted to being a thief. No matter that he had proven he could not be trusted. No! What mattered was the money, funds which could be used by the SS to perpetuate the nightmare of the Death's Head.

It was not a new story to Shaw. He'd seen enough of it before departing post-WW I Germany. Men of wealth, men of power, anxious to maintain their status, had used their wealth and prestige to obtain commissions in Himmler's fledgling SS. Himmler and the National Socialists needed money, and the affluent needed coalitions. Never mind that true alliances were forged between men of conscience, not purchased as marketable commodities; they had paid into the coffers of the SS.

And in some cases, the result had been power placed in the hands of fatuous buffoons, men such as the SS colonel next to Shaw. A colonel talking about U-boats—one at Kiel, two at Lorient. And an island mystery on Peenemünde.

Were they connected? Did one augment the other? The obvious answer was yes. The foolish man had said as much.

The train was slowing, and the men on board began milling around, confusion painted on their faces. Shaw peered out the frosted window. A light snow was falling. The trip north had taken them into the colder reaches of northern Germany, into the forests. The pine trees were passing more slowly, the train halting.

But there was no terminal. No station. Not one that Shaw could see. No signs of civilization intruded on the landscape of evergreens and leafless hardwoods and desolate snow.

The soldiers, sailors, and airmen peered out the windows, wondering about the unauthorized stop. Shaw checked his watch. Twenty minutes before their scheduled arrival at Wolgast.

When it came, the attack was sudden and deadly!

The shots came in volleys, barrages of lead reaching the men aboard the train. The sound of machine guns penetrated the closed environment of the coach where Shaw rode. Splinters of damaged wood flew in large slivers across the coach, themselves almost as lethal as the bullets.

Men screamed.

Chaos reigned.

Death intruded!

The fatal salvos continued, ripping at the interior of the coaches, tearing at the bodies of the men trapped inside. Those soldiers not wounded in the first assault fumbled with the weapons they carried. All had been unloaded for the train ride. The only rifles capable of returning fire were carried by the outside guards, two per coach. Six coaches. Twelve guards. Seven of them had fallen in the initial onslaught. The others desperately returned fire in the direction of the unseen enemy.

The carnage continued, screams escalating, and amplified in the closed quarters. Bodies fell like matchsticks as the large caliber weapons continued to rake the coaches with unerring accuracy.

Shaw dove for the floor. He landed on a Hauptgefreiter of the Wehrmacht, the three half chevrons on the soldier's sleeve already disappearing in the blood that soaked his uniform. Shaw felt a sharp intake of breath.

The noise was deafening! Horrifying! The scene was from a nightmare, a grisly replay of all the horror Shaw had seen in 1939.

The glass from the windows was transformed into lethal shards, invisible knives flying through the air, propelled by bullets fired by unseen hands.

Shaw crawled toward the exit at the far end of the coach away from the barrage of bullets; he marveled that he was still alive. He noted a change of pitch in some of the firing. The lighter caliber rifles of the few remaining guards made a distinctly higher pitch than the heavy caliber machine guns roaring from the forest.

Shaw hugged the floor as he made his way to the door. The train remained stationary.

Why was the engineer not moving?

Dead, perhaps. Or part of the ambush. Either option made sense, either equally fatal. For whatever the reason, the train remained locked in place, a static killing ground, a death trap.

Shaw could no longer hear the high pitch of the Wehrmacht rifles. The return fire had been silenced. The men who carried such rifles had died in a hail of steel-jacketed bullets, Shaw knew.

He reached the door at the end of the coach. The dead lay everywhere. Shaw was covered in blood.

The gunfire now sounded as if it was coming from further down the tracks, toward the engine.

Shaw grasped the door handle and opened the door. Moving onto the landing, still crouched, still vigilant, he looked first to the east, trying to locate the source of the assault.

He allowed himself a short smile. Efficiency. That is what had caused the death of the train. German efficiency. The train had run on time. It had been at this spot exactly on schedule. And the men behind the machine guns had used that efficiency against the Germans.

The staccato bark of the machine guns began again. Shaw realized they had been reloading. He scrambled from the landing, his feet slipping in the newly fallen snow as he landed; he hit the ground hard, rolling involuntarily, out of control.

The machine guns continued their deadly onslaught; the coaches were destroyed, the men within mangled. Others had escaped and were fleeing the killing ground, seeking shelter in the nearby forest.

Shaw bolted for the tree line, seeking the refuge of the solid hardwood trunks. A stray bullet kicked up the snow beside him as he ran. He reached the tree line and scurried behind the first large tree he came to, throwing himself prone on the ground.

He'd escaped the destruction, the death. Why? Others had tried and failed. Some—he could see them deeper in the forest—had escaped as he had. He, along with others, had made it, while still others lay dead or dying on the floor of the passenger car.

Voices.

Shouts.

Commands!

They were coming. The men behind the guns were finished; their deed completed. Death had been doled out in a wholesale manner. Shaw could hear the animated chatter of the killers.

Shaw realized he was thinking of the men who had perpetrated this deed as the enemy. In all likelihood, they were allies, friends.

But he could not take a chance. He would have to remain in character. He was SS. It had not occurred to him that as an SS member he might die in Germany at the hands of the very people he had come to save. And then he realized he was here to assuage his own feelings, seek his own revenge.

The voices were louder now. The gunfire had ceased, leaving behind it a stillness, a quiet so profound that Shaw could hear his heart beating beneath the uniform tunic he wore.

"Check the cars," a voice ordered.

Shaw realized the man was speaking Polish.

The Polish Resistance.

Partisans!

Boots crunched in the snow only yards from where he lay; they moved deliberately, purposefully. Shaw moved farther behind the tree, seeking its protection like a child behind its father's legs.

"They are dead. All dead!" a partisan on the far side of the train yelled. "Those that did not run like scared chickens," he added humorously.

"Be certain," another voice instructed. It was the voice of authority. "Do not let any of the vermin live."

A new sound filled the cold air, softly at first, then louder, more defined as it drew nearer, coming from the direction of the next village.

Vehicles!

Vehicles with troops!

"A patrol! From Wolgast!" a partisan screamed.

Shaw listened to the scramble of men as they sought traction in the snow. The partisans were escaping, running for their lives, their killing done for the day.

The sound of the patrol grew louder as it approached the carnage of the train. Several vehicles braked to a halt short of the train's engine. German soldiers scrambled from the cars, weapons at the ready.

"We have done our work this day," the bass voice said, almost as an aside, the man still close to where Shaw lay.

Shaw peered from behind the tree. The man was examining the outside of the coaches as if there were no approaching patrol, no racing cars of certain death. Shaw guessed his age to be in the mid-forties. It was hard to tell through the rough clothing of a peasant laborer. The man turned one last time before fleeing, and Shaw saw his face. But for the scar that marred the left side of the man's cheek, he was handsome, of rugged Polish ancestry. Then the man was gone, running with the rest as the German patrol closed on the killers.

Shaw emerged from behind the tree as the first of three tracked troop carriers pulled to a stop. The carriers had flanked the train, approaching from the forest. Gray uniformed Wehrmacht soldiers spilled from the carriers, rifles ready, not realizing the magnitude of the slaughter they would find.

A Wehrmacht Oberleutnant commanding the patrol saw Shaw. He approached, fear clearly showing in his eyes.

Was it the uniform he wore or his failure to save the train, Shaw wondered, that produced such a look of terror on the young officer's face. Probably both.

"Herr Sturmbannführer," the Oberleutnant fumbled for words. "What has happened here?"

"Ambush, Oberleutnant. That much should be clear. Check the coaches for any living. There are others in the forest. Help them. I'm afraid the men who did this were ruthlessly efficient. As if they knew this particular train would be at this particular spot at this particular time."

The Oberleutnant swallowed hard. Shaw's statement had sounded like an accusation. The train's security was the Oberleutnant's responsibility; he had failed. Recriminations would be swift and final.

Shaw toned down his accusatory tone. "Help those you can, *Oberleutnant.* You could not have known this would happen."

The Wehrmacht officer nodded and scurried away to direct his troops. Shaw moved to the entrance of the coach in which he'd been riding. He entered the same door he'd escaped through and was met with a slaughter of unbelievable proportions. He stepped over and around bodies of men he now recognized, moving toward his seat.

The side of the coach next to the seat where Shaw had been sitting with the SS colonel was pockmarked with large caliber bullet holes. The colonel was slumped to one side, his body blown toward the aisle. Shaw could see several large wounds that still oozed blood. The SS officer had taken the first volley full force from the side, saving Shaw's life in the process. The bullets that killed the man would have surely killed Shaw had the man not been seated next to the window.

Blood was everywhere. Wehrmacht soldiers from the patrol were scouring each coach, pulling those who were still living from beneath the dead. Corpses were carried outside to be identified. Gray, black, and blue uniforms dotted the snowbank just below where the machine guns had performed their bloody task.

Shaw noticed the Wehrmacht Oberleutnant stumble from the growing phalanx of dead and fall to his knees at the edge of the forest. He vomited.

Even the Nazis have their limits, Shaw thought. Then he remembered the reports of torture and torment that had come from concentration camps, and Shaw felt no sympathy for the young officer.

Shaw tugged and pulled at the body of the SS colonel until he had the body on the floor. His bag was beneath the seat and Shaw retrieved it just as a soldier removed the colonel's body.

"Is that his, Herr Sturmbannführer?" the soldier asked respectfully.

"Mine," Shaw answered. "That is his," Shaw said, pointing to another, almost identical bag.

"Perhaps I might have it. To aid in identification, sir. Unless you know his name."

"No . . . no I don't know his name. We'd just met on this train."

"The bag, then, Herr Sturmbannführer. This is a horrible day."

Shaw passed the bag to the soldier, wondering as he did so what kind of person talked to another for hours without ever knowing his name.

Shaw shook himself from his abstract musings, forcing his mind back to the world before him. He looked around the coach; most of the bodies were gone. He could hear the moaning and cries of the wounded. Shaw examined the bag; there was one neat, clean hole in its side. One bullet out of thousands had found the bag. It could have been worse, he thought.

Shaw opened the bag and checked the contents. The clothes were unimportant; they could be replaced. He dug through the bag until he came upon another, smaller bag. This bag held a shoe brush, polish, and assorted toiletries. Shaw pulled the shoe brush from the smaller bag. A splinter from its wooden handle dug deep into his flesh. He turned the brush over. The single bullet had pierced the wooden handle, destroying its utility. But that was not all.

A small object, its function destroyed by the impact of the heavy round, gleamed from the interior of the wooden handle. Shaw knew instantly that the radio components he had smuggled into Germany via the shoe brush were now useless. He would have to find another avenue to contact British Intelligence.

He'd made it to the right place at the right time. The conversation with the SS colonel, although obtuse, confirmed in his mind that something was happening. Something fearful, dreadful.

And Michael Shaw could tell no one.

CHAPTER
15

november 10, 1942
buckinghamshire, england

Malcolm Stanley had only one job as he sat in Hut 8 at Bletchley Park: intercept the daily key coming from B-Dienst, the radio intelligence service of the Kriegsmarine—the German Navy. Upon intercepting the daily transmission, Stanley fed the six-letter *bombe*—the coded text—and a probable clear text, into the proto-computers housed in Hut 8. The machines tested millions of possible permutations against the clear text, deciphering the daily key in as little as ten to twelve minutes.

With the daily key deciphered, it was entered into the German Navy's version of the Enigma, Germany's secret code machine. Unlike the Wehrmacht version, the Kriegsmarine version used six rotating drums instead of five, giving the navy version several million more permutations for every character.

Early on, it had become clear that the only way to decode the German Navy's transmissions successfully would be to acquire an actual Enigma. Bletchley Park already had a Wehrmacht version, but it was useless for decoding Kriegsmarine messages.

When the U-109 was captured in May 1941, the Enigma used by the U-boat radio operator had also been captured. Since then, the existence of the navy Enigma had been one of the most closely guarded secrets in British Intelligence circles.

A total of five people knew the machine existed. Malcolm Stanley was the lowest ranking man to be blessed—or cursed—with this knowledge. After all, he and two others were the ones actually receiving the daily key and doing the work to decode it, entering it into the Enigma and decoding the daily radio traffic of the German Navy.

Stanley had no doubt that others suspected the existence of the machine. It was only logical, given the accuracy of the data being sent to the British Navy's Submarine Tracking Room, allowing them to reroute convoys away from and around German wolf packs stalking the North Atlantic.

Stanley typed the coded daily key into the proto-computer and switched on the machine. The noise was almost unbearable as thousands of mechanical relays, switches, and contacts set about to break the daily code that would render the German Navy's Enigma impotent for yet another twenty-four hour period.

As the machine whirled and clanked and whined, Stanley poured himself a cup of steaming tea from the small ceramic pot his mother had given him years ago. It was one of the pleasures he allowed himself while on duty; the tea calmed his nerves and made him, at least in his own eyes, more productive as a cryptologist. Otherwise, life at Station X was little more than a grind.

With his tea poured and the permutations flowing through the system that would shortly spit out the decoded daily key, Stanley pushed away from his desk and rubbed his eyes. His watch was nearing its end. He would be able to crawl into his clean bed in the village of Buckingham and snooze away the next twelve hours. There was nothing the whirling machine next to him could do to stop that.

He thought.

The deciphered daily key came up almost instantly.

Never happened that bloody fast, Stanley thought, as he wrote the key onto his pad and entered it into the Enigma's six character key window. Each of the six characters acted as a further decoding key for the Enigma for the day. The Enigma was ready once again to reveal the inner secrets of the German Navy.

Almost as quickly as the key had come up, the radio began to receive the first of hundreds of messages the Kriegsmarine would transmit on this day. It was just luck—later on, Stanley would say it was God's will—that the first message was actually received by Stanley himself. With as many as forty radio operators assigned to Kriegsmarine radio traffic in Hut 8, it could have been as long as a couple of hours before the incoming message would have been entered into the Enigma.

Such was not the case on this day.

Stanley wrote the characters on a pad as he received them. When he was finished, the coded message looked like a jumble of German letters, arranged in word blocks with no meaning.

Stanley entered the coded words into the Enigma, much like typing a normal message; almost immediately the message began to appear.

```
Date: November 13, 1942
From: Joint Command BdU and SS
To: Commanding Officers, U-3009 and U-3021
Subject: Initiation of Omega
Begin immediate operations in accordance with
directives issued concerning Operation Omega.
Stop.
```

Stanley stared at the message for a moment before pulling his Auxiliary Directives book from the shelf. He opened the thin volume, found the numbered directive, and read it.

Dir. 6-7.43. "Omega" radio messages—Special distribution. All radio messages keyed with code name "Omega" ARE NOT FOR NORMAL DISTRIBUTION. Upon receipt of such messages, the number at the bottom is to be called within ten minutes, the contents of the message read verbatim, and the physical message destroyed in accordance with BI Directive 1254.3. Failure to follow these directions will result in disciplinary actions against the radio operator, the cryptologist, and supervisor as a military court martial may direct.

Stanley stared awestruck at the directive. When he recovered, he picked up the phone, dialed the number at the bottom of the directive, and waited. The phone rang only once before being answered on the other end. The cryptologist could hear the whirring and clicking that indicated a secure phone.

"Directives Desk," the voice said.

Stanley was not certain what to do. He'd been briefed on the possibility of the Omega messages, but he'd never considered that he'd ever receive one.

As a military court martial may direct.

The words stuck in his mind. "Omega message," Stanley said.

"One moment," the voice replied mechanically, then, "go ahead with the Omega message."

Stanley read the message exactly as the Enigma had decoded it. His palms were sweating despite the cold air that blew in and around the poorly lapped outer siding on Hut 8.

As a military court martial may direct.

"Bloody wonder," Stanley muttered as he waited for a further response from the Directives Desk. And that was another thing—*what is the Directives Desk?* He'd never heard of it. He made a note to ask his supervisor, one of the three cryptologists who knew the German Navy Enigma existed.

As a military court martial may direct.

Maybe he wouldn't ask.

"Your message is received. Your authorization to destroy your copy is Oscar–23." With that the connection was broken.

Stanley stared for a moment at the authorization—Oscar-23. Oscar . . . Oscar . . . O is for Oscar, O is for Oscar . . . O is for Omega.

O is for Omega!

Stanley felt his breath suspended; his head whirled in a gray mist. He lifted the cup of tea he'd not finished earlier and sipped the lukewarm liquid. Someday, he knew, this would be a story to tell his grandchildren. He touched a match to the paper and watched the coded message turn to ash before his eyes. He recorded the incident in the daily log, finished the tea, and glanced at the clock on the wall. Seven more minutes and he could head for his flat.

The man behind the voice who had received the Omega transmit made a notation on the face of the document that now represented the only copy of the message in existence. He opened a file folder and placed the numbered message in its proper place, in order, and shook his head. He would not want this responsibility hanging over him. He was thankful that burden lay on the shoulders of another.

CHAPTER
16

november 11, 1942
peenemünde, germany

Michael Shaw leaned back in the chair, a gesture of futility and weariness, the memories of blood and death still fresh. He could still smell the sticky odor of the spilled blood which had flowed over and through the floorboards of the train coach, staining the ground below—the stench of death.

Death, on the scale he'd witnessed, had been one of his desires for the people who'd killed Barbara. Merciful death was too good, too quick, too humane. He'd wanted revenge.

Retribution.

Vengeance is mine . . .

". . . and I'm your instrument," Shaw had said, as he recalled the Bible verse.

But death on the scale he had witnessed was unacceptable. It had been a massacre. The screams and moans of dying men still echoed in his ears; the smells still assaulted his nostrils; the *feeling* of death clung to him like a cloying perfume. He had not realized it until it was over, but he'd formed a bond with the men on the train. It seemed impossible, but the bond was there. At one point when he'd been fleeing the killing ground, he'd been calculating how he might save others. They had been soldiers—boys really—and they were the enemy, but he'd still felt a sense of loss at their death.

Shaw shifted in the chair, seeking comfort, a comfort that would not come. He'd remained at the massacre site long into the night as the Wehrmacht soldiers methodically cleared each coach of the dead and dying and administered medical treatment to the wounded.

Contrary to the Polish partisan's declaration that all the vermin were dead, more men had lived through the hail of high-caliber death than had died. Most, once free of the death coaches, had wandered around in shock; they'd seen battle for the first time from the interior of the train, and it was not the glorious victory promised by their Führer. Disillusionment had followed in the footsteps of defeat.

But that had been last night. Now Shaw sat in the office of SS-Oberstgruppenführer von Liebeman, the SS control officer on Usedom Island and the installation known to Shaw as Peenemünde. Von Liebeman's adjutant, Oberführer Diels, casually flipped through the folders Shaw had delivered upon his belated arrival at Peenemünde. Security had been impressive, bordering on oppressive, the SS and Wehrmacht guards almost gleeful in following their procedures. With the in-processing finished, Shaw had been assigned a temporary billet in the officers' barracks. But sleep had been elusive.

With the morning, he'd reported to von Liebeman's office, and now he watched the lean-faced Diels as he perused the documents. Shaw wondered if the documentation, most of it forged, would stand the Oberführer's scrutiny. Then he dismissed the thought. He'd examined the papers himself, comparing them to some he'd taken out of Germany on his leaving; it was impossible to tell the difference between the authentic and forged. Nevertheless, Shaw felt his pulse begin to race as Diels continued to examine the papers.

Shaw noticed Diels's furtive glance in his direction; Shaw remained erect in the chair, at seated attention.

"Impressive, Sturmbannführer," Diels said, not looking up.

"Thank you, Oberführer," Shaw responded.

"You have given all the information about last night's attack to the interrogation squad?"

"Yes sir, Oberführer," Shaw snapped back in what he hoped was typical German succinctness.

"Very well. Nasty business, last night. When we catch the partisans who did this, they will wish they had never been the sons of Polish women."

Shaw wondered how the man knew the attack had been carried out by Poles, but it wasn't important at the moment. It occurred to Shaw that he'd also failed to mention that the apparent leader of the partisans had a scar down the side of his face. But those men of death last night had been allies, men fighting Nazi tyranny as he was, and even if he'd experienced a fleeting pang of sympathy for those soldiers last night, it was gone this morning. He would not give up those partisans, even if he knew every name and every face.

"You will be assigned to the security division at the motor shop, Sturmbannführer. The work goes well there, but it is not quite where it should be," Diels said, closing the packet of information Shaw had given him. "Von Liebeman and I suspect sabotage." Diels leaned back in his chair, his arms behind his head. "The motors being developed there should have been finished months ago. They should be on the test stands this very minute. We have been thwarted at every turn. It will be your job to see that no one interferes with the progress in that shop. Also to ferret out any saboteurs, malingerers, and Jews that are aiding in the slowdown that is taking place there."

"If I may, Oberführer," Shaw began. "Is it permissible to ask the nature of the work going on in the shop? It seems to me that it would be to my advantage to understand what it is I'm looking for."

Diels leaned forward and eyed Shaw through narrowing lids. "You are telling me that you have been sent here and have not been briefed on the work that goes on here?"

"Yes, sir, I am," Shaw replied, a trickle of nervousness tickling his throat. Had something been overlooked? A missing bit of vital information he should have had?

"Good! Very good, Sturmbannführer! You were to be told nothing. Those were the orders. Every man here on this installation is here for the duration of the project. Himmler's orders. After the task is completed, we will be reassigned, but for now, we remain here as the eyes and ears of the Riechsführer."

"And the Führer," Shaw included.

"Of course, and the Führer. That goes without saying. But you should know that our orders come from Himmler. For the SS man, his word is law. And his word comes from the Führer."

"I understand," Shaw said. He could feel the hate building in him as Diels spoke of the SS as if it were the living church of God.

"As to what goes on here at Peenemünde, that is a difficult question to answer. I will answer it in general terms first, and then as it pertains to the SS." Diels rose from his chair, his hands clasped behind his back. Shaw knew the ploy, the superior teaching the inferior; the master to the student.

"Peenemünde is a research and development facility," Diels began. "What the Reich does here is invent weapons never before dreamed of in this world. Rockets, in a word. Flying bombs capable of raining untold destruction on distant targets. The proof of German superiority, a superiority that will be proved to the world on foreign shores."

"England," Shaw supplied in a whisper.

"England . . . and others," Diels said after a short hesitation. "Germans, true Germans, are the most advanced people on the face of the earth. We are destined to rule the lands. I say lands, because I include the areas we now own, France, the lowlands, the Scandinavian countries, and those to the east. Russia will very soon fall under our influence. Soon we will be embarking on even greater acquisitions. Greater endeavors. These weapons we build today will bring us the lands of tomorrow. They are simply the verification that God is on our side."

Of all the things Shaw had heard about and knew of the SS, God had certainly never played a pivotal role in their beliefs. But here stood an SS-Oberführer declaring the support of God to be on the side of the Nazis. It was an ironic—and perverted—twist on faith, Shaw marveled.

"As to the specifics of your position, Sturmbannführer, you will be the man in charge of seeing that the new motor for a completely new class of weapon is developed and finished within the next few weeks. The rudiments of the project have been completed. It remains but for you to ensure that the work is done without outside interference. Interference from groups bent on detaining, delaying, or completely halting the work. You will have full authority to use whatever measures necessary to complete your task."

Shaw absorbed the information, then asked, "What type of weapon are we talking about here, sir? I am not a propulsion engineer. I need to know what I'm looking for."

Diels walked back around his desk and returned to his seat. "The project is ultra-secure. The motor construction for which you are to provide security is the motor that will power a new form of rocket. The designation has already been made. It is to be the V-5. There are already two major rocket projects underway at this time. The V-1 and the V-2 are in the works. The V-1 will soon be ready for testing. The V-2 is much more sophisticated, more complex. The V-5 is a smaller version of the V-2. We have already launched a number of the V-5s using older, modified motors. But for our purposes, a much more powerful, specially designed motor will be needed. One which will withstand sea air and saltwater."

"To be carried onboard ships?" Shaw quizzed, his curiosity stimulated.

The Oberführer returned to his chair and pushed back in his chair, his hands once again behind his head, a smile of satisfaction splayed across his face.

"No, Sturmbannführer. Not to be carried on ships. To be launched from U-boats!"

Shaw controlled the sharp intake of breath he felt at the mention of the U-boat-launched weapon system. Such a weapon would bring devastation and havoc to coastal towns and cities. Supply line disruptions would be possible inland up to the limits of the rocket's range. Flying bombs for which no countermeasures existed or could exist.

Supersonic death carried on the winds of German genius.

"I see you are surprised. Do not be. We are Germans. What we can dream, we can build. This is a new concept, to be sure, but one that BdU Dönitz is anxious to have as soon as possible."

"Admiral Dönitz? U-boats?"

"The project initially was his idea. He was interested in interdiction of Soviet supply lines in the Baltic States. It was not possible to have the weapons in time for that purpose, but Dönitz has determined a better, much more sophisticated use for the system. He plans to launch them against the United States."

Shaw's mind raced! It was obscene! *Insane!*

What was to be gained by attacking the U.S. lands that could be reached by a U-boat rocket? Why risk the civilian casualties that were bound to result? If the idea had come from Hitler or Himmler, then he could understand better, but coming from Dönitz, it made no sense.

"Please pardon the curiosity, Oberführer. I realize that I am not a strategic thinker in this matter, but it seems counterproductive to attack the U.S. in this manner. What is it that Admiral Dönitz expects to achieve from such a mission?"

Diels smiled condescendingly. "No, you are not much of a strategic thinker, Sturmbannführer. But I will explain the problem as it was explained to me by the admiral." Diels repositioned himself behind his desk, moving closer to the desk and resting his elbows on the glowing wood surface.

"Last year, Operation Drumbeat fought the Americans in their own backyard. Dönitz's U-boats sank thousands of tons of shipping within sight of shore. The U.S. chose not to protect those ships close to shore. It was a slaughter. Not unlike last night on the train, you might say." Diels rose again, and poured himself a drink from the makeshift bar against the back wall. He ignored Shaw. Shaw was thankful.

"The Americans have learned some things in the interim. They are now protecting single ships within sight of their coast. They are becoming very adept at routing and convoy maintenance. The American and British destroyers provide shielding for the convoys. The British have updated their ASDIC. The self-defense capabilities of the merchant marines and the navies have temporarily halted our interdiction attempts on the open seas. Whole convoys escape without damage. All because the Americans are learning how to wage war."

Diels paused for a moment; Shaw watched the man move about the room.

"Admiral Dönitz believes the Kriegsmarine can hamper the American ability to escort convoys by attacking the U.S. coastal cities and military bases. It would force the Americans to assign more ship-ping to protect the bases and the people. There would be an outcry from the populace for protection on the home front. It is happening in California. The Japanese have seen to that. Ships would have to be pulled from convoy duties. Men and matériel would be ordered to pro-tect the U.S. coast. Convoys would go unprotected, allowing our other U-boats to again gain the upper hand in the Atlantic."

Shaw was sweating now, despite the coolness of the office and the light snow that was once again falling and blowing against the office window.

It made sense! Heaven forbid! It made perfect sense!

"With this new weapon, a single wolf pack of five U-boats will be able to effectively neutralize the abilities of hundreds of ships. Escorts, destroyers, subchasers, all would be reassigned. Dönitz has called it the ultimate deception. With these rockets, the U-boats will attack up and down the east coast. The Americans will know the war has come to them from three thousand miles away. They will demand protection! Security will be uppermost in every mind! Chaos will reign!"

Shaw's head swam. His eyes, once focused intently on Diels, now drifted to the ceiling, his concentration destroyed, his mind in turmoil.

Was it possible? The answer was "yes"!

Unthinkable!

"And I'm to be in charge of getting the motor ready for the system?"

"You have that privilege, Sturmbannführer. See that it is done. We do not have much time."

Time!

That was it! A time constraint existed! If he could delay the development further, then he'd have time to establish another communication link with Bletchley Park and relay the information.

". . . is Kurt Daluege."

"Excuse me?" Shaw said, realizing he'd missed some of the briefing.

"I said, Sturmbannführer, that the man in charge of the development process is a scientist named Kurt Daluege in the motor development section. You will be the SS representative. Daluege is the civilian in charge. You will need to work closely, but not too closely, if you know what I mean."

"I'm not sure I do, Oberführer."

"We are SS. We are the rulers. Remember that. You have ultimate authority in the motor development section. I stress the ultimate when I say this. Do you understand that?"

"Sir, yes sir," Shaw answered. He'd just been given permission to eliminate anyone or anything that stood in the way of the motor development. The same fate could await him should he fail. And failure was not acceptable. He would see Germany and the SS reduced to ashes in an attempt to avenge his wife's death. For that, he'd have to remain alive.

"I understand completely, sir," Shaw affirmed, rising to leave.

"One more thing you should know, Sturmbannführer. This rocket will be built. It will be mounted on a submarine and sailed to the east coast of the United States. What even the men of Peenemünde do not know is that the warhead will not be the conventional ton of high explosive. It will be, in the words of the SS-Riechsführer, 'more deadly to the people of the U.S. than the death camps are to the Jews.' It will be something to see, I assure you."

Shaw felt as if a horse had kicked him in the stomach. The pain radiated out and into his limbs. His breathing was short, his arms heavy. He wondered for a moment if the effects were obvious to Diels. He moved toward the door and away from the terrible revelation he'd just heard.

He knew he now had another assignment.

What was the warhead to be? What was so deadly, so obscene as to be compared with the death of thousands. What kind of mind propagated such madness?

CHAPTER

17

Located on the east bank of the Rhine River, the colossal manufacturing complex of I. G. Farben Industrie gave no outward indication of the horror produced within its walls.

Leverkusen, nestled between Bonn to the south and Dusseldorf to the north, was actually a suburb of Cologne. The population, accustomed to the smells and odors of the industrialized Ruhr region, went about their labors in the shadow of the great factory—if not in ignorance, at least in apathy.

The valley to the west was flat, rising as it progressed eastward across the Rhine. Through the huge, metal-framed windows of I. G. Farben, Reinhard Gluecks watched the Rhine flow past the manufacturing giant's headquarters. Gluecks, an athlete in his own right, wistfully envisioned himself rowing the river—single sculls were his choice. Then, as if the notion were a sin against the SS, he banished the passing fancy and turned to the task at hand.

"The demonstration went well, I trust?" one white-clad scientist said, uncomfortable with Gluecks's silence.

"It went very well," Gluecks answered succinctly, his gaze still upon the flowing waters of the Rhine.

"It is everything I indicated to the Reichsführer?" the man continued.

Reinhard Gluecks turned his classic nordic features from the river view and trained his ice-blue eyes on the scientist.

The white-coated man felt an involuntary tremor streak through his body as the cold eyes of the SS man fell on him.

After a momentary silence, Gluecks said, his cruel smile a delicate slash across his face as he spoke, "It is as you said. The Reichsführer will be well pleased. Well pleased, indeed."

The scientist released the breath he'd been holding.

"When can the . . . product be ready?" Gluecks asked, hesitating as his mind raced to define what it was he was talking about. The truth was, there really was no adequate description.

"It takes very little time to conform the . . . product to the necessary configuration," the scientist explained. "We can have it ready within twenty-four hours of your notification. Will that be sufficient?"

Gluecks smiled again, this time expansively, putting the scientist at ease. "That will be more than sufficient. I will report to Reichsführer Himmler that you have done all that he has asked, and more. It is a shame that it is all so secret at the moment. I have no doubt that he, and probably the Führer himself, would like to reward you for your loyalty to the Third Reich."

The scientist smiled, relaxing. It had been a long and dangerous undertaking. The product was finished, perfected for the use for which it was intended. Men had died in the process. Cruel, ugly deaths that haunted the scientist, thrusting their terrible realities into his sleeping nights and waking moments.

But it was over now. Terminated. All that was left was the application of the theory. The practical. The practicum. There could be no doubt as to that application, but the scientist justified himself under the mantle of scientific achievement. He was the theorist. Others were the strategists—those for whom application was everything. And if application far exceeded the standard morality of mankind, who was he to argue? In Germany these days, there was little that was either standard or moral.

"Thank you for those words. They are most appreciated. It has been a ghastly business, this. I will be glad when I can ship the containers away from here. I have had second thoughts about this facet. I'm still not convinced it is for the best. But it is for the Fatherland. That is enough."

"As it should be," Gluecks acknowledged, listening not only to the words of the scientist, but the tenor of his voice, the tone of his convictions. "This is, of course, to remain classified at the highest level possible. Only you, your workers, Reichsführer Himmler, myself, and of course, the Führer, know of its existence," Gluecks admitted, knowing full well that Adolf Hitler knew nothing of the plan, and feeling no guilt at the lie. "It is imperative that it remain so for the next few months. The Reich will see that you receive your just reward. You can be proud of what you have accomplished here," Gluecks finished, then uncharacteristically slapped the scientist on the back.

The scientist felt pride welling within him, a surge of nationalism that outstripped the clinging guilt he felt at having invented the horror resting before him.

"I must go," Gluecks said. "We will be in touch with you shortly," he told the scientist. *And,* Gluecks thought wryly, *you will receive your reward. The same fate that awaits every participant in this nightmare.*

CHAPTER

18

Sunlight streamed into the elongated room through the multi-paned windows lining the rocket engine research and development center. It was the first natural light to penetrate the oppressive cloud cover of Usedom Island in the two weeks since Michael Shaw had set foot on the spit of land in the Baltic.

He was still amazed at how easily he had penetrated the ultra-secret rocket base. The papers he'd been furnished, he decided, were not forgeries, not in the real sense of the word. The papers had come from Berlin, from SS headquarters, just as any other SS officer's had. They were only forgery in the sense of the name printed on the papers, for the man known as Schmidt here on Usedom Island did not exist. Shaw warned himself repeatedly to avoid becoming complacent.

Woe to them that are at ease in Zion.

Shaw had been familiarizing himself with the motor shop in particular and the rest of the huge installation as he had opportunity. The installation was huge, and two weeks had only provided a limited time to explore. But he had discovered most of what was going on here at Peenemünde, and it terrified him. It was an installation dedicated to the mass destruction of people, any people. Civilian, military, it made no difference.

Shaw snapped out of his ruminations and concentrated on his current situation.

The rocket engine research center was a narrow hallway-like structure; workbenches stood in the center of the room, various pieces of rocket motors cluttering the benches. Fully and partially assembled motors lined the far wall, their ducts and tubes appearing like metal intestines. With their massive framework and upright stance, the motors were almost four meters tall, reaching one-third the distance to the ceiling. High above on the opposite wall, a catwalk stretched the length of the building, offering a vantage point for the officials who were curious and held the necessary clearance. There were not many.

Straddling the room from one side to the other, another catwalk, complete with heavy-duty block and tackle to facilitate moving the motors, sat on steel "I" beam runners. The walk could traverse the entire distance of the research center on steel tracks. Green metal-shaded incandescent bulbs cast a slightly yellow glow over the room during cloudy and nighttime hours. But today, with the first glimpse of sunshine in two weeks, Michael Shaw knew there would be no need for the exposed lighting.

Two weeks!

It seemed more like a year. Fifteen days had passed since he'd met Kurt Daluege, the civilian in charge of the rocket engine center—the motor shop, as it was called by the workers.

Then, as he'd shaken hands with the sharp-eyed Daluege, Shaw had had a feeling, a sensation, about the man. It had been in his eyes, in the hate Shaw could see flowing from them in waves as the man stared at the black uniform and the silver death's head on Shaw's cap.

Shaw made a mental note to switch back to the field gray tunic. It seemed less intimidating to those outside the SS.

An ally. A friend, Shaw thought, though he was not sure why the thought occurred to him. Maybe the slowdown in the motor shop was not due to outside interference but to a master plan conceived and executed within the very pinnacle of the research center's brain trust. Perhaps Daluege was the source of the backlog.

Shaw had watched, waited, examining the shop, the motors, the research. Above all, he kept an eye on Kurt Daluege.

It had taken the full two weeks for Shaw to be certain, but he was convinced. There had been no overt tampering, no obvious malfeasance, only the assurance that Daluege was not what the Nazis thought him to be.

Shaw had been impressed with the man's intelligence, awed at the sight of the rocket motor Daluege was developing, frightened by the prospects of its use. He'd never considered the possibility that such a thing could exist.

Daluege had explained the theory patiently, demonstrating the various sections of the motor, explaining problems. In all of it, Shaw could sense the pride with which the man worked. He was convinced Daluege could produce a motor just like the one needed for the job at hand. Whether it would come about was a question Shaw could not answer.

"It's a controlled explosion," Daluege explained, describing what happened when the alcohol and the liquid oxygen came in contact within the rocket motor burn chamber. "There's no other way to describe it. We control it by the amount of fuel released into the chamber."

Daluege and Shaw were standing in the motor shop. Men all about were working feverishly on the refinements and corrections Daluege had issued in the latest set of blueprints. Giant milling machines groaned, lathes hummed, and workers shunted between partially assembled motors and workbenches.

"Sounds simple enough," Shaw remarked, his voice slightly raised over the din created by the workers in the shop, knowing the condescending remark would spark a conversation.

"Sounds simple, yes," Daluege replied testily. "But we have to consider the changing altitude and with that the changing temperatures and pressures. We have to take into account the constantly changing velocity up to maximum speed. Most of the rocket's speed is achieved in thirty seconds. The acceleration is tremendous. The 'G' forces are a problem that we must deal with. It is hard to get the leaders here to understand that. Perhaps, Herr Sturmbannführer, you would be good enough to explain our situation?"

Shaw laughed at the thought. "I don't think von Liebeman is looking to me for explanations. I think he is interested only in results."

As they watched, the huge overhead catwalk with its crane system moved along its railings, heading for a partially assembled motor. Shaw and Daluege watched as the workers secured the twelve-foot framing and high-temperature piping assembly to the crane, lifted it, and transported it to another portion of the shop, another demonstration of German efficiency.

"The encasement is the difficult part right now," Daluege continued, moving into the shop. "To enclose the motor within a casement that is impervious to saltwater is a difficult task. We are restricted by size and weight since this latest modification. Now we must find a way to get the same thrust from a smaller motor, one which will fit into the waterproof casing."

"I sympathize with your predicament, Kurt," Shaw answered. "But we must have this motor out and on the test stand within the week, or you and I may no longer be here."

"I do not think it is possible," Kurt Daluege said, shaking his head, a strange sadness in his voice.

"Pray that it is," Shaw responded, hoping for a response from the scientist.

"Pray?" Daluege responded. His reaction was unintentional, but he could not believe he was hearing a member of the SS speak of prayer.

Shaw felt a sense of satisfaction and anticipation. Stranger things had happened. He had gotten a reaction. Shock might have been a better description, he thought, but nonetheless, it was there.

"Pray, Kurt. That is what I said," Shaw repeated, this time in a lower voice.

"I thought the SS prayed only to Himmler and Hitler. That your only god was that death's head on your cap," Daluege responded, a note of disbelief in his tone.

"That may be true for some, but not for all," Shaw said, knowing he was about to put his life in the hands of Kurt Daluege.

"How so?" Daluege asked curiously.

Shaw turned to the scientist, his head turned from the assembly area, his voice low, intense. "There are some in the SS who believe that there are other values, other commitments. Not to Germany, not to a man. Others."

"You speak in riddles, my friend. Others? Commitments? Values? These are very dangerous words when spoken outside the context of the Reich. You are of course speaking of other powers. Externals. Those across the channel, perhaps?"

"I'm speaking of powers greater than those, Kurt," Shaw answered. "Powers that transcend this world. The U.S., Britain, and Russia are nothing compared to it." Shaw probed, delving into an area that could mean quick and painful death if his assessment of Kurt Daluege was wrong.

But time was precious. He had to test Daluege's loyalties, his allegiance. Shaw needed an ally. A communicator. He would push Kurt Daluege as far as he thought possible, and then beyond. He had to know.

"There are forces that eclipse even the power of the Third Reich. Even the power of Hitler," Shaw whispered, surprised by his own belief and certainty. It had taken Barbara's death and his insertion into a hostile land to show him how much he really did believe in a living God. It had taken two weeks of living with evil incarnate in the form of a Germany that had been compromised by murderers and henchmen. And the conviction grew stronger every day, every hour that he was on Usedom Island. When he thought about it, he could date the beginning of his changing beliefs to the day he'd met Wild Bill Donovan and Mark Daniels. It had not been obvious to him then, but in retrospect, he recognized the gentle hand of God in his decision to enter Germany.

Daluege nodded slowly, a painted mask of uncertainty on his face. It would not be surprising to find the SS using such a ploy, a perceived belief in the God of the universe, to smoke out believers and arrest them. He had to be careful. Yet there was a sincerity in this man's voice.

"That power will make this power . . . ," Shaw extended his arm, waving it to indicate the massive motors being built in the motor shop, ". . . seem like Chinese fireworks."

"And not the SS, I presume," Daluege smiled.

"Definitely not the SS."

"I can do all things . . ." Daluege began, stopping at that point. It was all he could think of on such short notice. It was not much, but it would have to do.

Shaw felt a sense of joy, of triumph. When he began this bizarre odyssey, he'd wanted nothing more than to kill Germans, kill the SS. But two weeks ago he'd seen men—German men, SS men, the *enemy*—die an agonizing death in the cold snow of northern Germany. It had not been the triumph he'd hoped for.

He must take the risk.

". . . through him who strengthens me," Shaw completed the biblical quote from Philippians.

Kurt Daluege peered at Shaw through narrow slits, examining the man in the SS uniform, alternately staring at Shaw's face and the death's head on his uniform cap. "I've heard that there are those who are religious in the SS. I find that hard to comprehend, Herr Sturmbannführer. It is not consistent."

Shaw hesitated. The game had begun. The feeling-out process initiated with the exchange of words. The game would continue until one or the other walked away or was convinced of the other's truth.

"Perhaps not consistent to the uninitiated," Shaw began. "An organization can demand membership; it cannot control loyalty."

"That may be true," Daluege said. "But even membership requires a kind of loyalty, wouldn't you say? A subconscious adherence to its laws? Its regulations? Did not Judas adhere to the expectations of the rest of the disciples while a member? That he was eventually a traitor did not render him immune to the influence of the rest of the men around him. And certainly that membership played a part in his eventual actions. Even as a traitor, he operated within parameters. Within expectations."

Shaw felt a warmth settle over him. A final assurance. "I think Judas was affected by the presence of the other disciples and certainly by the presence of Jesus Christ. No man could meet the Savior and feel less for such a meeting. Not even here, in this hellish environment."

Daluege lowered his voice. "You . . . you are what?" he asked in a shocked voice.

A week ago, two weeks ago, Shaw would not have answered as he did. But that time was past. Now was important. "I'm a believer, Kurt. You must decide in whom you think I believe. My words will not convince you." Shaw was rewarded with a gentle smile from Daluege.

"You speak of another power, of a Savior. Riddles, perhaps. You are here for some other reason than to see to it that my shop builds the necessary motor?"

"I am. But I am also worried that we are not showing enough progress. We must give our bosses a bone. Something to let them know we are serious here. We must keep them away from here until we can talk further."

"Yes, my friend. And we must talk further. Your revelation, while astounding, is, nevertheless, bothersome. We must talk," Daluege affirmed in a whisper.

"Yes, we must. I will meet you at your apartment tonight. It will seem nothing more than a meeting of the minds. You live in the family housing area, correct?"

"Building two-thirty-four. Room twelve. Tonight, after supper."

"Until tonight, Kurt," Shaw said. "And let's show some progress today. It may be the only thing that will keep both of us here and in charge. We must remain on this island and in this shop. We may be the only ones capable of stopping a nightmare."

"A nightmare, indeed," Daluege agreed.

"In Him, Kurt," Shaw said before walking off.

"Yes," Daluege nodded, too stunned to say more.

CHAPTER
19

Martin Saint-James scanned the instrument panel of his Mustang with casual exactness. He'd taken off from a fighter group base near Colchester in Essex, his orders specific.

For Saint-James, it was a dream come true. He'd been assigned as liaison officer to the RCAF weeks earlier. When some of the pilots had fallen ill with an undiagnosed viral infection, he had been asked to fly with the group. He had quickly agreed, and after less than four hours actual flight time in the P-51 model I Mustang, he'd been signed off as P-51 qualified. And now he found himself flying a reconnaissance mission into Germany.

For the first time in weeks, the skies were almost clear, a deep blue winking through high, scattered clouds. It was the kind of day reconnaissance pilots dreamed of and dreaded in one great well of mixed emotions. The clear skies meant good pictures. But the working statement of a reconnaissance pilot was: if we can see them, they can see us. The rapidly clearing skies offered both opportunity and peril.

Saint-James applied slight pressure to the left rudder, bringing the nose of his aircraft back to the east-southeast heading that would take him over the narrowest portion of Denmark and into the heavy flak corridor protecting Kiel harbor in northern Germany. He would line up as he crossed Flensburg, adjust his course further to the south, and overfly Kiel, his belly-mounted camera snapping pictures of the German shipyard as he crossed.

Let it be clear over Kiel, dear Lord, Saint-James silently prayed as he adjusted his prop controls to bring his manifold pressure back into the green. In the cold, thin air, his engine was running just slightly cold, and he reached for the vernier control to lean his mixture slightly. The P-51's engine smoothed out to a powerful hum that Saint-James could feel throughout the entire airframe of the Mustang. He checked the outside temperature with a quick glance at the thermometer mounted through the Perspex canopy and cursed silently as he recognized the small round face as an American-type Fahrenheit version and not the more familiar centigrade variety. The RAF had had the P51 since July and had changed most of the cursed Fahrenheit thermometers. A volunteer American pilot had made the first air-to-air kill with the British unit on a mission on July 27. But the RCAF had not yet gotten around to changing the thermometers in the ships they were flying. It showed minus twenty-two degrees.

Saint-James calculated the conversion in his head. Colder than he would have thought at eighteen thousand feet with a ground temperature hovering right at or just below freezing. The west coast of Denmark was just coming into view between the rapidly thinning clouds. Saint-James checked his watch and cross-referenced his flying time against the map in his lap. His dead-reckoned course had placed him almost due east of the North Frisian Islands. In minutes he would be over Flensburg, beginning his southerly turn into Kiel. He checked the trigger that would activate the camera and the small window that showed the amount of film used. He had a full canister. More than enough to map the German harbor installations completely. With the Mustang performing flawlessly, he had no fear that ground-based guns would shoot him down. The P-51 was simply too fast.

The buildings of Flensburg appeared on the horizon, and the Mustang gently banked in response to Saint-James's graceful manipulations. For Saint-James, the feeling of the powerful machine was almost a religious experience.

Less than fifty miles now. In seconds, the skyline of Kiel would be in view. Saint-James advanced the throttle on the plane and was rewarded with the deep-throated growl of the huge engine. The vibrations through the airframe increased, sending a comforting massage-like sensation through Saint-James's torso.

The altimeter's hand began to revolve around the face, indicating positive climb. He adjusted the trim control, stabilizing the aircraft in the climb configuration, and watched the vertical speed indicator settle at fifteen hundred feet per minute. He would shoot the pictures from twenty-five thousand feet. That height provided a general panorama of the shipyard and coastal installations surrounding the port city.

The first black puff exploded more than three thousand feet below, but Saint-James felt the shock wave of the flak as it passed over his ship. The Mustang jerked in response to the antiaircraft fire. More black clouds, deadly in their benign appearance, began bursting at every altitude. The small plane rocked and bucked as it flew through airspace where seconds before a shell had exploded.

Saint-James worried, not so much about being hit by the flak itself, but of flying into the shrapnel produced by the AA fire. The Germans had learned something about AA fire, and despite the speed of the Mustang, the air was becoming deadly.

Kiel appeared beneath his left wing, and Saint-James aligned his plane with the coordinates scribbled on the map attached to his right knee.

The AA fire increased; the small aircraft bucked and reared like a wild horse under its first saddle. Saint-James retarded the throttle, checking the climb, and let the plane settle in at twenty-five thousand feet. He toggled the camera switch and watched as the small indicator window showed that the camera was working.

Flak continued to explode, blessedly still thousands of feet below the Mustang. Occasional bursts reached the small plane, but always to the right or left. Saint-James touched the trim wheel, letting the aircraft fly itself.

It was a trick he'd learned long ago. The Mustang, with its inherent stability, would fly itself with much greater accuracy than a human could ever achieve, even without the aid of an automatic pilot.

The plane bucked once. Close. Too close. The small camera window showed the footage shot. Enough for the photo section to cull every bloody bit of information from the images, Saint-James knew.

He stopped the camera, banked to the west, away from the flak installations, and pushed the nose over as he advanced the throttle. He still had several hundred feet of film remaining in his canister. Shame to waste it, he thought. He glanced at his compass heading, adjusted it slightly in the bank, and slipped the aircraft into a westward heading. Usedom Island was less than a hundred fifty miles to the west. Why British Intelligence would want pictures of a Baltic island was beyond Saint-James. And not the entire island, at that, only the far northern tip of the island was listed on his secondary target list. A fishing village named Peenemünde.

A fishing village! If they wanted pictures of iced-over boats and dead fish, Martin Saint-James could bloody well provide them. And another opportunity like this might not come again for months. The P-51 I was the mainstay of the RAF and RCAF squadrons for whom he flew, but who knew for how long. Only the Mustang had the range necessary to accompany the bombers into and out of Germany, and this very Model I might be pulled for just that reason very shortly. Which meant, of course, that the airplane would get him to Usedom Island and back again. The island was close to the twelve-hundred mile range of the Mustang. Saint-James did some quick calculations as the P-51 droned westward. According to the numbers, he should be able to loiter over Usedom for two or three minutes and still have sufficient fuel remaining to reach Colchester with a slight reserve.

Saint-James checked his watch and compass once again. A hundred fifty miles. Not that far, he reasoned. He'd still have time to make the pub for the early evening dart game. Provided, that was, the debriefing did not last forever.

CHAPTER

20

The Schutzstaffel security team was in place. Most of the men had come from Munich, the Bavarian enclave of the SS. Other cities, other districts were represented as well. Some were from Stuttgart, Nuremberg, Dresden, and Hanover. The worst, the most cold-blooded of the bunch, were from Riga.

The security team consisted of one hundred men, all murderers, all with a misplaced sense of loyalty. They had moved into Lorient through Paris in the north and Lyon in the south. Orders had been issued, and the team had moved with German efficiency to carry out those orders.

Each man was dressed differently, yet each the same. Disguised as workmen in heavy peasant clothing, the men had infiltrated the French seaport with ease. Even in the clothes of workers, the men shared a sameness, a hardness about the eyes, a coldness nestled deep in their souls.

The leaders had met with the Gestapo agents in charge of shipyard worker surveillance. To the man, the Gestapo agents had informed the SS security team that none of the workers involved had disclosed the radical overhaul procedures they had performed on the U-3009 and U-3021.

Each U-boat, after overhaul, appeared to be no more than what they had been when they had entered the yard. No outward appearance, no telltale sign existed that would give a hint of their actual assignment. All was secure. Except for the workers.

Given time, some would talk of the strange work that had been done on the U-boats. The changes had been too drastic, too unusual for it not to happen. Men who drank had loose tongues, and every Frenchman drank.

The blueprints had already been locked away in massive vaults in the Hartz mountains, secure into the next century. The planers, the draftsmen, the engineers had all been transferred, their very existence dependent on the whim of those at Prinz-Albrechtstrasse.

Suppliers of exotic materials had been eliminated, often before the materials themselves arrived in Lorient.

Lists had been compiled—exactingly maintained, edited, augmented—to provide the latest information, the most timely documents reflecting current workers' status and location. These documents were turned over to the SS security team by the Gestapo agents.

The security team moved out, a metastasizing cancer which would invade and destroy in accordance with their edicts.

When Guy La Forche stepped out of the doorway of his century-old Lorient home, an uneasy feeling enveloped him like one of the gray fogs that so often shrouded the French coast in winter. He could not identify it other than to know something was not right. But, La Forche reminded himself, he was the consummate pessimist, at least according to his wife.

La Forche cut across two blocks to the train tracks that led into the Lorient shipyard. The French city was not that large, and La Forche was seeing faces he didn't recognize. He consoled himself with the fact that it was a shipyard, a military installation, and soldiers, sailors, and workers came and went every day, almost every hour. But there was something, a feeling lurking in the recesses of his mind that continued to prick his senses. He shook off the uneasy feeling and joined a small group of men walking beside the tracks, each making their way to the shipyard and the day's work.

"Another day, eh, Guy," Charles Fontaine called to La Forche as he approached.

"*Oui,* another day, Charles," La Forche answered, drawing even with and joining the small group of welders.

Charles Fontaine lowered his voice. "There are rumors, Guy."

"There are always rumors, Charles."

Fontaine shook his head. "Not like these. These rumors have to do with the U-3009 and the 3021," he said, indicating the two U-boats which had been overhauled in the Lorient yards.

"I have heard such rumors," another of the men added.

La Forche continued to walk, kicking at a single rock. "What are these rumors?" he asked, trying to ignore an increased gnawing in his chest.

"Something to the effect that there will be special awards to be made to the men who worked on the two boats."

"Doesn't make sense, Charles. We have done many overhauls on U-boats. There has never been a reward for such work, only more work and less pay. The Germans do not have a benevolent bone in their bodies."

Fontaine shook his head adamantly. "No. It is true. The rumor is that the men who worked on the boats are to receive a bonus of some sort. It will be announced today. Wait and see. We will be rich after this day."

"It's true, Guy," another said. "It is the only time such an overhaul has been done. The Germans are grateful for the cooperation and the work."

"The Germans have never been grateful for any work done. We are no more than slaves to the Third Reich. Have you all forgotten that? Do you so soon forget the invasion and rape of our country? No, my friends, such will not be the case," La Forche insisted.

The group joined with workers merging from all over Lorient and headed for the main gate of the shipyards. Each man in turn displayed his identification badge that hung from pockets, collars, and coats. Hundreds of bodies, all moving en masse, entered the huge shipyard, and then broke off, each heading for his respective assignment.

La Forche, Fontaine, and the men with whom they had been walking headed for the sub pens at the north end of the yard.

The uneasy feeling persisted, and La Forche shrugged the apprehension away. He donned his welding apron, gloves, and hood before crossing the wooden gangway connecting the dry-docked U-boat and the edge of the wharf.

All around him the giant cranes and equipment needed to produce the war machinery of Germany moved in a kind of synchronized ballet to the high-pitched melody of air tools and angry shouts.

La Forche was working on another U-boat, her snout flattened and broken from an encounter in the Gulf of Biscay with another German warship. La Forche smiled, thinking that the Germans could sink their own ships if just left to their own devices.

He'd just replaced his welding rod and snapped his protective helmet in place when he felt a tap on his shoulder. La Forche raised the hood and starred into the face of Henri Devereaux, one of the men with whom he'd walked to work earlier that morning. Charles Fontaine was at his side; both looked worried.

"What is it, Henri?" La Forche asked.

"Charles and I have been talking. There is something going on in the yard today. New faces. Some we've never seen before."

La Forche stifled an immediate feeling of disquiet. "There are always new faces. This is a shipyard. You and Charles are becoming worrisome."

"We're serious, Guy," Charles Fontaine added. "Something's not right. It's true there are always new faces, but today there are more than usual. And even if all the new faces we see are just new workmen, why aren't they doing any work? There are new men everywhere just standing around, watching. They pick up no tools, repair nothing, deliver no materials, *nothing.* I tell you, it is not the same."

La Forche removed his helmet and peeled off his heavy gloves. The wind from the Bay of Biscay was picking up. The weather was as cruel as the Germans, the open sub dry docks cold and uninviting. Yesterday had been an exception as the sun had broken through the clinging cloud mass, but now the wind was building again with the smell of snow in the air. The frigid air bit at La Forche's fingers.

He peered around him at the men working in the bays nearby, operating the giant cranes, carrying material.

Then he saw him!

Not men, but one man, hard faced, staring at him from the protection of one of the dockside sheds near the base of a medium-sized crane. He was dressed in the heavy clothing of a worker, but he didn't move. There was no attempt to work, no effort to disguise the fact that he was watching La Forche and the two men with him. La Forche felt a shiver run up his spine.

"—is not here today," Devereaux was saying.

"What?" La Forche asked, returning his attention to his friend.

"I said Schneider is not here today. None of the Gestapo scum are in the yard. It's like they all disappeared from the face of the earth."

La Forche recognized now that his friends were correct. That was the feeling he'd had earlier. No Gestapo! No Schneider! There was only one force on the face of the earth that could cause a Gestapo agent to neglect his assignment. The Gestapo agents had been replaced by these hard-faced men who only watched.

Watched and waited!

Waited, La Forche knew without any trace of doubt, for the men who'd worked on the two U-boats with the stainless steel ballast tanks. Waited for him.

"We've got a problem," La Forche said to his two friends. "Do you know the men who have worked on the U-3009 and the 3021?"

Fontaine and Devereaux looked at each other, perplexed. "All of them? There must be hundreds spread throughout this yard. It would be impossible to know them all."

"Every man who had anything to do with those two boats is in trouble. I can feel it," La Forche emphasized. "Get to the men you know. Tell them to tell others."

"Tell them what?" Fontaine asked.

"That the SS is here and their lives are in danger," La Forche said.

Fontaine and Devereaux's eyes widened at the revelation; fear spread across their faces as they looked at each other and back to La Forche.

"Even the Nazis are not that stupid," Devereaux argued. "They could never get away with it, would never try."

"Don't be ridiculous, Charles. You underestimate Aryan arrogance. We all have heard of the camps in Germany, Poland, the Baltics, and Austria. We know those who have been removed, even from France, and have never been seen again." La Forche shook his head in dismay. "We know it's true. Contact the men. As many as you can. Tell them . . . tell them . . . I don't know what. That men have been sent to silence us. That is all it can be."

If Devereaux and Fontaine doubted La Forche's sanity, there was no doubting his sincerity and conviction. Each man looked at the other, then at their friend. They were convinced. Both moved from the deck of the dry-docked U-boat as a light snow began to carry on the building wind from the Bay of Biscay.

La Forche watched as his two friends left, his mind operating, calculating, devising a plan of action to counter the madness he felt—*knew*—would strike at any moment.

CHAPTER

21

november 27, 1942
lorient, france

Admiral Karl Dönitz sipped the last of the cabernet, letting the wine slide down his throat gently, wishing it was a German Riesling rather than the French varietal. In his hand he held the latest Führerprotokoll promoting him from Befehlshaber der Unterseeboote (BdU) to Grossadmiral der Kriegsmarine—Grand Admiral of the German Navy—to become effective the first of next year.

Dönitz walked to the window of the Kernevel chateau and looked out on the mouth of the harbor. The U-boat bunkers at Point Keroman near the harbor entrance stood as reminders of how he'd begun this war. U-boats were his first love, his only love he'd admitted to himself during those rare times of introspection. As Grand Admiral, he'd insisted on retaining operational control of the U-boat fleet; Hitler had finally acquiesced. But even in his acceptance, Hitler was demanding more and more U-boats be sent to various locations to act in roles better suited to other, noncombatant ships. Dönitz had seen his boats rerouted to the Mediterranean and the North Sea to act as weather observation platforms supporting naval operations in those theaters.

Now, as Grand Admiral, Dönitz would be obliged to take a more strategic view as opposed to his preferred tactical one. And in that context, the overall strategic panorama, Dönitz picked up the order he'd drafted only hours earlier.

To: Kiel Naval Shipyard
Lorient Naval Shipyard
Peenemünde Research Center
SS-Reichsführer, Prinz-Albrecht Strasse, Berlin

From: Admiral Karl Dönitz, BdU, Lorient, France

Subject: Omega

Due to operational requirements and the necessity of maintaining every available U-boat possible in operational readiness, I am ordering the project known as "Omega" terminated and the U-boats assigned to this operation attached to the North Atlantic Fleet operation area force as soon as possible.

Signed
Admiral Karl Dönitz, BdU

Dönitz reached for his pen and scrawled his name at the bottom of the order and rang the small silver bell resting at the corner of his desk. The door opened and his messenger entered.

"Take this to communications and have it sent at once," Dönitz ordered as the man came to attention in front of the desk.

"Yes, Admiral," the man responded, clicking his heels and quickly leaving.

Dönitz contemplated placing a call to Himmler in Berlin, letting him know that Omega had been canceled, but thought better of it. Better, he reasoned, to let the head of the SS find out about it along with the rest of the commands. Trouble would come soon enough. Better not to court it.

Dönitz walked back to his desk and picked up the wine glass. It had been a difficult decision, but one that had been necessary. He would have loved to have attacked the United States on its home territory, but there were more pressing needs at the moment, and the three U-boats attached to the Omega project were sorely needed elsewhere.

He sipped the remaining wine, then in a fit of uncharacteristic rage, slammed the empty glass against the far wall. *The United States,* he thought. He would teach them a lesson. As soon as he could, he would return the three U-boats to Omega and attack the great coastal cities of the U.S. He would make them regret their involvement in the war. The development at Peenemünde would continue, as would his plans.

CHAPTER

22

The air was hot, rancid with the smell of burning oil; a macabre scene backlit by the fires of the dying ship; the air filled with the screams of the dead and dying.

Michael Shaw came awake. The room was dark and cool; the sweat that seeped from his every pore made the room feel clammy. He surveyed the small cubicle, his home for the last weeks. His gaze fell to where he remembered dropping the black uniform as he'd fallen into bed the night before. The black SS tunic was the prescribed uniform for the SS security detachment.

It was still there, the uniform; dark and heavy, a presence unto itself, a thing of malice and death. A narrow beam of light penetrated from the outside, reflecting off the silver skull that adorned the field cap. For a moment Shaw felt the obscene emblem laughing at him, taunting him for all his mighty ambitions against the Third Reich.

Barbara!

That's what had awakened him. The nightmare was back. The flames of death had been all around him, taunting him just like the silver death's head emblem.

It had sounded good when Wild Bill Donovan had first proposed the plan. He'd seen it as a form of revenge, a way to strike at the very heart of the evil which had snatched his wife from him. But here in the heart of Germany, he was fully aware of his shortcomings. He'd had the best of intentions, but he'd been ignorant. He'd had no concept, no idea of the magnitude of the German evil. Even the time he'd spent in Europe before leaving had not prepared him for the enormity of the degradation he had witnessed since returning to Germany.

Barbara!

Barbara could have explained it all, could have answered the questions, assuaged the doubts.

But Barbara was gone, and Shaw felt the loss all the more in the solitude of the dark room with the Totenkopf laughing at him from the chair.

He swung his feet over the side of the bed and let his head drop into his hands. It was these times—these dark times—when he wanted to cry, to reach out and strike at something—someone—in an attempt to stop the feelings he knew would follow the nightmare. The feelings of frustration, of lostness, of hopelessness. They were all present, eating at him, taunting him just like the silver death's head.

The death's head.

He walked to the chair where the black uniform of an SS Sturmbannführer lay. He picked it up, feeling the heaviness of the fabric, the coarseness. For the first time since he'd been at Peenemünde, he smiled. It was not the smile of delight; it was a smile of sorrow, a deprecating gesture born of frustration but also spawned from the realization that the black uniform would be used as an instrument to pierce the wretched heart of the Third Reich.

Barbara would have advised leaving retribution to God. God would, in his own time, right the injustices of this earth, she would say.

But Shaw couldn't wait on God. His lack of patience was a trait he would have to live with. Not one born of God, he knew, but one he'd learned to control and use.

What was happening at Peenemünde was abhorrent. The depth of evil had not surprised Shaw; he'd seen it as a reporter, heard it in the words uttered from his grandfather's and father's lips. What was a surprise was the ingenious form that evil was taking.

The rockets were the procreation of desperate men, men of little conscience who cared less for reality than for application.

The scientists!

Von Braun!

Daluege!

But, Shaw remembered as he moved to the small, single window in his room, Kurt Daluege was not as he appeared. The man had turned out to be the one ally on whom Shaw could depend. The man who was, almost single-handedly, responsible for the delay in the motor shop. The man who had kept the rockets grounded to this point.

Their first conversations had been intentionally fatuous, words and phrases with little substance, the probing of unknown allies. And Daluege had turned out to be just the ally Shaw was searching for. The man who, along with Shaw, could indefinitely delay the creation of the *Vergeltungswaffen*—the weapons of retaliation.

A light dusting of new snow covered the yard outside the field-grade officer's barracks just west of the family housing area of Peenemünde. Shaw gazed out on the white covering, letting his mind shift from the visions of the nightmare to the problems that faced him now.

He'd shared with Daluege the loss of his radio in the raid on the troop train. Daluege had told him how dangerous the attempt to communicate with the outside was. Shaw had attempted to repair the tiny radio but had been unsuccessful, even given his access to parts from various shops at the rocket center. Shaw had cursed his lack of engineering skills at that point. Communication with MI-6 appeared to be all but impossible. He would have to rely on himself and Daluege to stop the nightmare that was taking place in the Baltic.

The work on the new rocket motor had been delayed to the point of ludicrousness. The separate elements of the rocket known as the V-5 would be ready for testing the following week. Motors, guidance systems, electronics, and warheads would be mated, the resulting vehicle tested, refined, and produced. No delays would be tolerated; no excuses accepted. Orders issued insisted the rocket would fly within seven days.

Seven days!

Time was short, Shaw recognized. He had counted on several factors to delay the rocket construction, not the least of which was the involvement of Admiral Karl Dönitz, the soon-to-be Grand Admiral of the German Navy. The Führerprotokoll announcing the promotion had buoyed both his and Daluege's spirits. Dönitz was a man of conviction, possessing the logical thought patterns of a strategic commander. Both realized that one hope for the cancellation of the V-5 project lay in the overall weakness of the weapon and its means of deployment. Dönitz would realize that, be forced to admit to the shortcomings of the weapon system, and cancel it for the good of the Reich. But Dönitz was also a warrior. His U-boats had unmercifully attacked and destroyed shipping in the Atlantic. And thus Dönitz would be faced with a dichotomy of staggering importance. The V-5 project could provide time for Dönitz to rally his forces, redeploy scarce strategic forces and matériel. It was a toss-up as to what the admiral would do. Shaw could not wait.

The directives for the rocket to fly this next week notwithstanding, the program would have to be eliminated. It was necessary.

Shaw made his way back to his bunk, hesitating in the half-light to succumb to further nightmare-tortured sleep. He and Daluege were inextricably linked in the stanching of the rocket development. An investigation would reveal that. Shaw knew he could be gone within hours. But that would leave Daluege to contend with the horrors of retribution himself. It would mean leaving Daluege and the man's family, now housed in the civilian housing section of Peenemünde. Shaw had realized early on that he could not do that, could not leave the man to the vengeance of the German military machine.

The rocket would fly. It *must* fly to protect Daluege. Such a man could not be sacrificed on the pyres of German rocket development. Shaw had another plan, one that would assure Daluege's continued presence at Peenemünde yet stop the ultimate purpose for which the V-5 was being developed.

Shaw crawled into the bunk and pulled the covers up. He would not sleep, could not. At this point it would only bring back the nightmare.

Shaw would save Daluege, the man of God, the conscience of Peenemünde, the man for whom theory and practice had no definitive boundaries.

Shaw felt the warmth of the bed overtake him in his drowsiness; he fought it, but sleep won, its ally exhaustion.

As Shaw closed his eyes and his breathing slowed, the first yellow light of the fires returned. And with them came the memories.

CHAPTER
23

It was all Guy La Forche could do to keep his eyes from the man.
He was brutish looking, dark, and rough, wearing the clothing of a
French shipyard worker. But La Forche knew all too well the look in
the man's eyes.

He was SS.

La Forche had watched the same man throughout this second day
of surveillance. He'd first appeared last Friday. He'd not moved far
from the base of the crane near La Forche's work area. There had been
no attempt, except for the clothing, to disguise the fact that he was not
a shipyard worker. Once, when La Forche had checked, the man had
been gone and Guy had breathed a labored sigh of relief. But the next
time he looked, less than thirty minutes later, the man had been standing there, his gaze fixed on La Forche.

Now, with the workday ending, nothing had come of his fears,
and La Forche felt himself relax. The man remained, less obvious

than before, but there, near the supply shed that held the air tools.

The whistle sounded, ending the workday for his shift, and Guy La Forche quickly joined forces with the rest of the workers trekking homeward, away from the arctic blast that was now blowing in from the Bay of Biscay. Charles Fontaine and Henri Devereaux soon caught up to La Forche, and the three friends made their way to the main gate. Each man had a story to tell of the stone-eyed men who had watched them for the entire day.

"It's not right, I tell you," Fontaine said.

"It is nothing, *mon ami*," Devereaux joked. "I had one watching me also. He was no more than curious. I think perhaps the Gestapo has chosen to go underground," he laughed. "If you could call so obvious an attempt a form of subterfuge. But that would be like the Germans to think that we French are too stupid to recognize agents simply because they dress differently."

"I don't know," Fontaine argued. "What about your man, Guy?"

"He was with me the entire day. Once this afternoon I thought he was gone, but he returned. It was pretty obvious it was me he was watching. Once I left to relieve myself. He was right there outside the door when I came out." La Forche walked on, wanting to turn the near corner, knowing the wind that was biting at them would be tempered by the buildings of the street.

"Well, I'm not going to worry about it. I think the Germans have become paranoid in the extreme. This is just a way of keeping watch on us loyal Vichy," Devereaux joked.

Guy La Forche was instantly incensed. He grabbed his friend by the lapels, his powerful forearms driving the man into the nearest brick wall. Devereaux's breath was expunged by the force and suddenness of the attack.

"Don't ever call me Vichy, Henri," La Forche warned, the words spoken from between clinched teeth. His fingers were wrapped in the fabric of Devereaux's overcoat. He could feel his friend's body shaking as he held him pinned against the wall.

Henri Devereaux caught his breath and said, with effort, "I was just joking, Guy. Just a . . . joke. That's all."

"Do not even joke about that. I am no Vichy. My father was killed by those pigs in Paris along the Quay de la Tournelle."

Devereaux regained his composure. "Just outside Notre Dame Cathedral," he said, his voice low.

La Forche released Devereaux, straightening the heavy, soiled lapels of the greatcoat. "Yes, outside the cathedral," La Forche affirmed.

"I am sorry, Guy. I will never make such a joke again. Forgive me, my friend."

La Forche patted his friend's shoulder. "It is I who should be asking forgiveness, Henri. I have a quick temper. It is the one fault that most often gets me into trouble."

"It is good to know a man who has only one fault," Devereaux said. Both men laughed, the moment diffused by the sincere apology and the honest banter.

"This is where I leave you," La Forche said as he broke away from the threesome and turned left along the *rue de Rennes.* Here, as at the shipyard, the wind assailed the pedestrians unlucky enough to be caught out in the streets as the sun set. The cold knife edge of the ocean air cut at him as he walked. La Forche pulled the battered woolen coat tightly around him.

As he made his way through the dimming light, he thought again of the man who'd stood by the small shed at the base of the crane, his gaze fixed intently on La Forche. He had to be SS. There could be no other explanation. He had told Devereaux and Fontaine to warn the others, the ones who'd worked on the two U-boats that had required such drastic modification. But here, in the streets of Lorient, he was beginning to feel like a schoolboy trying to impress older children. As he walked, he thought.

It made no sense, what he'd suggested to his two friends. The Germans needed every able-bodied worker they could lay their hands on. Especially skilled labor like most of the shipyard workers. They were men who could not be replaced within a thousand miles of the Lorient pens. On them rested the responsibility of putting to sea the bulk of the Third Reich's U-boat fleet. Along the west coast of France, there were no better workers. The Germans knew this. It made no sense.

As La Forche rationalized away his fear, he heard the muffled steps of a man running. Almost, he thought, as if the man did not want to be heard. The steps were light, their cadence muted by crepe soles.

La Forche turned, curious as to the source of the sound. Just as his head swung to look back down the street, he felt the pressure as a man lunged at him, the dim light reflecting off the blade of an SS knife.

La Forche stepped to the side, a bullfighter avoiding the bull's lunge. The man with the knife flew by, his momentum carrying him well past the Frenchman.

La Forche squared up to meet the assailant head-on. The man turned, the last rays of light catching his features, especially the eyes. They were cold and black, dead, with only one purpose. That purpose, Guy La Forche knew, was to see him dead.

The man was the same one who'd been at the shipyard that day, waiting beneath the crane!

The man lunged again, this time in a more controlled, more deliberate fashion. The knife was in his right hand, the point thrusting, parrying, seeking the area just below La Forche's breastbone.

La Forche dodged away from the knife to his right. He felt the blade as it ripped at the dense fabric of his coat. His first thought was to run, escape down the street toward the one he'd just left, where there were more people, more lights, more protection. But this man was too fast, La Forche knew instantly from the looks of him. The killer was leaner than La Forche had first thought, more angular than he'd appeared on the quay. He would have to stand and fight and pray.

For a moment, La Forche smiled to himself at the thought of praying. He had not prayed in years. His mother was French Catholic, his grandmother Lutheran. He'd seen both of them pray. He'd even tried it once or twice, and when nothing came of it, he'd abandoned the idea as nonproductive. Now, as he stood facing this man whose only intention was to kill him, he found it singularly amusing that he thought to pray.

La Forche kept his eyes locked on the man with the knife. He stared at the man's midsection, knowing that where the stomach went, the rest had to follow.

The man moved with speed and agility, but he was smaller than La Forche, and, La Forche sensed, physically weaker. But the knife more than made up for the shortcomings, Guy knew.

The man was circling now, knees bent, the knife molded into his hand. He didn't flick at La Forche as he'd earlier done. He moved with deadly purpose.

La Forche moved in response to the man's circling. He felt the gash the knife had cut in his coat with the first attempt. The coat had saved his life, not in taking the knife blade in his stead, but by disguising his build, making the killer think he was actually larger than he was. Perhaps, he reasoned, he could use the coat to once again confound this man in front of him.

Circling to his right, La Forche began to remove his coat. His eyes were fixed on his attacker, his every nerve ready to respond to the next onslaught from the deadly dagger.

The man warily continued his movements, confusion showing on his face. He'd been assigned the elimination of this one man, and he'd been certain he could accomplish the task with few complications. But his first assault had failed. He'd wanted to kill the shipyard welder before the man had a chance to react. That had not happened. And this was not like the propaganda he'd heard spewing from the mouths of the SS elite. Here, in the dark streets of Lorient, France, he did not feel superior to the man he faced. As he watched the man remove the greatcoat which he'd slashed with his SS knife, he was beginning to wonder if he would be able to kill the man at all.

La Forche had his coat off. He partially wrapped a portion of the garment around his arm, leaving the remaining three or four feet dangling from his arm, much like the bullfighters he'd once seen on a visit to Spain. The fabric would work to conceal the bulk of his body and also deflect the knife-blade thrust. He could see the doubt reflecting in the SS man's face.

Pigs! They were all pigs, La Forche thought, competent only when the odds were in their favor. And as La Forche recognized the doubt, he felt his strength and confidence returning. Was this how prayer was answered? He wasn't sure, but it was possible, he reasoned.

La Forche matched the SS killer movement for movement, circle for circle. The knifepoint probed, bobbing in and out, but never committing to the final thrust. La Forche stared at the man, into his face. He felt no fear now, only anger. Anger that this man could so callously remove another human being from the face of the earth with as little regard for that life as a butcher in the meat market. Anger at the regime that bullied and threatened other countries as if they were no more than playthings to be stripped of their fortunes and discarded when no longer useful.

The killer was moving with the swiftness born of ineptitude, of desperation. La Forche recognized this. The blade was moving in small circles, the point intermittently thrusting and withdrawing. Once the knife cut into the fabric of the coat as La Forche parried the attempt.

La Forche could hear voices coming from the adjoining streets. But the shouts were in French, not German!

Running feet echoed down the corridor of brick and stone buildings. The killer heard the sound of approaching footsteps, the shouts. He would have to kill now or flee for his own life. He moved closer to La Forche, trying to get within range for his blade, trying to outmaneuver the Frenchman with the overcoat. He dodged right and left, feinted to his right, and drove toward La Forche with his right arm—his knife arm—extended before him.

La Forche, countered, sidestepped the knife thrust, and whipped the coat over and down in a sharp motion. The dangling four feet of the coat wrapped around the attacker's head and shoulders, blinding him. La Forche's left arm was in motion, the roundhouse left hook coming from his heels. The fist caught the killer in the throat, crushing his windpipe and sending the man to the ground, gasping for air, his face already purple in the French night.

"Guy," one of the running voices called.

La Forche looked up. Henri Devereaux and Charles Fontaine, accompanied by half a dozen other shipyard workers he recognized, were running down the street.

The would-be murderer writhed in pain at La Forche's feet; the SS knife glinted four feet away where it had fallen. The man would cause no more problems this night.

La Forche turned to the approaching men. "What is happening?" he demanded.

Devereaux was the first to reach La Forche. "You were right," he coughed, trying to catch his breath, his hands on his knees. "The men at the shipyard were SS. The same as this one," he said, indicating the man on the ground. "They have already murdered more than twenty workers."

"And?" La Forche said, knowing what was coming.

"They were all men who worked on the two U-boats. The SS is out to kill every person associated with them. That could be more than a hundred people! It's insane!"

"The SS is insane. It is led by the insane." La Forche looked around. He was no more than three blocks from his house. The weather was worsening, the snow beginning to fall in wet, heavy flakes; the wind was picking up.

"We must run," Devereaux said. "We must get away from Lorient. From these madmen."

"We cannot leave our families," La Forche reminded him. The other men had caught up with Devereaux and were standing around the now still figure of the SS assassin.

"We have no choice," Devereaux said. "We must leave them. Anything we do now will put them in jeopardy. We must get out of here and regroup, think this thing through. There will be another day."

Another day. La Forche once again smiled grimly, this time thinking of the day of judgment all men would face. The man at his feet would face his sooner than most, but all would face it. His prayer *had been* answered, he realized. He would live to fight the SS in another place at another time.

"We will run, Henri. For now. But we will stop running one day, and when that day arrives, it will be a sad day indeed for the men of the SS. That is a promise I make to you, to all of you," he said with a sweep of his arm, including the men surrounding him. "They all shall fall as this one here has." As he turned to follow the now fleeing men, La Forche spoke one last time, "That is a promise to God in heaven above. This evil will be defeated," he whispered to himself and the darkness about him.

CHAPTER
24

The black automobile crossed Budapesterstrasse and entered the Zoologischer Garten by its west entrance. This was Heinrich Himmler's favorite place in all of Berlin. The barren trees of the garden did little to dampen his mood. As he watched the snow fall and freeze to the trees in the zoo area, he anticipated the upcoming meeting with the leader of the German people, Adolf Hitler. He had much to tell his exalted leader.

Himmler forced his attention back to the papers he carried in the worn attaché case. The small stack of papers measured no more than an inch; the latest communiqué rested on top, as yet unmarked by the red pencil Himmler carried with him at all times. He read the order once again, his mouth twisting in a crooked smile beneath the pince-nez.

The communiqué was from UdB Karl Dönitz. It was the order to cancel Omega, return the three U-boats involved in the project to their original specifications, and return the boats to their original command in the North Atlantic. The order had been sent to the U-boat commands in Kiel and Lorient and to the rocket research center at Peenemünde. Himmler had chafed when he'd learned of the communiqué, and the fact that he had not been informed of its contents prior to its being released served only to exacerbate the situation. It made little difference now. The SS informant at Lorient in Dönitz's headquarters had typed the message and informed SS headquarters of its content even before it had been entrusted to the Kriegsmarine messenger.

The messenger had been intercepted on the outskirts of Nantes. The official report listed the man as being killed in an automobile accident. That report, along with all the papers carried by the messenger were forwarded to the Gestapo headquarters in Tours and from there to Berlin. It would be weeks, perhaps months, before Dönitz discovered that his order had not reached its destination. By then, Himmler knew, Dönitz would be the Grand Admiral of the German Navy and would have more on his mind than three insignificant U-boats.

Himmler replaced the file along with the copy of Dönitz's order just as the car turned toward the Siegessäule. The area was thickly forested by a variety of fauna. The cold winters of 1945 and 1946 would see this area stripped of every scrap of wood and used as fuel by the freezing Berliners, but now, in 1943, the woods were intact and beautiful with their accumulated burden of crystal snow and ice. A faint ray of sunshine was breaking through the overcast, and the radiant white of the reflected light left Himmler almost blinded.

The car sped on, headed for the Spree River crossing at Paulstrasse. Himmler leaned back, comfortable in the richly upholstered leather seat, and withdrew a silver flask from a holder on the rear of the front seat. He poured an inch of brandy in the small glass he'd pulled from another storage bin and closed his eyes, content, for the moment, to sniff the strong aromatic liquor.

He was on track. The SS was strong, the strongest arm of the Nazi party. He had, almost single-handedly, elevated the organization to the status of a religion. Every strategy, every concept, had been installed to render the mainline religions impotent in the face of the burgeoning SS. Religious practiccs, traditions long observed, had been replaced with those of the SS. Birth, death, and marriage were controlled by the SS. Obedience was demanded and punishment exacted for noncompliance. Hitler was god; the SS, his avenging angels; and Himmler, the favored son, professing the theology of Aryan supremacy.

Himmler sipped the brandy slowly, the liquid burning his throat. The SS had now extended its sphere of influence to include the U-boat command and the research center at Peenemünde. Life was good. Dönitz was tough, but soon he would have to rethink his positions, as he was already doing in the case of the three U-boats.

As the black automobile crossed the Spree River, Heinrich Himmler slumped down in the seat, his eyes closing against the harsh white light that penetrated the car's windows.

CHAPTER
25

december 2, 1942
leverkusen, germany

The two safety-clad I. G. Farben technicians handled the stainless steel container carefully, overcautiously, each sweating within the impermeable white latex suits. The container was no larger than the soccer balls the two men had played with as young boys and weighed exactly 18.5 kilos. Ten kilos of the weight was contributed by the container itself, the container manufactured to the strictest specifications from a single slug of stainless steel. The container was filled with exactly 8.5 kilos of an oily liquid that resembled used motor oil, sealed in an inner liner, its integrity additionally ensured by a vacuum within the container. The top of the container was held in place by twenty stainless steel bolts spaced equidistant around the circumference and torqued to exact specifications.

The two technicians gingerly lifted the container and placed it in a specially manufactured shipping vessel. The vessel was made of stainless steel and fitted with a small vacuum valve located within a recessed area near the right handle. The vessel contained a system of twelve steel straps with hooks at the end. Each strap was attached to an adjustable spring, which could be adjusted to preserve a preset state of equilibrium within a negative pressure environment.

The technicians attached the straps and released the container. It did not budge. Satisfied that the spring system was indeed set correctly, the technicians bolted the top to the vessel's body, taking care to check and double-check the torque pressures. With the bolts tightened, the larger of the two men moved to a workbench against the wall of the small enclosure, retrieved an electric piston vacuum pump, and checked the four-foot hose attached to the pump. He then snapped the hose's brass fitting onto the vacuum fitting located in the recessed area of the crate; he threw the switch and the pump hummed to life.

"Nothing to do but wait," he said, as he removed the protective hooded gas mask he was wearing.

"I wouldn't do that if I were you," the other, much smaller technician mumbled through his own gas mask.

"It's safe. I've worked with this stuff before. Once you get to this stage, with the vacuum pump running, it's as docile as pure water. Don't worry, you can remove your mask. The vacuum exhaust is vented to a special containment room should something happen."

The smaller technician unfastened the straps holding the mask in place and removed it. "I've heard about this stuff before. This is the first time I've ever been this close to it, though. Where is it headed?"

The senior technician gave the questioner a wilting glance to show his displeasure at the question, then relented when he saw the man did not really understand what he was asking.

"We don't ever know," he answered. "At least, officially we never know. But I can tell you that this is the first batch that has gone to a place other than the storage facility in the Hartz Mountain complex. That must mean the Führer has a use for it." Then the man lowered his voice and said, "But I've heard this order came from Himmler. Whatever that means." The man strode to the workbench where the vacuum pump sat working and checked the vacuum gauge attached. "Down to twenty-one. Won't be long now."

"So where's it going if this is the first batch to be shipped to a different place?"

The technician turned around, away from the pump and bench, his voice still low in the enclosed room. "A village on Usedom Island in the Baltic. That's about all I know except for the name. Place called Peenemünde. Someone told me it was a fishing village. Me, I don't have any idea. I just know that I don't want to be anywhere near this stuff when they open this canister."

The smaller technician walked to the vacuum pump. "It's as deadly as they say, then?"

"Worse. I've seen it in action. The scientists actually used people for the experiments. Came from Poland and Yugoslavia. Said it made for better testing. Ghastly is the only word I can use to describe the effects."

"The Poles I have no sympathy for. Good riddance. I would have liked to seen the experiments myself when they used them."

The bigger man shook his head. "No . . . I don't think you would have. It was horrible. Almost demonic the way those people died. I can't imagine a circumstance that would justify using this stuff, but then that's not my business."

"You've got that right. We're just here to ship this stuff. What happens to it after it leaves here does not concern us," the small man said as he checked the vacuum reading. "What are we looking for here?"

"Twenty-eight inches on the vacuum gauge. That's the best we can do with that old piston pump. It's enough."

"How much stuff is in the canister? I mean . . ."

"You mean, how many people will it kill?"

"Right."

The big technician shook his head. "That's hard to say. Depends on the wind, the atmospheric conditions, a whole host of other factors. Mainly it depends on the type of system used to distribute the liquid.

Theoretically there's enough in that canister to kill about a million people, but that's under ideal conditions. And I think most scientists exaggerate slightly when discussing their own inventions. I'd say probably a hundred thousand would be more like it."

The smaller technician was stunned. "That's still impressive," he said finally. "What would be ideal conditions as far as a delivery system is concerned?"

"That's hard to say, too. I've heard it said the ideal system would be one that could release the material anywhere from ten to fifteen miles above the earth."

The smaller technician laughed. "That's over twenty-five thousand meters! Impossible! Nothing in the world flies that high."

"I know that. Come on. Let's get this stuff out of here. Shut off the vacuum while I close the valve."

In two minutes the men had the stainless container sealed with a vacuum drawn and the special container on a dolly for transfer to a waiting truck.

As they watched the truck roll away from the I. G. Farben Industrie loading dock, each man thought the Farben scientists fools for inventing such a weapon and then overestimating its potential.

Twenty-five thousand meters! *Impossible!*

CHAPTER
26

december 2, 1942
peenemünde, germany

The skeleton of metal girders and reinforcement beams rising into the cold Baltic air reminded Michael Shaw of the Eiffel Tower in Paris. Test stand #5 was isolated, even more so than the other stands normally used for testing rockets and motors. Most of the stands were situated near the northern tip of Usedom Island, away from the prying eyes of Polish workers and others who might be interested in the origin of the strange sounds and booming claps of rocket engines igniting.

Test stand #5 was the exception, owing its existence to the persistence of Kurt Daluege. He'd argued—rightfully—that the motor shop needed a smaller, more accessible test stand, one nearer the center of the island. It was not as though the motor shop were going to launch its own rockets and needed the proximity of the sea as did the V-2 and V-1. The motor shop would be conducting static tests on experimental rocket engines, and a test stand hidden away in the pine forest of the interior island would serve as well, perhaps better, than the larger stands to the north. It had been a good argument, a logical one by German standards, and test stand #5 had been constructed under the direction of Daluege.

As a team of scientists and workers readied the newest motor for testing, Daluege approached Michael Shaw. Each man knew the concern of the other; each recognized the anxiety the other faced.

For Shaw, his battle was twofold. He, along with Daluege, had managed to delay the development of the V-5 for weeks. Shaw had been right in his assessment of the German scientist. Daluege *was* the one who had been stalling the production process, and together, they had managed to extend that time, but by only a few weeks. Weeks that had provided invaluable information concerning the small rocket, and weeks that had revealed the purpose of the weapon.

They had found each other as if it had been ordained of God, and they had worked together, seeking each other's counsel, fortifying, encouraging each other every step of the way. They made a good team, and Shaw was delighted with the progress—in this case, the nonprogress—that had been made under their combined guidance.

But Shaw, with his perfect German and practiced demeanor, fought another battle every night in the privacy of his quarters. A battle that erupted as sleep overtook him and exploded into his subconscious with the garish glare of burning oil and unearthly screams. Every night was 1939 all over again. Every evening the battle of the *Athenia* replayed itself within the confines of his soul. Every night he lost Barbara again and again until, as the melee escalated within, the inner conflict began to show outwardly.

Kurt had noticed it, had said something about it early on, about the dark circles under his eyes, the haggard, worn appearance, and the absence of life in his once-handsome face. Shaw had confided in the German scientist then, telling him about Barbara, about that night, and about his recruitment by Wild Bill Donavan. About the stress that had been building since the first day he had arrived at Peenemünde. Even his perfect German and his knowledge of German customs did not lessen the feeling of confinement. Sharing the tortured existence which came to him each night as he finally succumbed to unwanted sleep.

"She sounds like a great lady," Daluege had commented. "Such losses are difficult."

Shaw glanced toward the test stand at the workmen assembling the latest version of the V-5 engine for testing, remembering how, after Daluege had uttered those two, simple sentences, he'd broken down and cried and cursed a God who had let Barbara die in such a manner. Shaw had found himself in a dilemma. On one hand, he could see the providential hand of God in what he was doing, but he had only God to blame for allowing Barbara to die. It had been a German torpedo, but an omnipotent God could have stopped it, Shaw knew; thus the dichotomy of belief Michael Shaw battled every night in the solitude of his room.

"You blame God. He is used to that," Kurt had stated matter-of-factly. "But from what you say, Barbara was not the kind to do such a thing. She is with Him now, and I doubt even she thinks kindly toward you when you blame God for the evils of men on this earth. It is done all the time, it is true. But we are wrong to blame God, who gave us a free will, with the results of that will when we choose to use it badly."

Shaw felt the weight of the words Daluege had spoken. He knew his friend was right, that the emotions he felt concerning that night were directed at God because of the helplessness he felt. A noise drew him back to the present.

The wind began to whip through the tops of the tall pines that encircled test stand #5. The treetops swayed and bowed in response. The sound of the wind in the treetops was somehow soothing. Kurt was right. What happened on this earth was due mostly to the actions of men exercising the prerogative of free will. He had never thought of free will in such a manner. He would have to remember what Kurt had said.

The work crew had the V-5 rocket engine assembled on the test stand; control wires and fuel lines snaked over the frosted ground and connected to the engine at critical points. The engine resembled a mass of tubing gone askew attached to a large central pipe of about one meter in diameter and almost four meters high. Wiring was wrapped in and around the central core in what appeared at first to be haphazard fashion. Shaw knew the placement of the tubing and wiring was anything but random. Each wire, each tube, was strategically located to best serve its own peculiar function.

A small group of workmen gathered around the two fuel trucks. The trucks were positioned almost one hundred meters from the test stand and the engine but were connected to the motor by long umbilicals, each labeled with an identifying name: one read Alcohol, the other, Liquid Oxygen.

A nest of wires snaked from the control circuits of the engine, across the ground, and into the small, concrete bunker that served as the control booth for the engine test.

It was to this bunker Shaw and Daluege now walked. The bunker was no more than seven meters long by five meters wide and barely two meters high. Shaw had to stoop as he entered the structure; Daluege, a good six inches shorter than Shaw, could stand erect in the building.

Inside, five electronics technicians were already crammed into the space, each working at consoles lining the front wall. Above the consoles three individual slits ran the length of the structure, providing a somewhat restricted view of test stand #5.

Daluege walked to the center console and sat down, directing Shaw to follow him. Shaw took the seat next to Daluege and watched as the German scientist manipulated the various controls and switches before him.

The speed with which Daluege's hands flew over the master console never ceased to amaze Shaw. Shaw was careful not to touch any of the control switches or knobs in front of him. He'd been in the control bunker many times in his weeks at Peenemünde, but this was the first time he actually expected success. Until now, success was, for him and Daluege, when the engines failed. He'd seen explosions, combustion chambers burned through, even engines that failed to ignite. Each had been a form of sabotage, a way of hindering the rocket's development. Each failure had been orchestrated by Kurt Daluege in a manner so delicate, so painstakingly conceived, that no one had suspected tampering as the basis for failure. Each failure had been accepted as a matter of course, the cost of success, the price of perfection.

But time had run out. The motor that was now being readied for test would function perfectly, Shaw knew. Further delays—if there were to be further delays—would have to come from other shops, from other sources. He and Daluege had done all they could.

Kurt Daluege looked up from the console in front of him and sighed. Shaw caught the expression of reluctance on his friend's face and understood.

The work teams outside the bunker were scurrying for cover, from the rocket motor test as well as from the harsh elements of the Baltic winter. The last remaining technician, his uniform emblazoned with a large orange diagonal stripe, motioned toward the bunker.

Daluege caught the signal of the senior technician with the orange stripe as he motioned that all the connections were made, inspected, and cleared for testing. The scientist studied the people around him, noting with a certain satisfaction that each man had his eyes fixed on him, awaiting the orders each knew would come.

"Begin the clock on my signal. I want to know the exact duration of this burn to the split second. Karl," Daluege ordered the technician to his left, "monitor the fuel flow and pressure during the burn. It won't do us any good to have a good burn if the rocket can't carry the required amount of fuel. Martin, keep your glasses trained on the combustion chamber. Let me know if you see a hot spot. We may have time to stop the burn before it completely destroys the motor." Daluege directed his orders to every man in the bunker, knowing each would do his job. When he was satisfied that each man knew his task and was prepared for the test, he turned to Shaw. "This will be the last test. This engine will work. You know that, don't you?"

Shaw nodded.

Daluege gave the signal for the test to begin, and the men in the bunker flew into rehearsed motion, each instinctively performing his assigned task with no wasted motion. In seconds, each man had completed his pretest function and signaled Daluege.

Daluege gave one final look to see that all the workers had cleared the area. He thumbed the button to his right, and the test-warning siren blared its warning. Satisfied, he looked at Shaw, whose eyes were already glued to the rocket engine affixed to the test stand. The scientist's hand moved to the master switch and then the button that would send the oxygen and alcohol pumps into action. When both pressures stabilized, his hand moved to the red system-ignite button and began counting down from five. At zero, Daluege depressed the firing button; simultaneously the oxygen and alcohol valves opened, dispensing measured amounts of the volatile fuels into the combustion chamber. At that same moment, a tiny spark leaped across a three-millimeter gap at the head of the chamber, and the V-5 rocket engine roared to life in a contained explosion.

The sound reverberated off the face of the concrete bunker, but even so, Shaw could feel the pressure generated by the motor.

Test stand #5 was set in a clearing about one hundred meters wide, the stand centered in the clearing. The ground around the test area was completely devoid of trash, limbs, pine needles, and other debris that might be blown into the air by the test engine. As the engine ignited, dust—the only thing around the clearing that could not be effectively cleared away—blew into the air, reminding Shaw of a dust storm he'd once seen in Oklahoma.

Clouds of dust rose in the air, propelled by the fiery blast of the engine. Bright flame poured from the mouth of the motor like the tongue of an angry dragon.

Shaw was transfixed. He'd seen all the failures, and even those had impressed him. The utter power of the motors had been apparent, even in sabotaged failure. But here, before him, roaring and burning like an avenging animal, stood the attestation to German genius.

Shaw watched as the motor continued to burn. He was unaware of the others in the bunker with him, only of himself and the sound coming from the engine.

The sound!

The effect was chilling.

Dear God, he thought. *Forgive us.*

The motor was a living being, a thing of horror and of wonder. He'd never heard anything like it in his life. The sound continued, unlike all the other tests when, after only a few seconds, the sound had given way to an explosion, a burnout, or simple pump failure.

Shaw glanced at the wall mounted clock. How long had it been, now? He'd not checked the clock at ignition. One minute? Two? Ten? He had no way of knowing. Time was transfixed, stagnant.

Slowly he became aware of men's voices penetrating the bunker.

"Pump pressures normal."

"Exhaust gas temperature slightly elevated but within parameters."

"Total fuel burn approaching load limits."

"Total burn time exceeding specifications."

Shaw tore his attention from the burning monster fifty meters away and focused on the men in the bunker. Each was doing what he was trained to do, each functioning as a critical cog in the war machinery of Germany, each totally unaware that success at this point meant the death of people in the not-too-distant future.

And then, as suddenly as it had begun, the deafening sound of the engine was replaced with a silky quiet. A quiet so profound, Shaw wondered for a split second what had happened. He looked sideways at Kurt Daluege on his left. Despite himself, Daluege was smiling. Shaw recognized the sardonic grin for what it was. A mixture of pride and horror. He had perfected the rocket engine, within itself, a thing of beauty and mystery. But it would be used to kill people first and foremost, and that could never be justified, not even within the parameters of world war.

"Time?" Daluege said as he moved to shut down all systems of the motor.

"Sixty-three seconds," came the response.

Sixty-three seconds!

Shaw was dumbfounded. He'd imagined the motor had burned for twice that, three times that. He'd been completely and totally mesmerized by the roaring motor.

Daluege turned to Shaw. "We must talk, my friend," he said quietly. "Tonight. Come to my quarters. There are things I must tell you now that the motor is ready."

Shaw turned to his friend. "Sixty-three seconds is sufficient?"

Daluege nodded. "More than enough. If all the calculations are correct and the thrust figures we have from this burn are accurate, it will require only a fraction of that time to send the V-5 sixty miles into the sky. It is one of the things we must discuss."

"Tonight. Ten o'clock."

"Tonight is tonight. Right now we must disassemble the motor for inspection purposes. Come, the workers will already be at it."

Shaw followed Kurt Daluege from the protection of the bunker. The wind was picking up; it was cold already. It would be colder tonight. Both men approached the test stand around which half a dozen workers were busily dismantling the rocket motor.

Shaw held back as Daluege went ahead to direct the work. The motor had indeed functioned, well past the design parameters, well enough to launch the V-5 into the upper atmosphere. Sixty miles. That's what Kurt had said. What was the advantage of the sixty-mile altitude? Shaw wondered. Were the rest of the components so sophisticated as to allow the small rocket to pinpoint a target from that altitude? Was it the altitude necessary for a new type of warhead, perhaps? Shaw did not know. His own involvement with the V-5 had been nothing outside the rocket motor research center. The rest of the components, the guidance systems, the warheads, the electrical instrumentation, all of it was beyond his control.

He had tried on several occasions to wangle information from others working in the various areas of the V-5, but without much success. He'd been at Peenemünde for several weeks now, and the place was beginning to close in on him. The longer he stayed, the greater the chance of his being discovered. For some reason, he found that unsettling. He could have understood his apprehension if Barbara were still alive. He would want to be back with her, to hold her in his arms, to kiss her gently on the forehead the way she liked. But that was not the case. Barbara was gone; there was no reason to leave this place, nowhere he needed to go, and yet he had the feeling he needed to be gone from here.

Kurt was winding up his supervision of the motor work. The men had the engine dismantled. Elements of the motor were being loaded onto waiting trucks. The trucks would unload at the research center, and the scientists there would inspect the motor for flaws and design errors. Shaw knew they would not find evidence of either. The motor was ready. It could fly tomorrow if need be.

Kurt returned to where Shaw was standing. "It's ready. Let's get back to the shop. This weather is blowing up a storm, I fear."

Shaw looked at the darkening sky. "You are right, my friend. We will see some new snow tonight."

*   *   *

As Kurt Daluege and Michael Shaw entered a waiting car that would take them, along with the rocket motor, back to the research center, a lone man dressed in heavy peasant clothing moved from behind the test stand.

He had been right. The sounds that had come from this part of the island were of interest to the people across the channel. He'd sent his earlier information, and had, a few days after that, received a request to investigate further and find out more about the strange noises.

It had been easier than he'd expected. German security was impressive, but he had become an accepted feature at Peenemünde. He had only to present himself to the maintenance division of the rocket research center and he had been hired. Strong men were at a premium on the island. The Germans had processed him, taken his picture, issued him the necessary identification cards, and put him to work as a foreman with one of the assembly crews. His job was to assemble and disassemble the rocket motor test stands. It was hard work, especially during the winter, but no more difficult than building a road across the island. And here, within the heart of the German research center, he was bound to learn more than he could outside.

Already he'd made a discovery: The SS-Sturmbannführer who had escaped the train a few weeks back was part of the engine test center. During the train assault, he'd gone looking for the man in the gray tunic who'd fled out the back side of the train. The German army patrol had interrupted the chase just as he'd noticed the SS pig crouched behind a tree trunk like a scared dog.

He'd not had the chance to kill the man then, but now he would. He would see to it that one more black-uniformed SS man would become a martyr for his cause.

Walter Kolinsky rubbed the scar that creased his face, a reminder of what the SS did to their enemies. He smiled at the thought, for the SS was certainly correct. Walter Kolinsky was indeed their enemy. And he would prove it tonight.

CHAPTER
27

december 2, 1942
london, england

The traffic across Lambeth Bridge where Lambeth Road crossed the Thames was congested as the army sedan in which Sarah Collingsworth rode inched its way off the bridge and finally turned right onto Millbank Road. Sarah wondered why she had been summoned to the Cabinet War Room on Whitehall; she was nothing more than a primary photographic analyst attached to the photo reconnaissance squadron of P-51s flown by the RCAF. As such, her direct supervisor was a sergeant with the twenty-second photo/fighter squadron. His supervisor was a first lieutenant with the same squadron, and he, in turn, reported to a major. She'd never met the major, had seen the lieutenant infrequently during training sessions, and paid little or no attention to the sergeant, who was drunk most of the time. Sarah Collingsworth, for all practical purposes, acted as her own supervisor, analyzing the aerial photographs taken by the squadron and recording the results on the back of the photos and in the master log.

As Westminster Bridge appeared on the right where Millbank Road changed to Whitehall, Sarah realized she had never dealt with any person, army officer or civilian, higher than the rank of sergeant. Just who had summoned her to Whitehall she did not know. The reason she had been summoned lay in the brown folder beside her on the seat.

The building that housed the War Cabinet Room—in reality, a series of rooms—was no more than a block away. The request for her to appear on such-and-such a day at such-and-such a time had not come through the normal channels, arriving, instead, by special courier the day before. The courier was the man now driving the army sedan in which she rode. He had waited—orders, he'd said—until she was ready, and together they had left the air base late last night and raced through the night to reach London during morning rush-hour traffic. The trip had caused as much consternation within Sarah as the summons. Driving the narrow backroads of England with only marginally sufficient lighting had been a nightmare, but, she'd been told, blackout regulations prevented the use of unrestricted headlamps. The only available light had come from two small slits in the headlamp covers.

The sedan lurched to a stop on Whitehall. The traffic was heavier coming from Charing Cross and Piccadilly Circus, a few blocks away.

Sarah Collingsworth picked up the brown envelope, gingerly extracted the black-and-white photos from inside, and leafed through them once again, turning some over to review the notes she'd written on the reverse side.

It had all started with the photographs, she was convinced. Those stupid photographs.

Sarah had been working late, analyzing a set of photos taken earlier in the day in an overflight of the Kiel German naval installation. The weather had been superb, and the photos had been crisp, their details—and thus their secrets—present for the trained eye to uncloak. She had spent more time than usual on the photos, working into the night, recording several anomalies and noting them on the reverse side of the photos.

Following standard operating procedures, the photos had made their way to the next senior analyst, her findings either confirmed or challenged, and then the results forwarded to the local branch of military intelligence.

She had just finished with the last photo of Kiel when the lab technician entered her cubicle and dumped another set of photos on her desk.

"What do you make of these?" he'd asked curiously.

Sarah had taken the photos and quickly examined them under her stand-mounted magnifying glass.

"An island," she said.

"I know it's an island," the technician had replied, exasperated. "What island? Where? And why are these pictures from the same film roll as those others?" he'd asked, indicating the stack of photos she'd just finished.

"The answer to those questions are for neither you nor I to know," Sarah answered. "Our job is to analyze the photos. No more. No less." With that, Sarah had reached for the high-intensity lamp over her desk and flipped it on with one hand while still examining the new photographs. She stopped short, her hand resting on the lamp switch for long minutes as she continued studying the pictures. Time was suspended, reality frozen.

Slowly, with deliberate calm, she removed her hand from the switch, reached for the high-resolution magnifier, and positioned it over the northernmost portion of the island. As she examined the island through the optics, the buildings that appeared, and the strange objects, both prone and upright, seemed to grow from the surrounding terrain.

Some of the long, cylindrical, cigar-shaped objects were supported by what looked to be steel beam structures. Others she could clearly see still loaded on the trailers that had borne them to this place in the north of this island. Men were visible, appearing as no more than ants, working in and around the objects. It had been easy to determine the length of the cylinders—more than forty feet long—using the trailers on which they were carried as reference objects.

Sarah quickly scanned through the remaining photos. Other areas appeared: obvious housing areas, military barracks, factories, shops, and office buildings. It all added up to one thing—a complex, hitherto unidentified, at least by her, that was ostensibly producing the cylindrical-shaped objects so prevalent in the northern area of the island.

Sarah Collingsworth had never seen a rocket in her life, other than the kind sold at fireworks stands, the kind her brothers had shot off in the backyard, but it did not require genius to know that what she was looking at was a test facility and factory dedicated to the production of cigar-shaped objects that could only be some form of weapon. Nothing else made sense, and the Germans, for all their barbarism, rarely initiated a project of this magnitude for the good of mankind.

Sarah made all the notations she could on the reverse side of the photographs and then went to her typewriter and compiled a seven-page report describing what she interpreted as a new form of weapon. What its capabilities were, she could not determine. Her recommendations were that the photos be examined by the senior analyst as soon as possible and copies of the photos be forwarded immediately to Military Intelligence. She signed the bottom of the report, snapped off the light and left her office for the night, the images of black-and-white cigars running through her mind.

That had been only two days ago, and now, as the army sedan jerked to a stop in front of the War Cabinet Room building, she was beginning to wonder what she had started.

"This is it," the driver said without preamble.

Sarah got out of the car carrying the brown envelope in her left hand. The car wormed its way back into the Whitehall traffic and disappeared.

Sarah turned and walked up the stone steps of the building. She was challenged by an armed sentry and asked for identification. She removed her analyst ID and was surprised to note the sentry apparently knew who she was. He made a note in a logbook that rested on a podium to his right and returned the ID.

"Room 14, Miss Collingsworth," the sentry directed, holding the door for her to enter. "Down the corridor and to the right," he added as she disappeared into the warren of hallways.

Sarah could feel her knees begin to shake as she neared room 14. She stopped before the carved wooden door and knocked, the knock lost in the surrounding melee of clattering footsteps and shouted messages. Here, amidst the hubbub and clattering, the business of war progressed unabated.

The corridors were filled with people, in and out of uniform, hurrying about the task of making war. It was only when they neared the door of room fourteen that each stopped his own chattering long enough to give silent respect to those persons behind the door.

So obvious a self-subjugation served only to heighten Sarah's nervousness.

The door swung open, and a severely dressed woman motioned her into an outer office. It was large, overpoweringly so, decorated with heavy, dark wooden furniture. The oil-polished oak walls shone under the incandescent lamps that illuminated the early masterpieces hanging on every surface. A heavy walnut desk sat in one corner, the squat guardian of the only other door exiting the large room. Leather wing-back chairs were tastefully arranged in small groups, allowing the men already present to speak in relative privacy.

Sarah counted five men in all, each wearing the uniform of senior military officers. The officers stood as Sarah was shown into the room, each nodding in turn their acceptance of the photo analyst.

Sarah's mind was contemplating the intricacies of military protocol when the door to the inner office opened.

"This way," the austere secretary motioned.

The officers waited, making it clear that Sarah was to enter first. She swallowed hard, her pulse beginning to race, and, she knew, her face reddening at the acquiescent attitude of the officers. She walked into the inner office and stopped cold, a statue of flesh and blood, rooted in place, as she recognized the man behind the desk.

"Please," the prime minister of Great Britain said, getting up from behind the desk. "Sit down, Miss Collingsworth. Can I get you anything? Water? Whiskey, perhaps? Feel free to ask for whatever you need. You will be here in London for a while. We hope you find us accommodating," Winston Churchill said.

Sarah Collingsworth had heard the prime minister on the radio many times and seen his picture in the dailies. She had always supposed, when one got right down to it, that she actually worked for the man. Never in her most fanciful daydreams had she ever contemplated meeting the most important man in England.

"Thank you, Mr. Prime Minister," Sarah stammered, as she fell into the nearest chair. "Wa . . . water would be nice."

"Mrs. Granville," Churchill ordered the secretary, "a glass of water for Miss Collingsworth."

The military officers filed in and took their seats, none closer to Churchill's desk than Sarah. The prime minister moved around the desk and sat down.

"I see you've brought the envelope with you. Splendid. May I see it?" Churchill began, holding out his hand.

Sarah handed the brown envelope across, trying not to let her hand shake in the process. She noticed the man's hands were pudgy, yet delicate, and the incongruence amused her as Churchill smiled and took the quivering envelope and opened it.

"Ah, yes. These are the same pictures we received," he said as he turned them over and read the notes written on the back in Sarah's careful hand. For almost five minutes, Churchill alternately gazed at the photos and read the notes. "Umm . . . yes, I see," he continued. "You stand by these findings, do you?"

"Yes . . . yes sir, I do."

"No need to be nervous, my dear. It might interest you to know that every man in this room concurs with your assessment. So much so that we are at a loss to explain how it is that you were able to identify the . . . uh . . . shall we say articles in these photos."

"I'm afraid I don't understand, Mr. Prime Minister," Sarah began.

"What I mean is, you've identified some of the objects in the photos as rockets. How is that possible? To my knowledge, neither we nor the United States have anything remotely resembling a rocket. How can you identify them when you've never seen them?"

"Oh, . . . I understand," Sarah said, smiling. "No sir, you are mistaken. I never identified them as rockets. What I said was they resembled rockets, only much larger. The rockets I'm talking about are the kind you play with as a child. Fireworks. The Chinese invented rockets long before the Germans, sir. I have three brothers. All of them have stuffed gunpowder into cylinders and touched them off. Mostly they just blew up. Some flew, sometimes. But that's what I meant by rockets. The things in the photos *looked* like those rockets my brothers used to put together. That's all. If I've done something wrong, sir, I'm profoundly sorry."

Churchill glanced around the room, the small, twisted grin that was so much a part of his character displayed once again. "There you have it, gentlemen. Sarah has brothers. There is no deep, dark secret organization toiling surreptitiously within Military Intelligence for us to blame this on. She has merely identified these photos in the only vocabulary available to her." Churchill turned to Sarah and said, "And for that we are profoundly grateful, Sarah. You have done your job to perfection. Unfortunately, for that reason, we will have to ask you to remain in London for the time being."

Sarah looked at the five officers and the prime minister. "I'm afraid I don't understand, Mr. Prime Minister. I have my job in Aberdeen, my family, so much to do there."

"Yes, well, I'm afraid this puts all of us in a rather sticky position. I cannot explain to you the reason we cannot let you leave London for the time being without compromising certain strategic positions, as it were. That is all I can say at the moment. You have my sincerest apologies, Sarah, and I assure you that as soon as it is a viable option, I will personally see to it that you are returned to Aberdeen. I am sorry."

The five general officers rose as the door opened and the austere secretary entered, accompanied by two men dressed in the uniform of British Military Police.

Sarah stood, her mouth open to protest, but nothing would come as she was led from the office and out of the War Cabinet Room.

"Gentlemen, please excuse me," Churchill said.

The officers rose as one and followed Sarah Collingsworth from the office.

Churchill picked up the phone and spoke quietly into the mouthpiece. He waited a few moments for the connection to be made and said, "It's as we suspected. Peenemünde *is* a rocket research center. I don't see that we have any option, however. We *must* continue as planned," he said.

He waited for the reply to make its way across the miles of copper wire and finally said, "Then we are in agreement. So be it," he finished and replaced the instrument in its cradle.

Winston Churchill buried his face in his hands, a deep weariness overtaking him as he said, "Dear God in heaven, not again. Not again."

CHAPTER

28

The glow of the civilian housing area could be seen from where Michael Shaw grappled with the German staff car he had procured from the motor pool only minutes earlier. The military barracks on Peenemünde lay seven kilometers to the west of the civilian housing area where Shaw was to meet with Kurt Daluege. Too far to walk in the worsening Baltic weather.

The motor pool sergeant had offered Shaw a driver, which he had quickly and firmly rejected. He needed no third party to the meeting, not even a bored staff driver.

The road, normally an innocuous stretch of gravel and tar, had turned adversarial with the freezing temperatures and falling snow. Shaw struggled with the wheel of the small automobile, slowing his already dilatory pace.

Time was important. Shaw knew that Daluege would have had his name listed on the log at the outer security gate leading into the housing area. The meeting was normal, expected—a senior scientist meeting with his senior security counterpart. Such meetings were encouraged, Shaw knew, and no questions would be asked. And this meeting was important. There were strategies to be formulated, tactical exercises to be defined, discussed, refined, and put into action. The delaying tactics that would keep the V-5 rocket from murdering thousands of people would, beginning tonight, take a different tack.

The sound was sharp, piercing in the cold winter air! The wheel of the staff car jerked from Shaw's grasp as the car plunged off the road and into the shallow ditch paralleling the road. Shaw fought for control; the steering wrenched to the right and then back to the left. The car bucked up and over the small boulders concealed in the ditch, the undercarriage of the car protesting in a shriek of metal. It was all Michael Shaw could do to maintain even a semblance of control.

The headlights were suddenly extinguished, their filaments destroyed by the tortuous passage of the automobile over the uneven terrain. The dark countryside of Usedom Island turned even darker, a dense, silky blackness enveloped the car; the only hint of light came from the housing area. The car plunged on, finally coming to rest on the side of the road. Shaw could smell the gasoline flowing from the ruptured tank. His head had smashed into the wheel, and he could feel the slow ooze of warm blood on his forehead.

In an instant, all was quiet. Shaw struggled with the door handle, forcing it open with all his strength. He stumbled from the wrecked car and dashed for the cover of the nearby trees.

The smell of gasoline was stronger; he knew the car could explode at any moment, turning everything around the car into a giant fireball.

But what was that sound? A blowout? No, the sound had occurred a split second before the tire failure. A gunshot? It had sounded like a gunshot. A small caliber pistol? Perhaps a rifle?

Shaw ran, the edge of the pine forest within reach. Just as he made the tree line, he heard the low WHOOMP of spilled gasoline igniting. He turned to see the ground around the car burning. The flames, consuming the automobile at an alarming rate, reached the now half-empty fuel tank, and the car exploded, ripping the automobile in two. The doors of the staff car flew open in response to the force of the explosion. The interior of the car began to burn. Shaw dove for the ground and felt the initial shock wave wash over him in a tide of pungent warmth.

The car was engulfed now, the flames burning an eerie, soft yellow as the material of the seats fed the hungry flames.

Shaw was aware of the sound of cracking limbs over the distant roar of the flames. Heavy boots crunched over the frozen landscape, rushing toward him.

Shaw rose to one knee and turned in the direction of the intruders. He was conscious that he was backlit from the burning car, a perfect target; he scanned the area, looking for cover.

The footsteps changed. Desperate, muffled voices, urgent, demanding, came closer. Polish! The running men were speaking Polish!

A shot rang out.

It *had* been a shot. These men, whoever they were, had shot his tire out! Perhaps the headlights too. It had been no accident! His blowout and his subsequent wreck had been planned! These men were after him!

Shaw was up now, running to his right, away from the rushing footsteps and angry voices. As he ran, he could just make out movement in his peripheral vision. The movement took on a more organized effort, men who were only shadows in the night consolidating their attack. Shaw ran for the cover of the forest. If he could avoid detection for only a few minutes, the light from the blazing automobile would bring the security guards from the military barracks and most certainly a contingent of SS men. He was depending on the SS to save his life, thought Shaw wryly.

More men emerged from the forest; they had not yet seen him, their night vision ruined by the flames that licked at every combustible item of the staff car.

Shaw was into the woods now; the shadows changed to a deep purple. He could still hear the voices, the Polish commands uttered in muted urgency. He continued to run.

The Peenemünde civilian housing area—his original destination—was no more than a few kilometers over the next ridge. If he could make the security perimeter there, he would have eluded the men behind him intent on either capturing or killing him.

Shaw stumbled through the woods, fighting the deeper snowdrifts and the intense cold.

Who? Why?

The thought occurred to Shaw that the men seeking him were probably on his side. Partisans, freedom fighters. They were concerned only with the elimination of one more SS officer, this one an SS-Sturmbannführer. There was a certain irony to it all, Shaw realized.

He had come to Germany to fight the very thing these men of the night were fighting. He had successfully melded into the operations of Peenemünde. He had discovered the horrible secret of the island and the rocket research center. With the loss of his small radio, he had yet to contact the men waiting for word at Bletchley Park, at Station X. Communications was on the agenda tonight when he talked with Kurt Daluege. But communications were strictly monitored, in and out of Peenemünde. It would be difficult, if not impossible. He needed to get all the information to England, particularly the information on the V-5, the rocket that was almost perfected and waiting for deployment. Deployment to where, against whom, Shaw did not know, but the information he had was invaluable, even at this point.

But now, he found himself in the snow-covered forest of Usedom Island in northern Germany, fleeing for his life.

The voices faded as Shaw worked deeper and deeper into the pine forest. His eyes were becoming adjusted to the dark, his night vision taking over once clear of the blazing staff car. Pine branches slapped at his face, stinging painfully in the frigid cold. He could feel tiny

slashes where the limbs had cut him. Blood flowed from the cuts, min-
gling with that from the wreck, and quickly coagulated.

He fled.

There were no stars, no moon; the overcast skies that had
obscured the day now blotted out the night sky. Gradually Shaw eased
up, slowing to a crisp walk, gasping for air. He held his sides. He was
still moving through the woods in the general direction of the civilian
housing area, the area nearest to the ambush site.

A muffled spit kicked up the snow in his path. For a moment he
froze, slowly assimilating the sound. Another shot! This one from a
silenced weapon! A second shot struck the tree next to him. He reacted,
diving for the protection of the trees on his left. Three more shots in
quick succession followed on either side of where he lay in the deep
snow, the killer intent on success but unable to see in the darkness.

Shaw scanned the area quickly. He saw no one. No movement, the
element most easily detected in the darkness. The shots had come from
nearby, the silenced spits completely audible in the crisp air. The killer
could be no more than twenty meters away. Probably, Shaw realized,
moving in his direction this very minute.

Normally he would have been wearing his uniform holster and pistol, but he'd left them in his barracks room this night. Possibly a fatal
error in judgment. Just as quickly, he thought about the difficulty of
having to shoot men who were surely his allies.

The sound of the fire and cacophony of Polish voices had ceased,
lost in the distance, muted by the thick stand of pine. All was silent for
the moment, a stillness akin to death. The air was heavy, the forest
floor cold. His mind wandered for a moment, remembering the times
he'd played similar games during his childhood. Then they had been
nothing but games, versions of hide-and-seek, played out against the
chilled backdrop of coming winter. But this was different.

Another shot!

Shaw pushed himself up from the snow-covered forest floor and
ran, the pine boughs slapping at him once again. His legs protested.

The cold bit at him. He felt as if he were moving in slow motion. He could hear his pursuers as heavy boots broke through the frozen surface snow. His breathing was labored. His pulse accelerated as adrenaline pumped into his system. Shaw struggled to move his protesting legs, but it was no use. He was reaching his limit.

He had not been in this part of the forest before. His SS duties in the motor shop had carried him no farther than his barracks, the shop, the test area, and Kurt Daluege's apartment in the civilian area. The terrain was rugged, the ground uneven. The going was difficult, made more so by the deep snow and cold. Broken limbs littered the forest floor under the snowpack.

Shaw stumbled, fatigue setting in. He tripped on the snow-covered root of a nearby tree. His hand shot out in a frantic effort to break his fall. He struck the ground, his face burying in the snow, his ankle tangled in the hidden roots. Pain shot through his head and shoulders.

He listened. There were two . . . no, three footfalls, then silence again. He realized his pursuer had been following his sound. His running had exposed him to the killers. Lying on the freezing ground, he'd neutralized the men by stopping. But he could not stay in the chilling snow for long.

Shaw scanned the area he'd just traversed. Somewhere in the darkness, the assassins waited. He kept his eyes moving, not wanting to fixate on any one spot, giving his night vision a chance to catch movement, however minute.

There! To his right, no more than ten meters away. It had been only a shadow, but it had been movement.

Shaw fought to control his breathing, which still came in great gasps. His muscles were beginning to rebel in the cold, cramping his legs and stomach. The man had moved once and no more. Shaw scanned the spot where the man had been. He needed a plan. In his haste, he had abandoned the only place where he could have been assured of help. Here, in the deep forest, there would be no SS guards, no security force. They would see the burning car and congregate there, waiting for orders. The men who had burned it would be gone, escaping under the cloud of confusion. But the chance of the SS guards following him into the forest was almost nonexistent.

He was alone, stalked by killers with silenced automatic weapons. Men whose goal this night was to kill an SS-Sturmbannführer.

A match flared! Off to his right the tiny light had been ignited then as quickly extinguished. A warning? A signal? Both, perhaps?

There were two! Shaw rubbed his eyes, waiting for his night vision to return. He had thought about resisting, but that was impossible. Escape was his only option, his only hope. It would be only minutes before they would be on him. They had to know he was unarmed. He had not returned a shot during the chase, something he would surely have done had he been armed.

His breathing was returning to normal, his night vision regained. He would exercise his only option; he would run. He came up slowly, using the tree as cover and support. He took a deep breath, his muscles bunching beneath the black SS uniform, prepared for escape. His legs ached. His stomach contracted from cold and fear. He was ready to run when he felt the cold muzzle of a deadly silencer rammed into the base of his skull so forcibly that the skin broke and blood trickled down his neck.

"Run, Sturmbannführer. *Please* run," the voice said in perfect, but Polish-accented German.

Shaw turned around and stared into the eyes of Walter Kolinsky, the leader of the team that had attacked the train—the man with the scar!

CHAPTER

29

Footsteps echoing down the long corridor of the Reich Chancellery, Heinrich Himmler strode down the halls of power of Nazi Germany. The appointment with *Der Führer,* Adolf Hitler, had been made only hours earlier, and Himmler, in typical German punctuality, was precisely on time.

It was times like these when Himmler knew he'd been right, almost prophetically so. The SS had evolved, under his tutelage and care, into the ultimate German organization, supplanting even the church. Every contingency, every possibility had been anticipated and incorporated into the SS. If religion existed within the Third Reich, it was the SS.

Himmler approached the ornate double doors that led to Hitler's inner sanctum. The doors swung open, and Himmler felt the pride that went with being one of the elite, a leader. The SS *was* the religion; Hitler was the god; Himmler the archangel.

Hitler sat in the overstuffed chair that was his favorite and motioned Himmler to join him. Himmler obeyed, taking the chair directly across from the leader of all Germany.

"Heinrich. Good to see you," greeted Hitler.

"Mein Führer," Himmler responded, saluting in the traditional German manner. "It is good of you to see me on such short notice."

Hitler waved at the SS leader with the back of his hand. "Always time for you, Heinrich. What is on your mind this night?"

"Omega," Himmler said immediately.

"Omega. An interesting project. How is it going?"

Himmler handed Hitler the communiqué he'd received from Dönitz canceling the endeavor. "The admiral is well-meaning, I think," Himmler began. "But I think he lacks the intuitiveness to carry out the goals of Omega. As you see, he wanted to cancel the project outright. I had to put a stop to it. After all, there is as much SS money in Omega as Kriegsmarine."

"I understand your concern, Heinrich. Are you telling me that the SS has taken over the Omega plans?"

"Yes, *Mein Führer.* It became necessary when I received the order from Dönitz ordering the three U-boats back into traditional service. I did not think it a wise move."

"Admiral Dönitz will be upset when he learns of this. I would not want to be in your shoes when he learns what you have done. What justification are you prepared to offer?"

Himmler cleared his throat. It was the question he'd been waiting for. "The rocket is ready. That is to say, all the components are functioning properly. It will only be a few weeks at the most before the rocket is constructed. We have conquered tremendous problems in the construction of this weapon. I believe it would be a waste not to use it. Also, the V-5 will serve as a prototype for the V-2. Many of the technical problems are the same. The V-1, of course, is another matter. But the point is, the V-1 and V-2 are a couple of years away from deployment. The V-5 is ready now. We need to launch it, if for no other reason than to verify that certain technical problems have been solved."

Hitler cocked his head, listening, his eyes boring into Himmler, as was his habit.

Himmler continued solicitously, "I realize Admiral Dönitz will have objections to the continued deployment of the weapon on a strategic basis, and I understand his concern. But I believe," Himmler rushed on, "that it is imperative we strike at the mainland of the Americans. We must demoralize them, keep them on their side of the Atlantic. There is nothing more strategic than keeping the Americans occupied. Omega will accomplish this, I believe. The cost savings alone would be incalculable if we can force them to defend their shores rather than those of England. Even Admiral Dönitz would have to agree that mastery of the North Atlantic by our U-boats could again be achieved if we could force the U.S. to protect herself. In that vein, I am as concerned for the admiral as for the mission," Himmler said, feeling superior in his deception.

Himmler paused, his explanation succinct, direct, and effective.

"I see your point, Heinrich. Yes, it would free up our resources if we could force such a concession from the Americans. You have my permission to continue with Omega. But it must take place within two months. That I insist on," Hitler said, then added, "can you do that?"

"It will be done, *Mein Führer,*" Himmler assured the German leader.

"Good. Very good. Keep me posted."

Himmler rose, saluted, and left, knowing he'd have only a few weeks to put Omega into action. As persuasive as he was, Dönitz was every bit the diplomat, and, Himmler admitted to himself, the better tactician. The SS leader held no illusions on that score. As soon as Dönitz realized Omega was still functioning, he would address the issue with Hitler himself; and Himmler knew the all-powerful Führer would vacillate yet again, giving in to the admiral.

Himmler would allow himself two weeks to move all three U-boats away from the French and German coasts.

Two weeks to launch a most horrendous death on one of the most important areas on the United States' east coast.

CHAPTER
30

The pistol was jammed into Michael Shaw's neck just above his larynx. He could feel the bruised flesh and small laceration where Walter Kolinsky had forced the pistol silencer under his chin. Early morning light was beginning to break through the overcast, and the scar on the Polish resistance fighter's face glowed an ethereal pale white. The slash crossed his face and ended at the edge of a cruel smile. There was no doubt in Shaw's mind that the man intended to kill him.

He had been tied up in the corner for hours, a knot of filthy rag stuffed in his mouth to silence him. His captors had talked in low voices through the night, until the morning began to break. The scar-faced man turned to him, the legs of the chair scraping along the floor.

"One less SS swine, Sturmbannführer," the Polish worker spat. "This is for the family you animals murdered in the name of conquest. *My family.* May you die slowly, German," he said, pulling the rag from Shaw's mouth.

Shaw started to speak, but the Pole thrust the bulbous silencer into his mouth before he could utter a word.

"Not a word from you, or I will kill you on the spot and leave your body for the varmints when the spring comes. I removed the rag only to hear you beg for mercy before I kill you. Like my family begged."

Shaw nodded, and Kolinsky removed the silencer. A second man joined Kolinsky. Loathing was as evident on this man's face as on Kolinsky's.

"We have another one, Walter," the second man said.

"Yes. We will extract what information we want from this one and then see to it that he bothers no one else on this earth."

Shaw could see the crooked smile on the second man; there was no compassion in either man's face. It had come to this, he thought. He was about to die at the hands of people he was trying to help. But was that the truth? Was he really trying to help these people, or was he here for himself? He thought he'd known the answer to that question when he'd volunteered for Donovan's OSS. He was in it for revenge. But somewhere, somehow, something had changed, deep within him. He *was* in Germany to help these people, and the self-admission surprised even him. For a split second, Shaw wondered if this was a joke played by God, just to get his attention. But this was not the way God worked.

Strange, he thought, *that I should think of God at this time.* But then he realized he had been depending on God from the start; he'd just chosen not to acknowledge that simple fact.

The blow was swift, the butt of the pistol striking Shaw on the side of the neck. There was a flash of intense pain, and then he was engulfed by a blackness more profound than the darkness of the night before.

When Shaw awoke he gingerly touched the damaged area on his neck. The pain had subsided to a constant ache. He opened his eyes, searching for clues to his whereabouts. He was in the same, barren room.

A square wooden table surrounded by four chairs stood in the center of the room. Shaw lay crumpled in the corner. The two men sat at the table concentrating on something that lay on the surface. The light in the room came from a combination of weak sunlight and a kerosene lantern hanging directly over the table. There was little else. Nothing more was needed. Shaw knew now that he was looking at his death chamber. Pain slowly insinuated itself into his conscience; the pain of retribution, exacted by the man with the scar.

Barbara. He would see her soon if these men had their way. He realized he'd always thought of her as being in heaven, and then he wondered what it would be like. He thought about telling the men who he really was but knew that it would appear to be a pathetic ploy to save his life. The truth shall make you free, he recalled. But in this case, the truth will ensure a quicker, more painful death.

Shaw pulled his legs under him, his boots scraping on the wooden floor. The two men glanced up.

"About time, Sturmbannführer. I was beginning to think I had killed you already. I am glad I did not. It would have taken all the fun out of what we have in store for you. *After* you talk, of course."

"You are making a mistake," Shaw said.

Kolinsky laughed. The second man joined in.

"Perhaps. But you will talk, Sturmbannführer. For as long as we want about anything we want."

The silenced pistol lay on the table. Shaw locked on to it, seeing a slim possibility.

Kolinsky recognized the look in Shaw's face. He looked at Shaw and back to the pistol. "Please try it, Sturmbannführer. It will not bring me as much pleasure to shoot you, but you will be just as dead. I promise you that."

"Vengeance is mine? Is that it?" Shaw asked.

Kolinsky snorted, "An SS man quoting the Bible. It must be the Bible; you most certainly would not attribute that passage to the Torah, would you?" the Pole said, rising from the table. "What does an SS-Sturmbannführer know of God? Of the Bible? Of justice? Your form of justice is found in the camps. In the streets of Warsaw. I think God will look on your death as no more than the extermination of human trash," Kolinsky said, and returned to his seat.

"And your kind of justice is the justice of the righteous? You see yourself as the hand of God? What you do in the name of your God is justice, and what the Germans do is not. That's a convenient juxtaposition of the truth," Shaw countered. "I have even used the vengeance argument myself, not so long ago."

Shaw watched as the Pole fixed his gaze on him. Their eyes locked. From a heretofore untapped reservoir of understanding and will, Shaw stared into the eyes of Walter Kolinsky, the man with no family. He could feel the pain that resided there, beneath the harsh exterior and threatening words. It was the same agony he lived through each night as his mind seized on the events of that night in 1939. Then, it had been the last of his family. Here, in this hut, before these two men, it was the family of Walter Kolinsky that took center stage.

"We have much in common," Shaw said at last.

Kolinsky's head jerked up, his countenance terrible. He began to rise from the chair where he sat. The second man put a hand on his shoulder.

"Not yet, my friend," the man urged. "The time will come."

Kolinsky sat back down. "Yes, the time will come," Kolinsky said. "And the time *will* come quickly, if you compare the two of us again. Understood?"

Shaw knew the man meant what he said, but his response was no longer his own. "Have you heard of the *Athenia*?" Shaw asked.

"The British ship that was sunk in '39?"

Shaw nodded. "I lost my wife that night. It has taken me this long to understand how any good could possibly come out of that, but I am beginning to see the possibilities. I have no family, just as you have no family. In one way or another, I lost mine to the evils of the Reich, just as you. And I have just as much hate and loathing for those who did that as you do. We are alike, you and I. Why do you think it is taking as long as it is to perfect this weapon? It's because there are those of us who are working from within the Reich, just as you are working from without, to stop the nightmare."

Shaw stopped to take a breath. Kolinsky was frozen in place.

"You can kill me. It will do nothing but hamper your goals. For despite what you think, despite what you see before you, I am not as I seem. You are not as you seem. I suspected that when I first saw you at the train. And it is true."

"So, you saw me at the train?"

"You were the leader. It was you who issued the orders, and it was you who barely missed killing me when you came around to the back side of the cars. I was behind a tree, but I suspect you already know that. That is why you're going to kill me. You think I am part of this warped Nazi world."

"Hiding then as you hid tonight. A coward, perhaps, wanting only to save yourself."

"Just a man who has nothing to gain by killing his allies. Just as you would gain nothing by killing me."

"You wear the uniform."

"As you wear the uniform of a peasant laborer."

"A valid argument," Kolinsky relented. "But hardly conclusive. What else is there you can offer in your defense?"

Shaw shifted his body on the wooden floor. He had the man talking; there was hope. "I can tell you everything I know about what the Germans call the V-5 rocket. About the motor development, and about what I suspect the rocket will be used for. I can tell you I work for the organization known as the OSS. The United States. I can tell you about that night in 1939. Beyond that, there is nothing but trust and faith."

"Suspicions are not fact. Not proof."

"No. But you asked what I could tell you. My suspicions are part of that."

Walter Kolinsky rose from the table, pulled his chair closer to Shaw, and straddled the ladder-back chair. "Tell me what you know, German. Then I will decide what I am to do with you."

Shaw began, not with the attack on the train, but with the night the *Athenia* was sunk. He told his story in writer's form, short, direct, with facts used to bolster his contentions. He told of Barbara and Wild Bill Donovan. Of his being American. Of Canada and Washington and London. Of the ride across the English channel and of the demonic ceremonies he witnessed in Berlin.

"Himmler tries to abrogate religion," Shaw explained. "If he can do that, then the only values that will mean anything will be the values that he imposes."

"I have heard this before," Kolinsky agreed. "I am Catholic."

"I'm Protestant. But Himmler would destroy both of us for that. Once he has quashed organized religion, he can institute his own brand of worship. Worship centered on the man in Berlin. Values will be those imposed by the state. Morals will be judged by their acceptance within the government hierarchy. Most of the battle will be won if Himmler can annihilate organized religion."

"The people of Germany would be expected to worship Caesar," Kolinsky whispered. "That cannot be allowed."

Shaw nodded. "That is only part of it. Every facet of life will be controlled by the state. Those people found unacceptable will be banished—or worse, murdered."

"That is happening now."

Shaw nodded, "I have heard of the camps."

"But you have not seen them?"

"I have heard only the rumors of detainment centers for certain ethnic groups."

"They are death camps. I have seen them."

"Tell me about the camps."

Walter Kolinsky rose and began pacing, his hands alternately held behind his back or rubbing his temples to ease the pain that was building due to lack of sleep.

"They are everywhere. Dachau, Belsen, Auschwitz. Names that come from the very depths of hell itself. Places where women and children die if they cannot perform satisfactorily. Places where Jews die simply because they are Jews. The same with the Poles, the Czechs, the Slavs, the Gypsies. Anyone who is not pure is exterminated like an insect."

"They will have to answer for the evil."

Kolinsky laughed derisively. "These people do not recognize evil. They bow only to power and a warped sense of national pride. They are monsters."

"You are right, of course. And I'm here to try to stop just a small part of the madness."

"The V-5."

"Exactly. There are certain specifications that make the V-5 a particularly deadly weapon. I have never seen anything like the rockets being developed here, but the V-5 is a prototype for the V-2. In some ways, it is superior to the larger V-2."

"How so?"

"The V-5 has been fitted with a waterproof motor enclosure. The entire rocket will be impervious to salt water. What does that tell you?"

"They plan to launch it from ships and vessels," Kolinsky said. "There would be no country, no area within hundreds of miles of the ocean that would be immune to such a weapon. Including your United States, if, as you have said, you are American."

Shaw sensed the growing bond between himself and the Pole. It was an intuitive understanding, a belief that went beyond the circumstances. For Shaw, it was the confirmation he'd so long sought. The proof that there was yet a reason for him to be on this earth. But was it God's way of showing him the direction he should take? He looked into the Pole's eyes and saw the same confirmation reflected there.

"I am who I say I am. And you have just hit on a scenario that is particularly ominous. These rockets could be used against America." Shaw stopped for a moment, thinking. "If . . . if they could be launched against the U.S., such an attack would limit our involvement over here. Our military leaders would be forced to reevaluate American participation, forced to protect our own shores as opposed to those of England. It would be a massive accomplishment for Germany."

"Not to mention the number of people who would die on your very shores."

"That too," Shaw agreed. "We have large cities on the coast. These rockets could kill thousands of innocents."

"Then you have a plan to stop the killing?"

Shaw watched as Kolinsky reversed his course on the wooden floor, coming back to the chair and facing Shaw in the corner. "Then you believe I am who I say?"

"Let's say, I'm moving in that direction. Tell me about your plans."

"I'm not alone in this. Kurt Daluege has been doing all within his power to delay the development of this weapon. I came on the scene later. Most of the delays have been due to him. My plan necessarily leaves him in the clear to continue his work here on Peenemünde. That's a must. He cannot be exposed."

"That makes sense. I am new to the rocket center, but some other leaders have said they suspected that someone on the inside has been sabotaging the efforts of the rocket makers. I was sent to the center to find out who. It seems I have succeeded beyond my own expectations. What is to be done now?"

Shaw continued. "The rocket will be ready within weeks. The only way to see that it does not go into mass production is to instigate a failure so massive, so final, that the Germans will scrap the project themselves."

"That will have to be done at the source. An actual failure during deployment."

"I agree. But it has to be done away from the rocket center, to leave Daluege and the others in the clear. I will have to be aboard the vessel when the Germans deploy the V-5."

"And you will be able to stop the launch?"

"Not only stop it, but engineer a disaster of such magnitude that the SS will abandon all hope of ever developing the V-5 for general use."

Kolinsky was up and pacing again, his hand gently stroking the luminous scar. "You would have to be aboard the ship. That means that any disaster would involve you too. You could die."

"That has crossed my mind. I see no other recourse at this time. The V-5 must fail under actual combat conditions. Any other failure might bring undue pressure on Daluege and his men. I can't allow that. They need to be able to continue their subversion within Peenemünde."

"Agreed. What is it you need from us?"

"A disappearance."

"Of a particular person? That we can do." Kolinsky smiled.

"And I believe you will enjoy effecting this particular disappearance."

"Tell me what you have in mind."

Shaw began, the words spilling from his mouth in torrents. With each word, he realized he was placing himself in danger. Kolinsky had been right. He could die. But then, that would only mean he would be that much closer to seeing Barbara. He now had no doubts that she was watching him from the gallery on high. Death, under such circumstances, would be gain, as the apostle Paul had deemed it. Shaw laid out his plan over the next hour, directing Kolinsky as to his part, accepting the Pole's suggestions, and finally finishing as the sun reached higher into the sky.

"It will be done," the Pole assured Shaw.

"We shall pray that it goes well."

"As we shall pray that you will come through this alive."

"That," Shaw said, "is not as important as it once was."

"Possibly. What is important is that you return in such a manner as to make the SS guards and security force think you have been wandering in the woods all this time."

Shaw laughed. "You forget, Walter. I am an SS-Sturmbannführer. They will take my word for it. Besides," Shaw said, reaching up for the damaged flesh of his neck, "I have some pretty good evidence of my nocturnal wanderings."

"Yes, I suppose you have, and I suppose they will believe you. Come, we will get you to within walking distance of the car. You will have to take it from there."

"We will meet again, my friend. Soon."

"I look forward to it," Kolinsky said, rising to leave. "We will pray for you."

Shaw glanced at Kolinsky, wondering for the first time how such a prayer would be answered.

CHAPTER

31

Leitender Ingenieur (LI) Otto Reinertsen cursed softly as the U-135 made its way on an east-southeast course out of Kiel toward the island of Usedom. The trip should have taken no more than twenty hours steaming at normal cruising speed. Now, their third day into the passage, Reinertsen still had not been able to dive the boat with any degree of success. Every engineering trick he'd tried had failed, and Kapitänleutnant Günther Mohr was losing patience with his chief engineer.

The U-135 wallowed over an offshore shelf north of Usedom Island. Heavy seas and bone-chilling winds had combined to slow the transit pace to a crawl. The steel structure jutting from the afterdeck of the U-boat had proved to be a burden while running on the surface and a nightmare while submerged. The asymmetry of the launch apparatus caused every kind of imbalance above and below the surface. To compound his frustration, the Kaleu was looking to him for a solution to the aggravating problem.

Reinertsen stumbled aft from the conning tower. The deck of the boat was slippery with ice from the freezing spray that had plagued the type IXC boat since putting to sea. Three engineering mates were attempting, with little success, to secure a portion of the spaghetti-like apparatus that had broken in the choppy Baltic. Reinertsen made his way toward the three sailors, cursing the French welders who had built the strange apparatus. Even from a distance, he could see the look of disgust on each of the men's faces. Disgust mingled with fatigue. They had been at it for more than five hours now, fighting the bone-numbing cold, the roll of the Baltic, and the defective workmanship of the Deutsche Werke yards in Kiel.

The LI carefully crossed the last few feet of ice-coated deck, coming to a stop next to the launch stand. The three mates didn't even bother to look up at their boss. Each knew he was there and why. None of the three wanted to be the one to tell Reinertsen that they would have to put into port to repair the damage. Just as Reinertsen himself would not want to tell his captain.

The LI moved in and around the mechanism. The problem had come unexpectedly when the U-boat had accelerated toward its standard cruising speed of twelve knots. As the boat had passed through six knots, a sympathetic vibration had begun, sending vibrations through the pressure hull. Under normal circumstances, the vibrations should have been little more than a transitory annoyance. But the vibrations had turned out to be in the low frequency band, disrupting many of the analog instruments on the boat. At any speed above six knots on the surface and two knots submerged, depth, pressure, even engine instruments had vacillated to such a degree that true readings were impossible.

Kapitänleutnant Mohr had been livid. He had cursed the workers at Deutsche Werkes, the engineers who had drawn the plans, the French welders, and the politicians who had conceived the idea. None had escaped his wrath, including those of the crew who'd been in close proximity when the discovery was made.

The problem had been left to Reinertsen to rectify. He and his engineers had been working for two days on the problem. Nothing had remedied the situation. He had suggested to Mohr that they put into port at Peenemünde—their ultimate destination—and work on the problem there. Mohr had told him, quite correctly, that should such a problem arise while en route to the target site, they would not have the luxury of dockside assistance. So Reinertsen was stuck with what he had on board, which was little enough to solve such a complex problem of equipment-generated vibration.

"Anything?" the LI asked as he drew nearer the launch stand.

The senior engineering mate turned to Reinertsen. "Not yet, LI," he answered. "We've been over the entire structure. There is nothing loose. We have repaired the weld breaks and tightened all the structural bolts. It has quieted some but not enough."

"It is, as I thought, a structural malfunction. The architects and marine engineers failed to compensate for the vibrations set up by the diesels. The shockproofing they used is not adequate."

"What will the Kapitän do?"

Reinertsen shook his head in disgust. "I do not know. I have sailed with this captain many times, and each time I learn something about him I never knew before. One thing is certain, though. He will not take this boat out on patrol if it is not functioning properly. He has no death wish."

The three mates looked at each other and nodded. They had heard about Kapitänleutnant Günther Mohr before. He was hard but fair. A hero of Operation Drumbeat and as deadly a man with a torpedo as had ever sailed above and beneath the waters of the North Atlantic. They would settle for whatever decision their captain came to.

The LI turned back toward the conning tower. From the deck of the boat, the conning tower loomed like a great monolith of black steel. Just above the tower, the white sea cap of Günther Mohr appeared. Only three days into their journey and already Reinertsen could see the shadow of beard on his captain's face. It was a reminder of how grueling U-boat duty actually was.

Reinertsen climbed the ice-slick ladder attached to the outer skin of the conning tower and gently stepped down into the recessed area where Mohr stood. This time he did not salute. They were at sea; dockside amenities were sacrificed for expediency.

"Report, LI," Mohr said, his eyes resting on the aberration of metal that littered his afterdeck.

"It will be necessary to put in to properly repair the platform, Herr Kaleu."

"Can you do it, LI?"

"Yes sir, given a day or two. I will need to add additional metal in strategic places to lower the sympathetic frequency to an acceptable range."

Mohr turned to his LI. "You're telling me the addition of metal to the launch platform will stabilize it?"

"I believe so, Herr Kaleau. It is theoretically correct."

Günther Mohr smiled. "Then it is possible that we shall solve our problem with little effort." Mohr spoke into the communication tube mounted on the conning tower. "Number One, set our course for Usedom Island. How long will it take us to reach the northern tip?"

The reply came back in muffled words, their timbre lowered by the communication tube. "Seven hours, Herr Kapitän," the executive officer/navigator answered.

"In seven hours, LI, we will solve this problem by the addition of metal to the platform. Get your men below and get some rest. I will have you awakened when we reach Usedom."

"Thank you, Kapitän." Reinertsen motioned for his men to follow him below. Each man hustled out of the freezing wind and salt spray, thankful for the respite.

"And it will be more than mere metal we add to this platform," Mohr whispered under his breath. "We will mount certain death on that structure," Mohr concluded, his gaze fixed on the platform.

CHAPTER
3 2

december 15, 1942
south of peenemünde

The truck had traveled day and night, through Germany along the Rhine, turning north, and heading for Usedom Island. The orders carried by the men driving the vehicle were explicit, unquestionable, precise. Guards and transit officials who had perused the orders in insolent arrogance had stopped when they read the signature at the bottom of the transit papers and orders. When they realized the truck carried only a single object—a stainless steel security box—from the I. G. Farben Factory on the Rhine, they had hastily released the truck for further transit.

The truck had rumbled through western Germany and into northern Germany with little more than cursory glances at the orders. Each time the reaction was the same, and the men driving had made better time than even they had anticipated.

The truck rolled from the mainland and onto Usedom Island after only two days. This time the security checks had been exacting, verging on the paranoid. The papers had been scrutinized first by the outer perimeter security guards. Then the security officer—an Oberleutnant—had been called. He had examined the papers, recognized the signatures affixed to the papers, and called for his superior. The superior had turned out to be an SS-Oberstführer. With little formality, he had ordered the truck and drivers to a holding section within Peenemünde and placed his own call. This time civilians had appeared—one a small man and the other a round-faced man who could barely be out of his twenties. They were accompanied by an SS member, this time a Sturmbannführer. It was the most impressive display of security procedures the drivers had ever seen.

The round-faced civilian had immediately ordered the stainless steel container offloaded, taking care not to disturb the contents.

With that done, the truck drivers were dismissed and ordered to return to Leverkusen. The men had looked at each other, startled that this trip had ended in less than an hour at their final destination. They boarded the truck and left the island, each speculating privately as to the contents of the container.

The canister was enclosed in a specially designed carrier and transported to the warhead shop near the middle of the island.

Shaw, the Sturmbannführer, had never been inside the warhead design shop. Even as the handlers removed the canister from the smaller truck onto which it had been offloaded from the larger, he wondered what it was that demanded so much care and concern.

A hydraulic lift was attached to the loading loops located at strategic points around the canister. Laborers were in the process of removing the canister when one of the straps began to separate. The canister remained suspended for a moment, as if deciding whether it would succumb to the law of gravity or not. The men raced to lower the canister, its stainless steel glistening in the harsh white light of the warhead shop.

The canister was no more than twelve inches from the floor when the second strap parted. The canister teetered for a frozen moment, then, giving in to the superior force, the stainless-steel vault tumbled from the remaining straps and crashed to the concrete floor of the shop.

The SS-Oberstführer stormed forward, shouting orders and chastising the workers as incompetents. To Shaw, the canister was none the worse for the minor accident. The Oberstführer, however, was treating the mishap with the intensity Shaw would normally have reserved for explosives.

"Get the tools, quickly," the Oberstführer ordered. "All of you, stand back," he motioned to the contingent of bodies crowding around. They moved, Shaw among them, and watched as two of the laborers began removing the stainless steel bolts that secured the outer top.

In less than five minutes, all twenty bolts were extracted from their places and the top prepared for removal.

The men attached a small crane to the top and activated the electrically controlled hydraulics. The top slowly rose from the square container. When the top was clear, the men moved it to the side and set it down on the floor.

The men moved to the container and peered into the cavity. Each man nodded to the Oberst and proceeded to attach the now freed crane to another container inside the steel casement. Slowly the interior canister came into the light, shining in the same manner as the larger one from which it came.

When the smaller container was clear of the larger one, the men activated a transverse pulley system and moved the smaller canister horizontally until it reached a waist-high workbench. The man with the hydraulic controls slackened the tension on the hoist cable as the other man disconnected the steel hook from the transfer eye on top.

The second man reached for the hook, stopping to examine a spot on the outer skin of the container at the top seam. He touched the smooth steel with his finger as if testing a particular area.

Then it happened.

The man who had touched the canister recoiled as if he'd touched a hot stove. A split second later, he grabbed his throat, his eyes bulged, his tongue swelled, restricting his breathing. The scream that had begun deep within the man's chest was cut off by the combination of swollen tongue and paralyzed diaphragm. He fell to the floor, his face a hideous purple, the shade of a dark night, Shaw thought. No sound came from his mouth. His eyes pleaded with those around him.

Shaw rushed forward, his momentum stopped as he was restrained by Kurt Daluege. Shaw began to understand.

"No, my friend," he said quietly, "there is nothing you can do to help that man. He will die a most agonizing death. There is no hope."

Shaw turned away from the horrific scene; he could feel the bile rising in his throat, burning its way into his esophagus. He gagged once, twice, then raced from the room.

The man on the floor lay still, his face black. Death had come within a minute—sixty seconds of sheer agony. The muscles beneath the clothing twitched in death.

"Everyone out," the Oberstführer ordered. He turned to the remaining technician. "Get the chemical people over here with their gear. This was not supposed to happen. That container was supposed to protect the contents through an enemy bombing. I'm going to find out who is responsible for this error." There was no expression of sympathy for the dead man, only the cold evaluation of a containment system that had failed.

Shaw was outside as those from the warhead room filed out. He stopped Kurt Daluege with a hand on the smaller man's arm.

"What was that? What happened in there? That man died in seconds!"

"That is true. I have never seen it, but I have heard about it."

"About *what?*" Shaw demanded.

"That shipment came from Leverkusen. From I. G. Farben. Their main production weapons at this time are biological and chemical. What you saw was chemical. Biologicals don't work that quickly."

"You're talking about *chemical warfare!* That's against all rules of decency, not to mention the Geneva accords."

"German leaders obey no law but their own, Michael. What you saw in there, if I'm not mistaken, is the contents of the warhead for the V-5. The chemical that just killed that technician in less than a minute is to be launched in the rocket we built."

Shaw went white; the blood drained from his head, the color from his face. "It's beyond barbaric, Kurt. Beyond criminal. It *must* be stopped."

Kurt Daluege turned and walked from the warhead shop; Shaw followed.

"It will be stopped," Daluege swore quietly. "It is time for a meeting. Can you contact your Polish friends?"

"I can," Shaw answered.

"Tonight. The house you told me about, the one they carried you to that night."

"I will see to it. This has turned more deadly than I ever envisioned."

"More deadly, I'm afraid, than we even suspect."

"Tonight. Midnight."

Daluege nodded and trudged off. Shaw watched as the man disappeared from sight, the acid from the bile in his throat still burned.

CHAPTER
3 3

The room was the same; the ambience had changed. The same straight back chairs were gathered around the square wooden table. But this time Shaw sat in one of the chairs, rather than bound like a Christmas turkey in the corner.

To his right Kurt Daluege sat with an expression of interest on his face; on his left, Walter Kolinsky sat in the same chair he had occupied the night he had almost killed Michael Shaw. The room, but for the rough-hewn furniture and the three men, was empty. The three men were silent.

"Would you have killed him?" Daluege addressed Kolinsky curiously, breaking the silence.

Kolinsky smiled briefly, thinking about his answer. "That was the plan," he finally said. "But no SS member has ever spoken the way he did that night. We were surprised, to say the least."

"I can see how you might be."

"The Nazis have chosen to persecute many people. It is true they seek to destroy the Jews in Europe. They are death fanatics. They also persecute the Church, both Catholic and Protestant. They murder Jews, Czechs, Poles, Gypsies, Slavs—anyone who is not Aryan is subject to imprisonment, torture, and death. They even seek out the people known as Freemasons. It is an insane time."

"We are here to try to stop some of that insanity," Shaw broke in. "And in the context of this meeting, we have disturbing news."

Kolinsky shifted his gaze to Shaw. "Is this about the truck that arrived on the island this morning?"

"You are well-informed, Walter," Daluege said, surprised.

"It is my job."

"Yes," Shaw affirmed, "it is about the truck. The material for the warhead for the V-5 was in that truck. One man died unloading it. I have never seen anything as horrible in my life."

"This truck, where did it come from?" Kolinsky asked.

"Leverkusen."

"Chemicals," breathed Kolinsky, disbelieving. "The soul is being stripped from Europe."

Amazement flashed across the faces of Shaw and Daluege. Kolinsky was mildly amused at their reaction.

"Do not be surprised. Our organization has many arms, many facets. We delve into every aspect of the Third Reich. We have branches in every major city, every war production facility, here and in France, and every cabinet post up to, and including the heart of the Wehrmacht."

"Amazing," Daluege said with obvious respect.

"I had no idea the underground was so well organized," Shaw added.

"We do lack some organization as far as a central clearinghouse is concerned. We operate mostly on a regional basis, but certain things are too important not to filter through the rest of the organization. Leverkusen is one of those."

Shaw rose from his chair and walked to the lone window. Snow was beginning again, and the drifts piled against the side of the cabin walls acted as insulation. The cabin was quiet except for the breathing of the three men. There was no heat in the cabin; smoke from a chimney would have been too noticeable. Shaw shivered, wondering if it was from the cold or the subject matter under discussion.

"Reminds me a lot of my cabin on Missisquoi Bay," he said to himself.

"A lonely place, then," Kolinsky said, having heard the remark.

Shaw turned from the window. "Yes, it is. I don't think I realized how lonely until right now." He rejoined the others and said, "Kurt and I have been talking. We may have come up with a way to stop the V-5. We will need your help and the help of your people to carry it off."

Kolinsky threw his arms in the air. "That is why we are here, losing sleep and freezing to death in this rat hole. Tell me of this plan."

Kurt Daluege began the explanations. "The V-5 is completed. It is the only rocket of its kind. You know, I'm sure, of the other two, the ones that are now called the V-1 and V-2. The V-1 is simple, just a thousand pounds of explosives strapped to a pulse jet engine and pointed in the right direction. The V-2, on the other hand is extremely complex. It's a gyro-navigated missile over forty feet long. There will be no defense against it. It will shower destruction at more than three thousand miles an hour. It will never be heard until it's too late. But there are disadvantages to each weapon. The V-1 is slow and noisy. Interception is possible, even with English Spitfires. The V-2, while it can be mounted on railcars and moved within the country, is limited by the necessity to launch from land-based installations. That is where the V-5 comes in."

"The V-5 has no such limitations," Kolinsky interrupted.

"Exactly," Shaw said, amazed yet again at the depth of knowledge possessed by Kolinsky.

Daluege continued. "It is obvious from the design of the V-5 that it was made to be launched from ships. It's all there, from the encased motor system to the protected guidance and sealed warheads. I've seen most of the plans from the shops. The V-5 will be half the size of the V-2, carry two-thirds the weight in its warhead, and will be impervious to salt water."

Kolinsky was mesmerized as he listened to the scientist's explanation.

"The V-5 will be a ship-launched weapon. The idea came from the Kriegsmarine, from Admiral Karl Dönitz. He wants a rocket to use against supply lines and landing forces. The V-5 will do that."

Kolinsky held up his hand. "But the warhead was supplied from Leverkusen. That suggests that at least one rocket will be launched using chemical weapons. You speak of multiple rockets launched against supply lines. That would mean launched against forces here on the continent. What of the chemical warhead?"

Daluege glanced sideways at Shaw. Shaw nodded. "We believe the chemical warhead is a one-time venture. A psychological weapon."

"Against whom? For what purpose?"

"To regain dominance of the North Atlantic."

Kolinsky's face changed to a pallid gray. "That would mean . . ."

". . . that it would be launched against the Americans, against the nearest target. The east coast," Shaw finished his sentence for him.

"Civilians!"

"Exactly," Daluege confirmed.

"But how?"

"U-boat. That would explain the pains with which Peenemünde has sought to seal every operating system of the V-5. It would also explain its size. The V-2 is large, but not so large that it could not eventually be deployed for shipboard launch from some of Germany's larger vessels. The size of the V-5 suggests it is to be deployed by smaller vessels, U-boats. Class IX boats can easily accommodate the rocket."

Kolinsky let his head rest in his cupped hands, his elbows on the table. "They are not content to destroy a single continent; they must carry their madness to the rest of the world," he said quietly. When he raised his face from his hands, the look of despair had been replaced by one of determination. "What must we do to stop this . . . this *insanity*?"

"The problem, as we see it, is target selection. The odds are in our favor that the rocket will be launched against a high profile target on the east coast. But we can't be absolutely certain. It could be fired against England from the Channel, Russia, North Africa, or any number of targets in the Mediterranean, but none of those targets would accomplish what launching against the U.S. would. It will be impossible to determine the target before deployment. We must have a man on board whatever ship deploys that rocket. It will be up to him to see that it is never fired."

Kolinsky shifted his gaze from Daluege to Shaw. "This is what you were telling me. You are to be the man on board the ship, yes?"

Shaw nodded in answer to the Pole's question. "It is the only way to neutralize the rocket and not compromise Kurt and the rest of his team here at Peenemünde."

"You are a brave man."

"Bravery is nothing more than action born of necessity. I see no other option."

"You spoke of a plan that would entail the use of my men."

"Kurt will explain that part," Shaw said.

Daluege pulled his chair closer to the table as if the snow-covered walls were listening. "Whatever boat or ship deploys the rocket, there is one factor that will not change. With the rocket must go a five-man technical team. Their responsibility is to see to it that the rocket is maintained in peak condition during the transit, to program the target site into the gyro guidance system, and to launch the rocket. The head of the team is an SS-Sturmbannführer Meyer, a sixth man. His only purpose is to protect the investment of the SS in this project. It was one of Himmler's conditions for funding Omega, as this project is known."

"And," Kolinsky began, peering once again at Shaw, "since we have our own SS-Sturmbannführer, it would be advantageous for us to remove this Meyer and insert our own man into his position. That I can understand, but I do not see how one man, especially a nontechnical one, can stop the launch of the rocket."

"There are many ways to stop the launch," Daluege explained. "Guidance systems go awry, fuel pumps fail, turbines overheat, wiring burns through. Those are all possibilities. But since Shaw has been assigned to the motor shop, we thought it better that we come up with a malfunction directly connected with that portion of the rocket he is most familiar with."

"A rocket motor failure."

"Precisely. To be exact, a combustion chamber failure."

"If, as you say, you can manufacture such a failure, for it to occur on a U-boat would mean almost certain death. An explosion on the deck of so small a boat would almost guarantee the boat's destruction as well."

"I have thought about that," Shaw said. "It's a job that must be done. I will find a way to survive. I'll be in God's hands."

"Of that I have no doubt, my friend. But we would be presumptuous to attribute to God our own myopic view of such a venture."

"The launch must be stopped. I will do what must be done."

"Yes, I believe you will," Kolinsky sighed. "What is it that I and my team must do?"

"Eliminate Meyer. With him out of the way, the next logical choice to accompany the rocket technicians will be Sturmbannführer Schmidt here," Daluege motioned to Shaw.

"And you will sabotage the launch."

"I will. Kurt has engineered the combustion chamber shroud in such a manner as to allow access to the outer portion of the chamber," Shaw explained. "With such access, I will be able to create a defect in the chamber. That defect will cause the chamber to burn through. At the very least, the motor will have a limited burn."

"And at its worst, it could explode before clearing the launch platform," Daluege interjected.

"There are risks that have to be accepted. If there was any other way, I would take it," Shaw surmised.

"That same idea was put forth two thousand years ago by another."

"How do you mean?" Shaw asked.

"Our Lord Jesus Christ in the garden. 'Remove this cup from me; yet not my will, but thine be done.'"

"An interesting analogy. There is, of course, another analogy from your example."

Kolinsky looked questioningly at Shaw. "And that is?"

Shaw released a breath and said, "There was no other way."

"Yes," the Pole agreed. "I see your point. I will remove this Meyer. You must do the rest."

Shaw and Daluege locked eyes, both knowing that Shaw had just been condemned to death.

CHAPTER
34

december 21, 1942
lorient, france

It was only four days before Christmas, and the daily codes had just been entered in the two Schlüssel M code machines aboard the U-3009 and U-3021 when each machine sprang to life. The radio operators aboard each of the boats quickly scribbled the messages onto separate sheets of top secret paper, folded them, and headed for the small berthing areas of their respective captains.

The captains took the messages, reading the contents in each case with a mixture of fear and excitement. Under normal circumstances, they could expect to be at sea for three to four months, supporting the operations of the smaller U-boats from their massive stores of fuel and ammunition.

This patrol was different. Each boat carried one component of the two fuels necessary to launch the V-5. They would rendezvous with the U-135 at a designated point in the mid-Atlantic to refuel the smaller U-boat, then proceed in wide formation to a predetermined point off the coast of the United States, fuel the V-5, and return to France. All-in-all, no more than forty-five days.

The Ultra message was the order they had been awaiting—the order to initiate Omega.

The crews of each of the large type XIX boats sprang into frenzied action. Engineering spaces were manned; navigation equations and dead-reckoning plots were begun; the supplies that could not be put onboard until the last minute were hastily secured in any available space; and deck hands stood by the moorings, ready to single-up and ultimately release the lines that tethered the boats to the wharf.

For the men of U-3009 and U-3021, the superiority of the German Navy was about to be demonstrated. The first direct assault on the shores of the United States was underway.

Omega had begun.

CHAPTER
35

As the message was received aboard the U-3009 and U-3021, the same message was being decoded at Station X, northwest of London. Unlike the routine radio traffic that made up the bulk of the naval decoding section, the mention of Omega in the message sparked an intense interest inside the white clapboard building.

The job had been boring; there had been few transmissions over the Kriegsmarine Ultra communications system. Not because the German Navy suspected that their codes had been broken; in fact, all other forms of Ultra communications had been prolific. It was just that, until this very moment, there had been no Omega transmissions.

The analyst on watch dutifully transcribed the message as it exited the Enigma machine, flipped through the directives in the notebook that lay on his desk, and found the updated entry concerning Omega transmissions. Every analyst in the Ultra section had been briefed concerning the handling of Omega messages, but it still came as a shock to the man when he read the directive. He transcribed the message, grabbed his hat and coat, and called for the duty driver.

In minutes, the military sedan was headed for Whitehall. The analyst gently held the envelope that contained the message, as if excess handling might cause the paper to burst into flame or explode. The orders had been simple and straightforward: the message was to be delivered to the Cabinet War Room on Whitehall.

The ride was a blur, the analyst concentrating on what he would say once he arrived in Whitehall. He'd been with the cryptoanalytical section for over two years, and in all that time, he'd never so much as seen the Cabinet War Room from the outside, much less the inside. Now the message he delicately held in his hand was his ticket to the inner workings of the building. He began to sweat despite the cold slush and ice covering the roadway.

The driver pulled to the front of the stone building and the analyst got out. For a moment he looked around, wondering what it was he felt. Then he knew; it was fear.

He entered the building, passed through the security checks, and was ushered into an outer office. He did not have a chance to take a seat before the door opened and he was ushered into the inner office by a stately looking secretary. She motioned for him to take a seat facing a large, ornate desk. He did so.

From a small room off to the right, the door opened, and the analyst felt the breath expunged from his lungs. Breathing became difficult, his gasps evident to the man who'd entered.

"Please, calm yourself. I assure you nothing drastic will happen here," Winston Churchill said in a soothing voice.

"Yes, sir, Mr. Prime Minister," the analyst answered.

"You have an Omega message?"

The analyst dug into his coat pocket, feeling silly for not having had the message at the ready, and handed it to Churchill.

The analyst looked at his watch. "An hour ago, Mr. Prime Minister."

"And you have not recorded this in your log? Is that correct?"

The analyst swallowed. "No sir, there is no record of its receipt."

Churchill smiled. "Very good. There is, of course, no need for me to remind you that this is a top priority message and that you are not to discuss it with anyone, not even your immediate supervisor. Is that clear?"

"Yes sir, perfectly."

Churchill nodded and reread the message once again. "Thank you. You may go," he said offhandedly.

The analyst rose, feeling as if he'd been to court and had been exonerated for crimes against the state.

Churchill waited until the door closed behind the analyst and picked up the phone on his desk. "This is an Omega call," he said into the mouthpiece. He waited as the call was placed and the other end was picked up.

"It has begun," he said gravely, and replaced the receiver. "God be with us," he prayed quietly.

CHAPTER

36

SS-Sturmbannführer Otto Meyer cared less for his assignment than might have otherwise been the case had he been assigned to a full combat unit or one of the Waffen SS support battalions. The fact that he was stuck on the desolate island of Usedom in the Baltic was just further proof that the SS hierarchy did not appreciate his experience and abilities.

True, Meyer recognized, as he studied the reports before him, he was to be the head of the contingent to board the U-boat that was, this very minute, en route to Peenemünde. The men who knew what was happening—the ones who would make it happen—were the five technicians he would accompany aboard the craft.

And Meyer had heard service aboard a U-boat was nothing more than prolonged intense tedium punctuated by moments of sheer terror. Not to mention the extreme discomfort in which U-boat crews operated. And to add insult to injury, the rocket that would be embarked was nothing more than a grand experiment, one which had a greater chance of failure than success, at least in his view.

Meyer removed his glasses and rubbed the bridge of his nose between thumb and forefinger. He'd been at the reports for the last three hours, enough for one night, he decided.

He rose from his desk, grabbed his overcoat, and started for the car that waited in the small courtyard just outside his office. While others had to make do with makeshift office space, he had been assigned a private space. Space, particularly private office space, was a rare thing on Peenemünde. Almost every square foot had been given over to rocket research, which, in Meyer's mind, was a vast waste of resources.

He pushed through the outer door and into the cold night. His car sat five meters away, motor idling, meaning it would be warm inside. That was another thing he hated about the Baltic—the unrelenting cold. He would have preferred the southern coast of France, where the Mediterranean was warm and the women were beautiful. After this assignment was over, he would check into a transfer. Maybe he would relent and consider Paris.

Meyer opened the rear door of the car and folded his tall frame inside. His driver, one of the amenities he enjoyed because of his position, was at the wheel.

But there was something strange this night. Meyer had become accustomed to his somewhat small driver, but this man was husky, broad shoulders showing above the rear cushion of the front seat. The shape of the head was wrong, the manner in which the driver gripped the wheel . . . everything was different.

"Where is Franz tonight?" Meyer asked, slamming the door behind him.

"Ill, Herr Sturmbannführer. The transportation sergeant assigned me to your car a half hour ago. Is there a problem?"

"No." Meyer relaxed. He knew the transportation sergeant. This was just another example of the man's efficiency.

"Ill you say. What is his problem? He said nothing about it earlier today."

"Perhaps," the driver answered as he shifted into gear, "he did not want to burden the Sturmbannführer with personal problems."

Meyer relaxed into the deep cushions of the staff car. "Perhaps."

The automobile lurched forward on the slick surface, rear tires spinning, throwing ice in their wake, the driver's gaze locked onto the road as he drove.

Meyer, remembering that he'd left a report on his desk that he wanted to read in his room, came up out of the cushioned rear seat and tapped the driver on the shoulder. "Stop. I have to go back and get a file from my desk. I won't be a minute." With that, he reached for the inner door handle to let himself out. What he found surprised him.

The door handle was gone! Someone had removed it!

Quickly he dove for the opposite door. That handle, too, was gone! Meyer felt his heartbeat slamming against his chest, mini-explosions of light illuminated in his brain.

The front door!

Meyer leaned over the back support of the front seat, scrambling for the handle of the front door. It was there! He grasped the handle, pulling himself forward with its support. The handle gave, the locking mechanism operating, and the front door opened an inch. Before he could force his body into the front seat and out the door, he felt the ugly muzzle of a Luger automatic pistol driven into the sensitive area below his left ear. He froze, hand on the door.

"Return to your seat, Herr Sturmbannführer. *Now!*"

Meyer contemplated resisting but banished the thought. He'd been an accountant before joining the SS. None of the training he'd undergone had prepared him for physical combat. His desire for combat was something he dreamed about only because he knew there was little chance of such an assignment. He pulled the front door shut and fell back into the seat.

"I have this pistol pointed at you through this seat. You are perfectly framed in my rearview mirror. Do not move one centimeter, or I will be forced to shoot you right here."

Meyer's eyes strayed to the mirror mounted over the windshield. He could see the eyes of the driver and what looked like the beginning of a scar illuminated by the lights of the dashboard. He'd seen that face, that scar, somewhere before, but he could not remember.

The car passed the checkpoints with little trouble. Every guard knew the car and could see Meyer in the rear seat.

Once out of the security area, Walter Kolinsky headed the staff car toward the east coast of Usedom Island and a remote inlet just at the border where the island joined Poland.

*   *   *

Kapitänleutnant Günther Mohr could see the docking area where he would moor the U-135. There was a good harbor entrance here on the northern shore of Usedom Island. He could see two large cargo ships moored side by side, in the protected area of the natural harbor. That was good; the weather was horrendous. It would be good to get to more southern latitudes.

The harbor pilot stood next to Mohr, more a formality than an official pilot. Mohr had allowed the man onboard to brief him on the harbor approach but had informed the man in no uncertain terms that he, as captain, would pilot his boat into the harbor. The harbor pilot had said nothing.

The U-135 was within half a mile of docking, and the pilot grudgingly had to agree that he could not have done better than this U-boat captain. The U-135 moved like a ballet dancer in response to Mohr's orders.

Within minutes, the first line would come aboard the U-135, and the last phase of Omega would begin.

Neither man knew that, at that very moment, fifty kilometers to the south, SS-Sturmbannführer Otto Meyer was being escorted from the staff car and to a remote inlet of those same Baltic waters. Meyer would next be seen in public in a place called Nuremberg.

CHAPTER

37

Long shadows crept over the dark hull, distorting reality, painting the U-135 with alternating stripes of light and dark. The sleek hull sat low in the water, its engines quiet, menacing even in repose.

Michael Shaw stood on the quay in his black SS winter tunic, a light dusting of dry snow falling, staring at the sinister object. Men swarmed over every foot of the U-boat. It reminded Shaw of a rotting carcass covered with ravenous ants. But this was not carrion on which to feed; it was a machine of war, provisioned and made ready for its deadly journey. Even as the men worked, loading the remaining supplies from the quay, Shaw could not take his eyes from the long cylinder now mounted on the rear portion of the U-boat's deck.

Supported by a complex design of metal beams and hydraulics, the V-5 rocket lay horizontal, its body secured to the launch stand. Five rocket technicians checked and rechecked every system, making certain that the rocket would survive the upcoming voyage.

Shaw felt the dry chill of fear wash through his body. He shuddered. It had all been so easy. Walter Kolinsky had been as good as his word, and Otto Meyer had disappeared the night the U-135 tied up at the Peenemünde wharf. After a search and the conclusion that Meyer had deserted, Shaw was appointed to replace Meyer as the SS representative on the Omega mission.

Christmas had come and gone, honored only by a few of the families in the housing area. For Shaw, it had been a reminder of what he'd lost in this life. The days had been filled with work and preparations, but the nights had been claimed by tedium, boredom, and, worst of all, loneliness. Shaw realized he was almost looking forward to putting to sea in the dark shadow of the U-boat.

That had been one week ago. The V-5 rocket had been assembled, the warhead mated to the body, and the rocket loaded onto the launch platform of the U-boat. The last of the provisions were being stuffed into the limited space aboard the boat.

Shaw had not known what to expect, but what he saw when he first went aboard the U-boat had made him want to flee.

One long corridor ran the entire length of the boat, fore to aft. Sleeping quarters gave way to weapons systems, propulsion power plants, torpedoes, and diving and trim controls. To his horror, he discovered only two toilets in the labyrinth of steel tubing and insulated wiring, and one of those, he was told, would be used for storage on the Atlantic crossing, leaving only the aft toilet for a crew of fifty-seven men.

Supplies were stuffed into every available space. Upper bunks in the aft and forward torpedo rooms were rendered useless; loaves of bread occupied the spaces and skins of sausage were suspended from the overhead like round bats gone to roost. The smell of black bread and heavy spices wafted through the interior, combining with the odor of sweat, grease, and diesel.

Shaw had been shocked when he'd been told he could bring only what he wore, nothing more. There were no showers, no means of ridding the boat's closed quarters of the smells of men and machinery. A smell that would turn rancid only a few days after deployment.

Shaw shifted his gaze from the men performing last-minute chores to the man standing in the conning tower of U-135. He'd met Kapitänleutnant Günther Mohr the first day the submarine had docked. That had been his one and only contact with the stern-faced captain, and Mohr had made clear that he did not like having to give up six of his seasoned crew members to accommodate five rocket technicians and one SS observer. Mohr had argued, quite correctly, that the boat needed each of its fifty-seven crew members to ensure a successful voyage. Shaw had feared that his logic might well mean he, at least, would be left behind. But it was not to be. Mohr had abandoned his argument when the necessity of the five technicians had been explained. The protocol issued from Berlin ensured the attendance of the lone SS officer.

Mohr had glared at Shaw, turned on his heel, and stomped from the room. Later, when Shaw had tried to smooth things over with the U-boat skipper, Mohr had ignored him and had gone about his business.

To quell his nerves, Shaw continually reminded himself that he was on this voyage only because it was God's plan. That was the only explanation for the success he had enjoyed thus far. By all accounts, he should not be on the U-boat. He should, if fate played a part at all in life, still be in England, perhaps even at the bottom of the English Channel. Or lying dead on a cold road just outside the family housing area where he'd first encountered Walter Kolinsky.

Certainly his meeting Kurt Daluege could not be attributed to mere fate. And the inclusion of Walter Kolinsky was no toss of the dice, either. From beginning to end, this mission had been overseen by someone greater than all of them.

Shaw watched as Günther Mohr directed the men under his command with practiced precision. There were no questions, no rebuttals, only acceptance and performance. He could see by the crew's actions

that they were an experienced group of sailors with only the completion of the mission on their minds.

Shaw's gaze was drawn once again to the rocket. The technicians
were finishing with the preembarkation inspections. Every system,
every wire, every vulnerable nut and bolt had been secured, made
watertight for the voyage. The senior technician, whom Shaw knew
only by sight, walked to the base of the conning tower and shouted
something to Mohr. The captain turned around and nodded his
acknowledgment.

Then, with deliberate control, he looked at Shaw and motioned
him to come aboard. Shaw crossed the ramp onto the icy deck of the
sub, shinnied through the forward hatch, and lowered himself into the
bowels of the steel monster.

Kurt Daluege watched as his friend disappeared through the hole
directly forward of the conning tower. Had anyone cared to notice,
they would have seen a small tear in the corner of one eye. "Go with
God," he whispered before turning from the quay and walking away.

In the background, the ignition of the twin nine-cylinder, 2,170-
horsepower diesels drowned out all other sounds.

CHAPTER
3 8

The apparition came from the sea, from the freezing mist that was forever lingering in the narrow straits. Like a ghost emerging from the grave, the gray shape materialized almost silently, crossing the open water as if resting on, not in, the murky depths. The only sound, a deep-throated thumping, was masked by the heavy, moist air.

Erik Swenson had seen German naval vessels come and go. The German Navy's superiority in the Baltic was almost absolute. Swenson had relayed untold numbers of messages from his vantage point to British Intelligence. Keeping track of German ships was what he did best. But of all the ships that had passed his coast watching station, none had carried the graceless bulk of metal framing and the tube-like device that now filled the field of vision of his binoculars. Whatever it was, it was a weapon of war. The type IX U-boat to which the device was mounted told him that much.

Swenson watched the boat until, just as it had appeared from nowhere, it disappeared into the light fog and freezing drizzle. The conning tower had carried no number, consistent with German wartime policy. He could see from the profile that the U-boat was larger than the normal type VII boats that frequented the Baltic. A type IX, no doubt about it. But what was the apparition that rode the sub's back like a malignant cancer?

Swenson shook himself from his thoughts and dragged his eyes from the point where the sub had disappeared. This, he knew, was worth reporting.

CHAPTER
3 9

january 1, 1943
north atlantic

There was no indication within the vessels that a new year had begun. The two U-boats were traveling together, maintaining an interval of just under two miles. The U-3009 led, and the U-3021 lolled in her wake to starboard, following three thousand meters away. The twin lookouts on each boat shared the critical responsibility of identifying enemy aircraft or surface vessels before being identified by them. With the two boats two miles apart, they had an effective observation range of just over seventeen miles, in good weather.

But the weather was anything but good. Winter in the North Atlantic provided perhaps the most hostile operating environment a U-boat could venture into, and today was a prime example.

Standing orders restricted surface speed to less than eight knots, and the charted route took them well to the north of the great circle route leading to the shores of North America. Such operating limitations could only mean that they would surely rendezvous with one or more U-boats before the week was out.

Neither captain had voiced his concern to the other, but each knew that the sooner they could offload the fuel they now carried and return to France, the happier they would be.

CHAPTER
40

january 3, 1943
north atlantic

Michael Shaw had known misery, both physical and mental, in his life. Some, he now knew, had been self-imposed. Of the two, the mental was the more profound. Before he knew God, he had experienced an intense lostness. And then the small girl from the hills of Virginia had entered the picture.

Barbara.

They had fallen in love, he at first glance, she after several weeks of his undivided attention. They had been married, spent a honeymoon in Hot Springs, Arkansas, and loved each other with a passion that Shaw had thought impossible. It had been a love that could only have been possible within a God-ordained institution, and he had been ecstatic.

Barbara had dragged him to church. He had gone willingly, content to be near her regardless of the location. But he had listened to the Word of God, and that Word had supplied the final piece of his being deep within him, and he had accepted Jesus Christ as his Lord and Savior. He'd not known what all the words meant, but he'd never been happier or more fulfilled.

The misery had started the night Barbara died; but, as he looked back on it, she had left him with a lasting legacy of love that even death could not completely eradicate. He was just beginning to realize the hollowness he'd known before Jesus. He'd not been deserted in his time of need.

But misery comes in different forms, and the physical wretchedness to which he was now exposed was beyond anything he'd ever envisioned.

The U-135 was making its way north and east, following the great circle route between Europe and North America. The crowded conditions aboard the submarine bordered on the unconscionable.

Fifty-seven men were crammed into the narrow pressure hull with as little regard for comfort as cattle being led to the slaughter. Every available space, including many of the sleeping berths, was full of supplies, food, and assorted equipment. Men slept only at the end of a sixteen-hour watch, and then only briefly. It was the sleep of exhaustion, not the deep, therapeutic sleep they so desperately needed.

The innards of the boat stunk of sweat, and waste, and decaying food. Shaw's black tunic lay next to him. He could smell its fetidness. The men wore one set of clothes from start to finish. That meant, on most patrols, a minimum of three months without bathing, shaving, or laundering clothes.

The inside surfaces of the U-boat sweated constantly, the moisture beading and running in rivulets down the pressure hull. Every inch of the interior reeked of mildewing cloth and molding bread and cheese. The temperature that had hovered in the high fifties plunged into the thirties as the boat made its way into the northern latitudes.

The Atlantic changed temperament. It had gone from the giant rolling swells off the French coast to the battering surface waves that imbedded themselves in the giant swells. The boat not only rolled and pitched in the extreme seas but rattled and shook with each rise and fall along the face of the waves. Half the men on the boat were seasick, and the by-products of their sickness added to the stench that permeated the U-135.

The five members of the rocket crew were strapped into bunks in the after torpedo room. Shaw feared that he might die before he ever had opportunity to stop the launch of the deadly missile strapped to the U-boat's deck.

His stomach had turned on him only hours out of Peenemünde. He'd not been able to eat. Eventually, there was nothing left to throw up, and he had tried to eat but to no avail.

He peered through the gloom of the torpedo room, staring at the water droplets as they accumulated, joined others, and ran down the side of the hull next to him. He would have to force himself out of the bunk and into some kind of action if he expected to play an active role in the demise of the V-5. He had just pushed himself up onto his left elbow when the speaker in the room blared to life.

"This is the captain speaking. We have now cleared friendly waters and are north of the western approaches to England. We have not been spotted by any English or American vessel, which, as each of you know, was vital to us in fulfilling our assigned patrol duties. We have been running on the surface and will continue to do so as long as we do not come in contact with enemy shipping. At this point, I am about to open our sealed orders and read them. Stand-by one."

Shaw swung his legs over the edge of the cold bunk, instantly alert, the misery radiating from his stomach temporarily forgotten.

The U-boat struggled up a mountain of water, the deck inclined upward. Shaw grabbed for the nearest handhold. It took all his strength to keep from falling from the berth. As quickly as it had begun its climb, the boat's nose tilted over and began the long dive into the deep trough.

Shaw was amazed as he looked around him at the complacency with which the more seasoned submariners went about their work.

Weapons mates were busy checking circuits and settings on two of the torpedoes stored in an overhead rack.

The speaker came alive again, and Shaw turned his attention to it.

"The orders read: The U-135, under the command of Kapitän-leutnant Günther Mohr will proceed to the coordinates designated as 'Omega' on the master plot, arm, and launch the V-5 rocket, and return, via the great circle route, to Lorient, France, on or before the twenty-eighth day of February 1943. Under no circumstances are the officers and crew of the U-135 to proceed to any landfall other than Lorient on or before the specified day. Should any factor, whether natural or manmade, result in the detection of the U-135 on or before the launch of the rocket designated V-5, the officers and crew are to scuttle the U-135 with all haste, ensuring in the process that the rocket is destroyed and all evidence of said rocket in no way falls into the hands of England, the United States, or any allies of the two countries. The orders are signed by Adolf Hitler, Chancellor of Germany."

Shaw was shocked by the cheering that went up within the boat at the completion of the reading. It was all there. They were to launch the V-5. The chemical in the warhead would be used to kill people, and by all indications, the target specified Omega was located within the boundaries of the United States.

Shaw felt his head reel as the submarine fought its way up and over the crest of a giant roller. His stomach felt as light as his head.

He'd have to get a look at the master plan. That meant forcing himself to act in spite of the sickness, in spite of the fear that had suddenly overcome him.

God be with me, he prayed silently.

CHAPTER
41

Admiral Karl Dönitz detested Berlin. It was a constant reminder to him that he had stepped from the world he knew best—the world of U-boats, and strategy, and war—into a world for which he was less suited. Even as the supreme commander of all Germany's warships, he was nonetheless reduced to limited tactical responses to the enemy's advancing strategic moves. To make matters worse, the Führer continued to siphon off valuable shipping for uses elsewhere.

To compound the problem of a lack of viable combat vessels, Himmler had gone behind his back and pulled three of his top-line U-boats from the war and sent them on an insane mission halfway around the world. True, initially he'd supported the concept of Omega, but tactical assets were becoming scarce, and the three U-boats of Omega were sorely needed elsewhere. What should have been a joint decision between him and the SS had turned into a mishmash of subterfuge. All to the detriment of the war effort. Unbelievable!

For that reason, he was in Berlin, away from his beloved Lorient, and about to do battle with the master deceiver of all time—Heinrich Himmler, head of the SS. This was the part of war he hated most—the politics.

The staff car wove its way down Prinz Albrechttrasse as Dönitz reviewed his plan of attack. It all would be so much easier, he knew, if Himmler knew anything about the art of war. But the SS-Reichsführer was no more than a glorified policeman in the service of the National Socialist Party and Adolf Hitler. A politician promoted beyond his capabilities.

Dönitz snorted derisively at the thought but quickly reined in his growing anger. Men like Himmler were the reason Germany was losing the war—the reason they had lost control of the shipping lanes in the vital North Atlantic. The reason the Afrika Korps had been humiliated in North Africa. The reason the rumors of an Allied invasion were now beginning to surface as plausible fact rather than puerile fiction.

The driver threaded the car through to the curb and braked to a halt. Dönitz looked up at the stone edifice, took a deep breath to calm his building anger, and mounted the steps. He would have to be diplomatic, and he despised that affectation. But he needed his three U-boats; and what was worse, if he was correct, he desperately needed them not to be doing what he suspected they were.

As Dönitz pushed into the building, soldiers came to rigid attention. The admiral casually returned the Nazi salutes as he made his way deeper into the confines of the SS headquarters.

An essence of oppression settled over Dönitz. A heavy quality that seemed to cling to his very soul. It was a black feeling, a reflection of the uniforms he saw about him.

Himmler's office was on the top floor, and Dönitz walked up the winding staircase of the SS headquarters. His two aides trailed one step behind their master and to the right and left.

Heinrich Himmler had adorned his office in the style he thought befitting a master planner or regent. The fact that he was neither had not halted the acquisition of plundered artwork from conquered lands.

Dönitz entered the Reichsführer's outer office and was pleasantly surprised to see the clerks' and secretaries' startled looks. They had not been notified of the Grand Admiral's appearance, just as he had wished. Surprise was a strategy he had used to perfection in the early days of the war and one that worked equally well in war or politics. Dönitz's senior aide approached an opened-mouthed clerk.

"Please inform the Reichsführer that Grand Admiral Dönitz is here to see him," the man said. "He has exactly thirty seconds."

Dönitz smiled inwardly. Another trick had just been employed by his aide: set a time limit, but leave the results of that limit ambiguous.

The clerk rose, rather shaken Dönitz noticed, and disappeared through the ornate door just behind him. In less than thirty seconds, the man was back. The short man trailing the clerk wore pince-nez and a small mustache.

Himmler.

Dönitz would have burst out laughing had the occasion been any other. But he was here to tackle one of the most influential men in the hierarchy of the Third Reich.

Himmler skirted around the clerk and moved toward Dönitz with his hand outstretched. "Admiral. Good to see you. You should have informed me that you were coming. We would have accorded you the appropriate honors," Himmler said rather obsequiously.

"There was not time, Heinrich," Dönitz replied, intentionally using the Reichsführer's first name. He could see immediately that the informal term of address flustered Himmler. Another trick of the trade. Keep the enemy off balance until you are able to unleash a well-organized offensive.

"Shall we go into my office?" Himmler motioned with a wave.

Dönitz walked past Himmler and into the elegantly appointed office. The aides remained in the outer office. This would be a clash of titans. No place for lesser mortals.

Dönitz marched to the front of Himmler's desk and stood at rigid attention. Himmler moved around behind the desk and sat down. Dönitz remained standing. He looked down on the Reichsführer, his gaze intense, unwavering.

"You have commandeered three of my U-boats. I want them back immediately," Dönitz began without preamble.

Himmler was surprised by the tone of the rebuke but did not let it show. He could play the game, and waiting was a part of it.

"You have exactly twenty-four hours to send a message through the Ultra communications network and inform those three captains that they are to return to port in Lorient and report to me. I will be taking a plane back to France as soon as we are finished here. Do I make myself clear?"

Himmler sat back in his chair, his initial shock over. He glared back at the Grand Admiral of the German Navy and said, "The Führer has himself given permission for the continuation of Operation Omega. Any change in plans will have to come from him, but I can tell you right now that he is in favor of us striking at the heart of one of the Third Reich's most efficacious enemies." Himmler leaned back further in his chair, his gaze locked on Dönitz, his fingers interlaced behind his head. "Please, Admiral. Feel free to call the Führer if you doubt me." Himmler pointed to the phone on his desk, hoping he had not overplayed his hand.

Dönitz felt his fury building, but he held it in check. He had no doubt that what Himmler had said was true. He had been outmaneuvered by a purely political mind.

Dönitz placed both fists on Himmler's desktop and leaned toward the weasel-faced man. "Do you have any idea what you have done? Have you taken into consideration what the consequences of such an action will be?" Dönitz whispered harshly.

"Admiral . . . ," Himmler began smoothly.

Dönitz cut him off. "Of course, you haven't. You don't have the brain to calculate the indescribable damage you might do to the war effort."

Himmler was on his feet screaming. "I have the brain to calculate exactly what will happen when our rocket lands on its target. We will have struck a blow for Germany. For the Third Reich," Himmler bellowed. "We will have shown the Americans that they, too, can be reached by the long arm of Germany's *Kriegsmarine* and the SS. They will quake in their shoes! They will grovel before the might of the Third Reich! They will be forced to defend their own shores! I know exactly what I have done!"

Dönitz ignored Himmler's condescension. He leaned in closer. "What you will do, Herr Reichsführer, is what only Admiral Yamamoto has been able to do up to this point. You will fill an industrial giant with a terrible resolve. Do not think for one moment that a single strike such as Omega will halt the American advance. *I* want to strike at the heart of the United States, also. But there are other contingencies to consider, other priorities, both military and political. At the very least, it will point up a weakness—which they will fill with even more production of war material. They do not even know there is a war going on for the most part. They go about their daily lives as if nothing were happening. You will disrupt this temporary complacency at a great cost, I fear."

Dönitz, his weariness now manifesting itself in his face, let himself sink into the chair that fronted Himmler's desk.

Himmler sat, red faced, searching for words of rebuttal. "It's a calculated risk, I admit. But one we must take."

"And you shared that with the Führer, that Omega *is* a calculated risk?"

"Of course not. That is not the way to get things done with our Führer. I promised him a great victory. Which is more, I might add, than his general staff is able to promise."

Dönitz rose, a tiredness lining his narrow face. "Then for your sake, I hope such a victory materializes." Dönitz moved toward the door. Just before exiting the office, he turned to Himmler. "But, I have to tell you, Heinrich, it will never happen. I fear we have miscalculated where the Americans are concerned."

"It was your plan, too, if you will remember, dear Karl."

Dönitz smiled now. "Yes. It was. But I have since learned a great deal about the Americans. They are not the weaklings I thought they were. That much has been proved. We could have defeated this continent and even the British, but I am not so certain about the Americans."

Himmler sat, confusion showing on his face. This was the scourge of the Atlantic, the originator of Operation Drumbeat, and he was worried now about the Americans and the possible consequences of Omega. Had he, Heinrich Himmler, miscalculated?

CHAPTER
42

Freezing spray broke over the bow as the U-135 lunged into the face of a North Atlantic swell. Already the running lines and antennas that protruded from the conning tower were coated with ice. The two lookouts—starboard and port—were having to break a thin patina of ice from their oilskins every few minutes. The binoculars they were using were virtually useless in the gray atmosphere. Sea and sky had melded as one; the horizon was nonexistent. Great ocean swells lifted the U-boat up and over a crest, only to force the boat down the following face and into bone-wrenching shudders as its nose plunged beneath the sea.

"Report, starboard," Günther Mohr ordered, looking up at the lookout perched precariously on the right side of the conning tower.

"Contacts negative, sir."

"Port."

"Contacts negative, sir."

Mohr held onto the ice-covered railing of the conning tower just to the right of the deck-mounted combat binoculars. Number One, his executive officer and navigator, stood by him. "You have verified the coordinates, Number One?"

"Yes sir. We are well within the target area. According to plan, the milk cows should be here waiting for us."

"In this weather, it will be difficult to spot a U-boat riding low in the water. Refueling is going to be a major undertaking."

Number One nodded agreement. Nothing had been said, but every man knew the chances that would have to be taken to achieve success on this patrol. Every factor concerning the rocket was an unknown. The effects of temperature, wind, freezing rain, and unstable launch platforms were yet to be learned.

Mohr raised his Zeiss binoculars and scanned the distance. Nothing. The boat plunged once again into a deep valley of water as Mohr, his number one, and the two lookouts clutched at the freezing metal surfaces. The U-135 rolled slightly to port, righted herself, and headed up the face of another swell. Mohr had his binoculars to his eyes before the boat reached the crest. This time, with the advantage of height, he saw it.

"Antennas to port," the lookout called.

Mohr had already acquired a fix on the approaching U-boat.

"Antenna to starboard," the other lookout called.

Mohr shifted his gaze from port to starboard and immediately his field of vision was filled with the cold gray hull of another U-boat. Both had made the linkup, each no more than a kilometer from the other.

"They were waiting on us," Number One said.

"That they were," Mohr agreed. "Get a signal mate up here on the double. We will use lights. No radios."

"Aye, aye, Kaleu." Number One spoke into a speaking tube just to his left, relaying the captain's orders.

In seconds, the head of a German signal mate appeared through the hatch at the feet of Number One. The man scrambled through the hole and onto the bridge of the conning tower, a signal light in his hand.

"You have the messages," Mohr said. "Send them."

The signal mate stepped to the outer railing and began sending Morse code to first one, then the other U-boat. Replies were returned in like manner. The signal mate wrote the responses on a tablet and handed it to Mohr.

Mohr nodded, approving the sequence in which the refueling would take place.

"Commence the refueling, Number One."

The first task scheduled was the actual refueling of the U-135 herself. Although the submarine had enough fuel to complete the entire mission, Mohr always felt better with full bunkers. The boat from which they would refuel also carried the liquid oxygen in her converted ballast tanks. The oxygen would be pumped into the rocket's fuel chambers, all hoses secured, and the boat would back away to a safe distance. The second boat, containing the alcohol, would then approach, link-up with the 135, and fill the rocket's alcohol tanks. Both boats would be free to begin their return passage to Lorient, France.

In theory, with the fueling of the rocket, the U-135 would proceed to the coordinates labeled Omega on the master plot. The trouble, Mohr knew, was that nothing ever went as planned, especially in the North Atlantic.

Refueling and rocket fueling were scheduled to take no more than four hours. Four hours of terror and misery in a raging sea of mountainous waves and below freezing temperatures could easily mean six or even eight hours. Even six hours would push the availability of daylight at these latitudes.

The first U-boat was almost in position, ten meters off the port beam of the U-135. Crew members of the larger milk cow were struggling with the refueling hoses, snaking them from deep within the boat and onto the deck.

Number One was issuing a steady stream of orders to maintain the southwest track of the U-135 and keep the boat within the operating parameters necessary for a successful refueling.

The fueling hoses were manhandled aboard and made fast, the connections slipping into place, and the diesel fuel that was a U-boat's lifeblood began filling the bunkers of the U-135.

Michael Shaw had become accustomed to the growing stench that pervaded the narrow confines of the U-boat. He had even fought to overcome his seasickness and for the most part was ambulatory for the first time since leaving Peenemünde.

He worked his way forward, passing through the electric motor room, battery storage, and the diesel engine room.

Mohr was topside. Number One was at his side, directing the refueling process under Mohr's watchful eye. That meant the plot room and attack bridge were manned by junior officers. Shaw knew he would not get another chance like this.

He had to see the master plot to know what the intended target was.

Shaw turned sideways in the narrow corridor, allowing two torpedo mates to pass. Each man eyed the SS-Sturmbannführer with slightly veiled hostility but said nothing.

Shaw felt their eyes on him, recognizing the loathing coming from the two men. He wondered briefly how an organization such as the SS could exist when it seemed that all around were those who hated what it stood for. But then he remembered the harshness with which the SS forged its hold first in Germany and then the rest of Europe.

The control room and the master plot room were located in the same space, separated only by function and the master plotting table and the dead reckoning tracer. Shaw had seen the DRT in action only once, days earlier. It had been no more than a drill, one designed to relieve the tension as well as sharpen performance.

Shaw had found one man on board who would talk to him. He'd learned that the master plot was a group of identical squares superimposed on a grid map. Each square was then subdivided into nine squares and each of those divided yet again. Thus, the target area was represented by two letters: The designators for the larger square, followed by two numbers. The first number indicated the first subdivision; the second number further refined the target site.

He'd also learned that the executive officer—Number One—was also the navigator and was responsible for correctly plotting the coordinates. Rumor had it that Omega was already plotted on the master plot. If he could sneak a look at the plot, Shaw thought, he would know the target. With that, he could also know the relative final position of the U-135, and with a little luck, he could get to a radio and transmit the final coordinates to shore batteries, or naval coastal watches. Subchasers and destroyer escorts would steam from the east coast, intercept, and sink the U-135 before she could launch the rocket.

Failing that, he would sabotage the combustion chamber the way Kurt Daluege had shown him and hope the engineer was right about the abbreviated burn time.

As he neared the plot room, Shaw stepped through the last door leading to the control room. Heads turned in his direction as he entered. One junior officer was gazing at the plotting table with interest. Shaw walked over to the table.

"We are refueling?" Shaw asked the young officer.

"Yes, Herr Sturmbannführer," the man replied.

The boat was rising and falling with the running sea, and Shaw could feel the nausea returning as the boat moved and bucked.

"I understand Number One has completed his calculations for the launch. I am curious. Are we close?"

"Another two days. Maybe less."

"Rumor says we will attack the city of Boston, with its rich homes and arrogant population. I would have preferred Washington, D.C. It would be what the American Congress deserves for declaring war on us."

The young officer smiled. "Either would be a fine target. But neither is the target. Come around here. I will show you."

Shaw skirted the edge of the plotting table and moved around behind the young officer.

"Here is the east coast of America," he pointed out, indicating the broken shoreline of the United States. "We are here, just south of Newfoundland. We will approach through the south corridor of Nova Scotia, then turn south to here," he said, indicating a blocked-off area with his finger, "and launch the rocket from here."

Shaw examined the plot. He knew the range of the rocket was limited to just over two hundred miles, in ideal conditions. He retrieved a navigation compass, set a two-hundred-mile radius, and centered the point on the launch site. He circumscribed half an arc, intersecting the coastline, noting the population areas that fell within the arc.

There it was! There could be no doubt! A small, colored-in area fell within the arc of death.

Insanity had overtaken sanity! It was madness, but madness with a logical conclusion. The arc had superscribed several population centers, but only one was indicated by the color highlight. The target was neither Boston nor Washington D.C.

Not even Kurt Daluege or Walter Kolinsky could have guessed at the depth of madness to which Heinrich Himmler had sunk.

Shaw stared at the plot, praying it was not so, but knowing the truth. It was propaganda at its worst, but it also made strategic sense, in a perverted manner. Hundreds, perhaps thousands of innocents would die if the rocket were launched. It all made sense—morbid, fascinating sense.

The target, Shaw knew, represented all that was wrong with the world. The V-5 would rectify that. It would fly against the perceived heart of the United States. Not against the politicians or the industrial giants but against the force behind such men. And the death rained down from the skies would be multiplied many times over when the rocket struck home.

Shaw felt beads of perspiration pop out on his forehead despite the chill in the control room.

He would have to stop the launch, stop the madness!

Shaw took one last glance at the plot, memorizing the coordinates and the small darkened area representing the target.

The coordinates overlaid New York City. But the city itself was not the target. At least not the city proper. The small colored-in area was nestled on the southern tip of Manhattan. The launch trajectory would carry the weapon from the North Atlantic, over Staten Island, splitting the Upper New York Bay in half as the rocket's gyros guided the twenty-foot cylinder of death unerringly into the financial capital of the free world: Wall Street.

CHAPTER
43

"It's confirmed?" the voice on the other end of the line inquired.

"From several sources. One of our watchers on the east coast of Denmark detected the submarine slipping through the straits several days ago. He described it perfectly. Right down to the miniature Eiffel Tower lying on its side, with what appeared to be a twenty-foot log strapped to it."

"You said several sources."

"Another from a Polish resistance member working on the island. He confirms that a submarine configured in exactly the same manner departed about the same time. And the boys at Bletchley intercepted a coded message over the trunk lines. Same information."

"But nothing ever came from our man?"

"Nothing. We can only deduce that something happened to his radio before he could reach us and he was unable to replace it."

"A plausible explanation."

"What we haven't figured out is why he did not use the same trunk line as our man inside. We know the two of them talked, and from what we were told, your man is on that U-boat as part of the launch team. Still, it would have made sense for him to have placed a long-distance call, perhaps to the German Embassy in Mexico and used a basic code. We know he knew that all the overseas phone lines run through England and that we have men monitoring them day and night. It would have been the easiest way to pass information on a one-time basis."

The voice on the line coughed, a hacking, debilitating rattle that caused the man in England to hold the phone at a distance. "Perhaps there were extenuating circumstances that either prevented or precluded such a contact."

"You need to take care of that cough," the caller said in exact, syncopated English. "And you are probably correct in your assessment. There must be some overriding factor which necessitated his inclusion in the launch team."

"He is aboard the submarine, then. Confirmed?"

"Confirmed by the same sources which relayed the other information. As you say, that would explain why we never heard from him. He might have worried that even a single contact might jeopardize his standing. If he knew he had a chance to be aboard the boat, he probably opted for that rather than possible exposure through contact."

"Perhaps. It would explain a lot. Do you believe he will be able to stop the launch?"

The English voice was clipped, precise. "The source contact on the island says he has a fifty-fifty chance. The problem seems to be that on such an infinitesimal launch platform, the possibility of his dying in the process is almost assured. I suppose we will have to wait and see. Our source says he will do it."

"Suicide," the voice whispered over the transatlantic trunk line.

"So it would seem," the English voice agreed.

"Where do they come from, men such as these?"

"From a God who knows that this life is not the final chapter, but only a beginning."

"You believe that, don't you?"

There was a pause. "Yes, I have to. It's the only thing that makes any sense of days like these. It is certainly the only way you and I can justify what it is we are doing right now. God is the only one who understands. If this deception were revealed, we both would be vilified in every court, every legislature, every public forum in the free world."

"Yes, you are correct, of course." The voice stopped again, interrupted by a hacking cough that exploded from diseased lungs. After the interlude, the voice asked, "Do we know the target, yet?"

"No. It went aboard in sealed orders from Prinz-Albrechtstrasse. It could be anywhere from the southern coast of Newfoundland to Cape Hatteras. There's no way of knowing."

"New York?"

"Possibly. *Probably.* Such an attack has no military value. It would be a psychological strike, pure and simple. Meant to assault the psyche of a nation. To put your people on the defensive."

"It won't work."

"Of course not, but Himmler and Hitler don't see it that way. One of our men in Berlin, who happens not to be a man, by the way, relayed the details of a meeting between Himmler and Dönitz a few days ago."

"Grand Admiral Dönitz?"

"The same. He went to Prinz-Albrechtstrasse. Confronted Himmler in his own office. Dönitz was in on the beginning of this madness. Apparently he finally saw the light and tried to cancel the operation. Himmler undermined him, went directly to Hitler, and took control of the operation. Apparently you could hear Dönitz castigating Himmler from the Tiergarten to the Volkspark. Seems he told Himmler that it would in all probability blow up in his face."

"History will show that our best allies will turn out to be the men in charge of the Third Reich."

"True. If Hitler listened to his generals instead of his politicians, Germany would be spread from the Urals to Central Africa."

"Then we wait."

"Wait and pray," the reply came.

"God help us," the coughing voice managed.

"Yes, I think that may be our only chance," Winston Churchill said as he hung up the phone.

CHAPTER
44

january 8, 1943
north atlantic

Shaw sensed the rhythm of the boat changing. The mechanical cadence that had carried the U-135 across almost three thousand miles of the North Atlantic was slowing, the boat beginning to roll with the swells, the interior becoming more miserable as the boat lost headway.

The refueling of the submarine and the fueling of the V-5 rocket had been accomplished forty-eight hours earlier, south of Newfoundland. The primary circuits had been checked and initial coordinates entered into the guidance system. The only thing left to do was to refine the gyro settings to coincide with the final launch window.

That, Shaw had determined, was when he would have to make his move. He had already ruled out using one of the U-boat's radios to notify American coastal forces. There was no time when the radios aboard the U-boat were not monitored. He would have to be on deck with the technicians and access the shielding around the combustion chamber to ensure that the chamber was damaged according to Kurt

Daluege's instructions. The damage would limit the burn time and thus the effective range, causing the motor to fail before effective apogee could be reached.

Shaw looked around the aft torpedo room where he had just spent the most miserable time he could remember. He and the five Peenemünde technicians had been banished to the few bunks that lined both walls of the aft room for the duration of the voyage. Günther Mohr had made it known that he did not like having nonrated men replacing valuable, qualified submariners. The six men who'd been left on the beach to allow the six from Peenemünde to board had created extra work for the rest of the crew, a fact each submariner had not been shy in sharing as the opportunity arose.

Shaw could see the tension in the faces of the five technicians as they tried to find a little room on the boat. Most days had been spent in the bunks, trying to stay out of the way of the men who ran the U-boat.

Shaw now found himself feeling fear, confusion, and anger. He was angry at the men who had conceived the insanity of which he was now a part. Fear and confusion surfaced at odd moments when he finally realized he was the only person on earth who had a chance to stop the launch of the V-5 against an innocent population.

"The boat slows, Herr Sturmbannführer," one of the technicians said.

"What?" Shaw asked, rousing himself from his thoughts.

"The boat. It is slowing. Some of the crew have said we are within a few miles of our launch site."

Shaw sat up on the bunk. "That is so. I heard Number One tell the captain. We will be entering the final launch coordinates shortly. Are all of you prepared?"

The technicians looked at each other and nodded their heads. The senior technician spoke. "We are prepared. I must say we have some concerns, though."

Shaw was instantly alert. It was the first time he'd heard of such concerns. What were they? Moral uncertainties? Mechanical difficulties? Had the technicians considered what the launch of such a weapon would do? Were they becoming incapable of mass murder?

"What concerns?" Shaw asked.

"The weather."

Shaw did not understand. "We have launched rockets on Peenemünde in such weather. Surely that is not a major factor."

The technician nodded slowly. "It is true we have launched rockets in similar temperatures and atmospheric conditions. That is not what concerns us. Hantz, the mechanical technician, is concerned about the amount of ice that has formed on the outside of this boat and the rocket. We have never launched a rocket with an ice coating. It will surely change the trajectories and flight times, if, in fact, it will fly at all. It is something for which we have no previous data. We simply do not know. A rocket is not an airplane. It does not require lift generated by the air flow over the wings, but the ice is bothersome, nonetheless."

Shaw felt buoyant, his spirit lifted. Was it possible? Had he come all this way thinking only he could stop such a diabolical plan only to find that the weather had done a much more effective job?

When he thought about it, it occurred to him how much in control of this world God was. He was acutely aware of a presence within the steel confines of the U-boat. Not the demented, evil presence he'd come to know since becoming part of the V-5 project, but a feeling of light and life. It was the same feeling he used to get just being around Barbara. The feeling of certainty, of love.

Barbara!

He could almost feel her with him. Was he losing his mind? He was in the midst of his enemies, encompassed by all means of evil, and yet, he felt at peace. It was a peace born of certainty.

"What do you think will happen?" Shaw asked the technician. "Surely such factors have been taken into account. Von Braun would not have sent this rocket on such a mission with such a tremendous possibility of failure."

"Herr von Braun was not in control of the project toward the end. It was your SS men who retained jurisdiction toward the end of the project. Certain tests results were ignored; other tests were not even performed. This rocket was put together with the barest minimum of testing. Theoretically, it should perform according to predicted parameters. All the systems are basically the same as the V-2, only smaller. But even the V-2 still has problems. Von Braun warned the people in charge of such a possibility. He was ignored."

The U-boat was turning now. Shaw could feel it. The boat heeled to the right; Shaw grasped at the bunk railings to steady himself. The men around him did the same as the boat changed course to the south.

Without warning, bells began ringing to the background of a blaring horn. Men began running in response to the signal. The torpedo room was instantly filled with sweating, grunting torpedo mates. Shaw glanced out the watertight door in time to see the same pandemonium taking place throughout the rest of the submarine. Men were moving in excited frenzy, donning sound-powered phones, powering up electronic equipment, arming offensive and defensive weapon systems.

Michael Shaw felt his heart begin to beat a nervous tattoo within his chest. He looked around once again; every eye of the five-man technician team was on him.

CHAPTER
45

january 8, 1943
east coast of united states

The chaos was orchestrated, every movement precise, defined, organized. Worn, bearded men raced to their battle stations as the blaring horn offered a counterpoint to the activity.

Michael Shaw was up and moving forward in the pell-mell bustle of sweating bodies and German curses. He reached the aft torpedo room door and had to stand aside as three torpedo mates crashed through the opening into their designated stations. Shaw was through the door and moving deliberately forward. He could feel the boat roll further to the right. The nose bent downward sharply.

They were submerging!

Shaw scrambled through the electric motor and battery spaces heading for the diesel motor room. The sailors ignored him, each concentrating on the gauges, valves, and switches that were their primary responsibility during the dive sequence.

Shaw sidestepped past the senior diesel mate. The man had already secured the twin engines and was in the process of closing the outside vents. Shaw felt the pressure change; his ears popped as all outside vents were closed, isolating the submarine from the outside atmosphere.

The deck beneath his feet increased its downward angle; Shaw felt himself losing his balance. Around him men went about their business as if they had lived all their lives at acute angles. These were sub-mariners. Shaw felt his respect building for such men.

He was through the diesel motor room and into the corridor lead-ing to the combat center, the heart of the U-boat. As he pushed his head into the center just before the watertight door closed behind him, he heard a hard-edged voice address him.

"Herr Sturmbannführer. I see you have overcome your seasick-ness. It is amazing how fear will cure even the most desperate cases, is it not?"

The words stung Shaw. He heard the muted laughs of the control room crew at the words of their captain, Günther Mohr.

Shaw glanced at the depth gauge just to the right of Mohr. It read twenty meters and was still falling. He tried to recall the crush depth of a class IX U-boat but could not. "I am concerned only for the safety of the mission, Captain," Shaw responded automatically. He had not considered until now what it would mean to die. Nothing, not even the attack by the Poles on the train months ear-lier, had held any fear for him. Now, as the U-135 slipped deeper into the waters off the coast of North America, he felt a dread build-ing within him.

He did *not* want to die. That much he was now sure of. What he wanted he could not say. He had not come that far, but he knew death would be a coward's way out.

For the first time since she had died, Shaw was able to understand Barbara's death. It was amazing now, as he stood in the combat cen-ter of the submarine, just how clear everything had become.

Had Barbara not died, he would not be here. There was little doubt that the V-5 project would have continued, been carried out to its culmination with as little regard for human life as he had witnessed. Perhaps another would have been recruited to take his place; perhaps not. That was difficult to answer. What he did know was that he was the only person on the face of the earth at this very moment who could halt the inevitable launch of the chemical warhead-equipped rocket. It had fallen to him, an ex-journalist, to save thousands of people. The realization weighed heavily, but for some reason, he accepted it, *sought* it. Should it bring death, that was acceptable, but he would not seek it.

The U-boat's deck began to level out, and Shaw shot a glance at the depth gauge once again. One hundred meters! More than three hundred feet! It had to be close to the limit.

"Do not despair, Sturmbannführer," Mohr said, seeing the look on Shaw's face. "I have taken German U-boats to much greater depths. I do not think it will be necessary in this case, but it is possible."

Shaw was about to respond to Mohr's statement when the length of the boat began to shake violently.

"All stop," Mohr ordered. "LI, what is that?"

Leitender Ingenieur Otto Reinertsen turned from the manifold gauges which he was monitoring. "Without a doubt, Kaleu, it is the rocket and the framework causing the vibrations. We never had the opportunity, as you know, to test the apparatus at this depth. It is probably caused by strong cross currents in this area. I recommend minimum turns to maintain slight headway. Otherwise the currents might act as wind in a sail and rotate the entire boat along its long axis."

Günther Mohr turned to Shaw, his eyes blazing. "You see, Sturmbannführer," he said vehemently, "what happens when politics mix with the military. We may well die down here before we even get the chance to deliver your secret weapon." Mohr moved from his station and around the master plot table. "We have submerged because some freighters were spotted. Normally, we would attack and sink those ships, but we barely have minimum maneuverability while we are saddled with that monstrosity topside. LI," he continued, turning to Reinertsen, "I want you and your men to be prepared to cut away that abomination after we have launched that rocket. I will not endanger these men or this vessel any more than I have to. We will not sail back to France with that mass of grotesque steel attached."

"It will be done, Herr Kaleu."

Mohr turned to Shaw. "As for you, get your men ready to launch the rocket. We are within fifty miles of the designated area. As soon as we can resurface, we will launch this thing and be out of here. I do not want any wasted motion, either. When we surface, tell your men as much."

Shaw nodded. Fifty miles. Five hours running on the surface, no more. The time had come.

CHAPTER

46

They had been submerged for six hours. In that time seven ships had passed overhead. Shaw had stood the entire time, off to the right, out of the way. There was no place to sit. He'd been isolated in the combat center when he'd moved forward. Mohr had gone to general quarters upon returning to the control room and had refused to violate watertight integrity to let him return to the after torpedo room.

Now his legs were beginning to feel like rubber. The air in the sub was becoming increasingly saturated with carbon dioxide. The smell of sweating bodies, even in the chill of three hundred feet, festered like a suppurating wound. Shaw's headache was compounded by a feeling of light-headedness.

"That last ship is down Doppler, Herr Kaleu. Moving away. Single screw. A merchant, no doubt. No up Doppler," the single sonar mate reported.

Shaw had been in the combat center long enough to know that

down Doppler referred to the sound of a ship moving away from the U-135 and *up Doppler* meant one moving toward the U-boat.

"Very well," Mohr said, glancing over at Shaw. "Put us on the top, LI. Pump the tanks dry, do not blow. Let's do this as quietly as possible." The captain turned to his number one. "Number One, what is our position?"

"Hard to say, sir. Dead-reckoning calculations put us about here," he said, indicating a spot on the master plot chart. "It's still daylight, Kaleu," the navigator whispered.

"No more than two hours of surface steaming to reach the minimum launch window, less perhaps."

"Yes sir. That will put us south of the inlet, in perfect launch position."

Mohr glanced up from the chart, looking directly into the eyes of his first officer. He knew—everyone knew—the danger of surfacing and proceeding toward their target during daylight hours, but it could not be helped. The exact positioning of the rocket was critical to its accuracy, and that could only be accomplished with clearly defined reference points. Mohr knew he could use his periscope to maintain a course for another hour and a half, but the air in the U-boat was reaching unbearable stages. He needed to run his circulating fans. They would need the fresh air when they submerged after the launch. If they got that far.

Shaw had not been cognizant of the time of day. They'd been down almost seven hours. He glanced at the depth gauge. It was moving slowly in response to the negative buoyancy created as the electrical pumps forced the water from the ballast tanks. It took longer to empty the tanks in that fashion, but it was much quieter and provided for an extra measure of control during the ascent.

"Get your men ready, Sturmbannführer," Günther Mohr ordered without looking up from the chart. "You can enter final coordinates and gyro settings while we steam toward the launch point. I want to launch and be gone before that rocket ever strikes the earth."

The deck of the boat tilted upward. The interior walls were sweating from the accumulated humidity. Shaw felt the effects of the moist chill through his body. He was not sure if the reaction came from the temperature in the boat or the apocalyptic words of Mohr.

"Ten meters," a voice rang out.

"Sonar?" Mohr automatically recited.

"Sonar negative."

"Surface," Mohr ordered.

Within the bowels of the submarine, Shaw could hear the water-tight doors being opened. The circular handle on the door nearest him rotated and the door swung open.

"Less than two hours, Sturmbannführer," Günther Mohr reminded Shaw.

Shaw was through the door heading for the after torpedo room. Just as he passed through the diesel motor room, the nine-cylinder twin engines roared to life. Shaw felt the boat accelerate as the twin screws bit into the water. The rolling and pitching that had characterized the North Atlantic crossing resumed but with an abated ferocity. The waters were shallow over the continental shelf, the wave action decreased compared to the unrestrained pounding farther north.

The five technicians were sitting or lying on the bunks of the aft torpedo room. They sat up when Shaw stuck his head through the opened watertight door.

"Less than two hours to make final settings and launch coordinates," he told them. "Captain Mohr wants it done while we are steaming."

"That's impossible," the senior technician retorted. "The gyro settings are too delicate. We must have a steady platform from which to input the final settings and from which to launch."

Shaw shrugged, feeling better and better. Maybe, just maybe, the launch could be averted with little risk to himself. From the way the technicians sounded, the tossing and bucking the boat was now doing would be enough to negate the launch.

"Orders. On this boat, Mohr is the captain. We do what we can," Shaw suggested. "Let's get topside."

Each man emerged from the electric motor room escape hatch, one at a time, safety lines lashed to their waists. The technicians moved up and out of the submarine. The deck was shining, the deck plates encased in a layer of ice.

The weather was only slightly more tolerable than the confines of the submerged U-boat. The wind whipped at the oilcloths worn by each technician and Shaw. The sky was low and gray, even with the morning sun. There was no snow or rain, but the odor of pending precipitation was in the air. Snow or rain or both could begin at any moment. The U-boat rolled and pitched in response to the swells and waves assailing the outer hull of the boat. The men moved with difficulty to the rocket launch apparatus bolted and welded to the deck no more than three meters from the hatch.

One by one they began their individual checklists. Shaw was the last to emerge from the relative protection of the U-boat's lighted interior. A gray light still filtered through the overcast.

Shaw took one look back into the submarine's pungent interior and then scrambled onto the slick deck. Each technician carried a small pouch of tools designed for specific purposes. Shaw had to wait for his eyes to adjust to the light. The technicians were already clustered around the weapon, removing inspection plates, connecting necessary gauges, adjusting critical settings.

Shaw approached the senior technician. The man was standing back from the rest, holding onto the framework of the launch platform, directing the actions of his subordinates.

"How long for the final setup and launch?" Shaw asked, moving alongside the technician.

The man looked at Shaw. "We will finish within the time frame allowed. I must reiterate, Herr Sturmbannführer, that this is not an acceptable platform for an accurate launch."

Shaw felt his pulse race once again. "Explain."

"The guidance system is basically a two-dimensional system, not a three-dimensional one. We rely on a stable launch platform to give us the initial heading and trajectory. Once launched, the gyros adjust pitch and roll only. Distance is governed by the burn time of the rocket motor. It is imperative that we maintain a stable platform at launch if we have any hope of hitting our target."

Shaw's feeling of elation waned. He had just realized what the technician was explaining. "What you are saying is that we can launch the rocket, but we will have no way of knowing where it is going to land. Is that it?"

"Exactly, Sturmbannführer. This rocket will fly. But I cannot be sure where it will land."

Shaw calculated in his mind. He knew the launch area. He knew the target area too. The launch would occur almost at noon New York time. The area around Wall Street would be packed with New Yorkers intent on lunch. Given the weather conditions, there would not be as many outside as if it were a nice spring day, but there would be those hearty souls out for the noon meal and they would die first. Later, as the sarin penetrated the board rooms and offices, others would die too.

Flight distance was dependent solely on the duration of the motor burn. If the rocket flew, people would die. It might not kill the people it was intended for, but it would still murder unsuspecting, innocent people. It was still left to him to stop. Staten Island, perhaps. New Jersey? Brooklyn? All were possibilities. Success meant death.

"You're saying that we will hit something, then?"

The senior technician smiled. Shaw saw the malevolence in the man's eyes. "It will fly, Sturmbannführer. And it will land somewhere. Where, I do not know. But wherever it lands, it will kill."

It will kill!

There could be only one option. The rocket must not fly. He would have to reach the outer portion of the combustion chamber. He would have to disable the motor as Daluege had directed. He might still die. His mind was made up.

"Let's have a closer look at the rocket," Shaw said, moving toward the launch stand. The launch derrick was still folded in its transport position, the rocket parallel to the deck. Hydraulics would raise the rocket into position after the final settings had been set in the guidance system. For a few minutes, the U-boat would have the upright rocket protruding from her after deck like a whale with a huge harpoon stuck in its back.

What if the motor were ignited before the launch platform was raised? There would be no launch. At least, not one of any consequence. The rocket motor would burn until the horizontally launched missile buried itself in the cold, black sea.

That was the answer; he would activate it before it was raised in position. An accident? Carelessness? Malfunction? All would be possible explanations.

Shaw had seen the launch procedures, knew the pattern of switches, the sequences. "Have you completed the launch sequence connections and the control connections?" Shaw asked the technician as they moved about the rocket. The severity of the weather seemed to have lessened in the last hour. Shaw checked the time. They'd been topside almost an hour. It didn't seem possible.

"Not yet. That will be the last thing we do. That's a little like hooking the plunger to dynamite before setting the charges. It's just not done."

"Do it," Shaw ordered, hoping his SS rank and curt manner would frighten the technician into obeying.

"Herr Sturmbannführer, I cannot do that. It is against all accepted procedures."

"I will take responsibility for it. The captain wants this thing launched as soon as possible. We will have to take shortcuts to accomplish that."

"Herr Sturmbannführer . . . ," the man began.

"Do it!" Shaw demanded.

"It will be done," the man said, resigned to the madness.

Shaw scanned the immediate area. What was surprising was the lack of shipping in the area. While it was true Mohr was keeping the U-135 north of the normal shipping lanes, there should have been at least a coastal patrol boat or tramp steamer. The ships that had passed over the U-135 had been merchantmen by the sound of their propellers. Where were they now? It seemed that the U-135 was having an inordinate amount of luck. One sighting by a single steamer would have been enough to activate the Coast Guard. But there was nothing for as far as Shaw could see.

In the gray light, Shaw could see the argument taking place with the other technicians. He looked away, knowing that each man was telling the senior technician that the SS man was crazy. His gaze drifted to the conning tower. There, along with the two lookouts, stood Günther Mohr, his white sea cap glowing in the dim light. Shaw thought for a moment he could see a look of amusement on the captain's face. Then, as if the man knew exactly what was about to happen, he shook his head and disappeared from view.

The technician made his way back along the pitching, icy deck with the launch box in his hand. He handed the box to Shaw; his expression revealed his true feelings.

Shaw took the box. He examined the switches. They were all there, just as he remembered them from the launch bunker. The same switches he had seen Kurt Daluege manipulate in sequence prior to firing the motor.

The two pump switches that controlled the liquid oxygen and alcohol pumps were in the upper right corner. The preignite switch dominated the upper left corner. Three pressure dials looked back at Shaw like the eyes of a mutated Cyclops. One pressure gauge each for the twin fuel tanks and one gauge to monitor the combined pressure as the fuel fed into the combustion chamber. The final launch switch was in the lower right-hand corner, enclosed in a red safety cover.

Shaw reviewed the launch sequence in his mind: both pump switches to on; liquid oxygen and alcohol pressure in the green;

preignite switch to on; combustion chamber pressure to ignition point; final launch switch to fire. It was simple. He'd watched Daluege do it numerous times.

Shaw glanced up from the launch sequence control; his gaze locked with that of the senior technician. He could see the concern in the technician's eyes. What else was it he saw? Fear? A realization of what was about to occur? The man went back to his work directing the other four technicians.

High in the conning tower, Shaw heard a shout. He looked toward the source. The U-boat's number one was gesturing wildly from the tower. Shaw felt a brief moment of anxiety. Had the man lost his mind?

The senior technician worked his way along the icy deck to just below the conning tower. Günther Mohr's white cap appeared beside his number one. Mohr gestured in the same manner as his navigator. The technician turned from the conning tower and made his way back along the slick deck of the U-135.

"We are within thirty minutes of the launch window, Herr Sturmbannführer. Number One's calculations show us that close. It is time to raise the derrick. It is time to strike a blow for the Fatherland and the Führer!"

Shaw felt his stomach knot at the news. Had he waited too long? Was there still time? Could he begin the launch sequence in time to finish it? As best he could remember, the pumps required several seconds to build to the proper pressure. What would happen if he activated the final ignite switch early? Nothing? Would there be time for the technicians to overpower him and launch the rocket anyway?

There were too many things he did not know. There was no time to reach the combustion chamber and disable it like Daluege had planned. He had failed.

*   *   *

The *Mary Glen* fought the building seas. The wake of the escort vessel a thousand yards ahead was clearly visible in the gray light. Jon McDowell sipped at the steaming cup of coffee and marveled at the chameleon-like demeanor of the ocean. One day it was a tiger, lashing and clawing at a ship as if to drag it to the ocean floor. The next it was like a quiet kitten sleeping at the foot of a bed. Today, McDowell wished for the kitten. He was thankful that the escort vessel appointed to escort his ferry was not a renovated minelayer but a new destroyer escort doing double duty today. The escort trip for the *Glen* would be the DDE *James Ballard's* final shakedown cruise before joining the fleet for convoy duty.

The pounding vibration of the *Glen's* engines echoed through the steel decking, the one aspect that was comforting and reassuring. McDowell had come to love the *Glen* these last few months. He had almost forgotten the strange sight of the dead SS man picked up by one of his escort vessels five months earlier. What a day that had been. A day he did not want to repeat.

"Keep him in sight, quartermaster," McDowell gently reminded the helmsman. He liked the young man at the wheel. He'd taken him on when the boy had been turned down by the navy for medical reasons. He was glad he had. The young quartermaster had the eyes of an eagle and the reflexes to match.

The gray sky and lowering ceiling combined to flatten the rising sea, despite the increase in the height of the waves.

The *James Ballard* rode easily in the rough seas, not like the smaller escorts he was used to. This was a ship of war. The presence of the ghostly looking ship was comforting.

Suddenly, as if an alarm had gone off, the stern of the *James Ballard* dug into the choppy water. The white foam beneath the fantail churned as twin screws bit into the ocean. A sound drifted back over the surface, signaling exactly what was taking place. The *James Ballard* was going to general quarters.

The captain of the *James Ballard* had ordered battle stations.

*   *   *

A humming sound penetrated Shaw's thoughts. The rocket was rising on the hydraulic cylinders, the cylinders powered by small electrical motors. The twenty-foot rocket pointed into the night sky.

Shaw heard the locking pins as they slipped into place along the base of the launch platform. He was aware of the rolling sea, the dark waves, and the vertical shaft of death that loomed above him. Suddenly he was jarred back to reality as the senior technician wrestled the control sequence box from his hands. He was too stunned to react. The man had the launch box! He was going to launch!

Shaw reacted. The technician was moving toward the conning tower, the box and its connecting cords trailing behind. Shaw leaped. He was on the stunned technician instantly. There was no more thought, no more deliberation, only action. The launch had to be stopped!

The technician slipped to the frozen deck under the suddenness of Shaw's attack. They went down together, the control box slipping along the deck, pulled up short by the trailing wires.

The technician was stunned. Shaw dove for the box. He would start the sequence. Perhaps, God willing, he could hold out until the launch was actually activated. He could only hope that the U-boat had not yet reached the point from which the rocket could reach land. Just a few minutes would make the difference. New York was a port city. The launch calculation had been made to put the U-boat at the outer distance of the launch. That meant any early launch would result in the rocket falling into the Upper New York Bay. The chemical would be diluted by the seawater, the damage mitigated. Perhaps death could be prevented.

Shaw could hear shouting. He raced for the control box. It lay near the base of the launch tower where it had ended up. He was on it, his feet slipping from under him on the ice. He went down; his head hit the hard surface. He could feel the control box in his hands; his fingers fumbled for the twin pump switches.

Other hands were on his! Voices! Shouts! The hands were over his, clawing at his own hand, delaying the launch sequence. The other technicians came to the senior technician's aid. Two had scrambled back onto the deck as Shaw had attacked the man. Now they were wresting the control box from his grasp. The pain was excruciating as they bent his fingers from the box.

Shaw kicked, his right foot contacting the soft flesh of the technician on his right. The man grunted and fell away, his hand grasping at his injured stomach. The other technician struck out. Shaw felt a fist connect with his jaw; stars flew into the night, his brain on fire. Another fist to the jaw. His head snapped in the opposite direction. He was losing consciousness. His head exploded in pain! He felt the box jerked from his grasp. He struck out at the hands clutching the box. His fist struck. He felt his wrist shatter under the pressure of the impact. Shaw rolled back onto the deck, holding his damaged wrist, his eyes searching for the box, the pain in his wrist forgotten for the moment.

Hands were all around him, holding him, preventing further attack. His eyes cleared. The senior technician stood two meters away, the control box in his hands. The two technicians who had come to the man's aid were nursing their own wounds near the base of the launch tower. Three burly U-boat sailors had Shaw in their grasp. He could not move. His wrist was on fire, his head exploding.

"I never did trust you, Herr Sturmbannführer," the senior technician said. "Seems I was right. Well, you shall see this launch firsthand. We will allow you to remain on deck during the launch. Please, tell us what you think when it is over," the man said malevolently.

The two technicians slipped down the electric motor hatch and off the icy deck. The three sailors released Shaw; his legs failed him, and he slipped to the deck just below the conning tower. The senior technician and the control box were up the ladder of the conning tower. The relative protection of the structure would act as a launch bunker.

The rocket loomed above Shaw, the outline darker against the dark sky. Black against black. A dark angel.

Shaw's temples pounded; his jaw was bruised. He held his wrist limply, the arm was useless.

He could hear the voice of the senior technician as he began the countdown. The pumps in the V-5 activated. Shaw could hear the muffled whine of the impellers as they propelled the oxygen and alcohol into the combustion chamber.

*　　*　　*

The *James Ballard* was coming to flank speed as its bow tore into the choppy water. Its gray shadow heeled over as the ship changed course, heading for an unknown destination.

Jon McDowell reached for the microphone, but just before thumbing the talk button, the voice of *James Ballard's* captain came over the external speaker.

"Hold your position, *Mary Glen.* We have a U-boat sighting, and we are moving to intercept."

McDowell felt the hairs on the back of his neck stand up. It was the first time since he'd been captain of the *Mary Glen* that he'd actually heard of a U-boat being this close.

"*Mary Glen* holding course and position. Good hunting," McDowell radioed, then replaced the microphone. When he turned around the young quartermaster was staring back at him.

"Watch your course," McDowell said, hoping his voice was calmer than he felt.

*　　*　　*

In seconds, the icy deck of the U-boat would turn into a flaming pyre. Shaw knew he would be burned alive by the white exhaust of the rocket motor. He hastily scanned the deck. With two good hands, he could work his way around the conning tower to the front portion of the U-boat. Then the structure of the tower would protect him from the exhaust. But he only had one good hand. Was it possible?

Shaw stood. He could hear the increased whine of the twin pumps as they reached maximum pressure. He began working around the conning tower. Metal ladders were welded into the structure. He grabbed the first of the rungs and began pulling himself along the narrow deck that skirted the center structure. As he moved along the narrow deck, the waves and wind combined to overpower the high-pitched whine of the pump motors. It didn't matter. Shaw knew what was coming. The pumps would reach maximum pressure, the preignite switch would be thrown, and the pressurized fuel would begin dumping into the combustion chamber. When the chamber pressure reached its maximum, normally within seconds, the fire button would be depressed and the rocket motor would ignite, sending white flame from its gaping aperture. The thrust would increase geometrically until it exceeded the weight of the rocket, and the rocket would launch. It took no more than ten or fifteen seconds after the pumps were started. He had five seconds remaining to reach the protection he sought behind the conning tower.

*   *   *

The captain of the *James Ballard* concentrated on the low-riding hull of the U-boat. A sharp-eyed lookout had spied the boat. How, in the dreadful weather, the young captain was not sure, but he was thankful for young eyes.

He ordered the crew to battle stations, donned his combat helmet, and stepped out onto the small flying bridge of the ship.

It had taken him a few minutes to locate the U-boat. Even after spotting it, the small boat was difficult to see in the ragged sea and flat, gray light. Then something happened the young lieutenant had never seen in his life. Something began rising from the deck of the U-boat.

At first, he thought he was seeing things, but whatever it was, it continued to rise until it was vertical on the boat's deck, twenty feet in the air. One thing was certain. Whatever the U-boat captain was up to, the young captain of the *Ballard* was going to stop.

"Come to one-seven-five," he ordered, feeling the ship roll slightly with the course change. "Forward battery standby."

The orders were relayed instantly. The destroyer was alive and in its element.

"Steady up on one-seven-three. Forward battery, commence firing when we get within range."

The first salvo echoed from the forward gun of the *James Ballard*, announcing to the rest of the ship's company that the newest destroyer in the fleet was a warrior even before it had gotten out of sight of New York City.

The first shell fell short. The forward battery gun barrel came up, adjusting for the range, and fired again. This time, the shell struck home.

*   *   *

A sudden boom announced the final ignition of the rocket motor. Shaw was hanging onto the final rung of the ladder with his good wrist.

A second boom followed the first. What was happening? Shaw wondered. The second boom had shaken the U-boat. Shaw lost his grip.

Lord, he prayed, *be with me.* Shaw planted his foot against the deck and pushed against the slippery surface, knowing he had no chance to make the relative safety of the boat's aft deck. Miraculously his foot did not slip. He was propelled behind the conning tower. The rocket exhaust exploded from the rocket motor, melting the ice on the after deck.

Shaw counted. Ten seconds.

The rocket sound changed, indicating the weapon was leaving the launch platform.

Shaw could feel the heat as it snaked and wrapped itself around the protective tower. He thought he heard shouts coming from above, from the area where the senior technician had initiated the launch sequence.

The motor continued to roar, its powerful belching noise obscuring everything else. Time was suspended.

There it was again. Voices. Voices raised in distress. Words shouted in rage, in desperation.

A third boom echoed over the waves. The sound was closer. Microseconds later the U-135 lurched, as if mortally wounded.

Screams filtered through the rocket's roar. Shaw recognized the hysterical voice of the senior technician.

Shaw heard the sharp clanging sound that marked the closing of the hatches. He felt the boat lurch beneath him again.

Shaw was on his back when he saw the rocket streak into the air. A sense of utter desperation enveloped him. He had failed. Failed all those who had counted on him. Failed the people who would die when the rocket struck. Failed Wild Bill Donovan, and Kurt Daluege, and himself. And he had failed Barbara, for he was now certain that she watched from a great gallery on high. Despair took over.

Michael Shaw never knew how far he was blown when the U-135 exploded south of New York. The second and third salvos from the *James Ballard* had found the bunkers of the U-135, igniting the diesel fuel. The fuel exploded seconds later, ripping the U-boat in half. The U-boat went to the bottom of the Atlantic, taking every member of the crew with her.

Michael Shaw was blown clear of the dying U-boat, the only crew member to survive the devastating eruption.

His life expectancy in the freezing waters was only ninety seconds longer than that of his shipmates.

The rocket flew unerringly toward New York City and Wall Street.

CHAPTER

47

january 8, 1943
atlantic ocean, south of new york city

The explosion of the U-135 could be seen from the deck of the
Mary Glen. McDowell ordered his young quartermaster to change
course, steering for the explosion.

"Something in the water, Captain McDowell," the young quartermaster said.

McDowell moved to the front of the bridge and peered over the
railing. He saw nothing.

"Five hundred yards ahead, dead in the DDE's wake," the helmsman said, knowing his captain would not pick out the single, floating
object without the context of the wake.

"I see it," McDowell acknowledged. He reached for the ship's telegraph and rang up all stop, then, as an afterthought, full astern. The
Mary Glen shuddered as her engineers reversed valves and rerouted
high pressure steam to fulfill the wishes of their captain. "Come right
ten degrees."

The young helmsman spun the circular steel wheel, his eyes glued to the compass in front of him. Jon McDowell moved to the rear wall of the bridge and pulled a microphone from its resting place. "Make ready with port lifeboat. We have a body in the water."

On deck, the senior boatswain's mate, an ex-navy man, directed the actions of four deck crewmen. The port boat was swung over the side, the coxswain at the ready in the stern. The boatswain directed his gaze toward the bridge. McDowell was out on the flying bridge now, looking aft. "In the water, Chief," he relayed through the megaphone in his hand. "Looks like he's wearing oilskins."

The ex-chief waved an acknowledgment, directed his remaining three men into the boat and followed. The boat was in the water in seconds, the chief in the bow acting as lookout. He had no trouble spotting the oilskin-clad figure in the water. The coxswain moved the boat alongside, and the three sailors manhandled the body into the boat.

Jon McDowell stood on the flying bridge wondering how many bodies he would see pulled out of the North Atlantic. This was his second inside six months. He leaned out over the bridge railing. The lifeboat was returning; it had disappeared beneath the structure of the flying bridge, and McDowell changed positions to keep the boat in sight. He watched as the crew drew alongside the now stationary *Mary Glen.* The boat davits were swung out, and the lifeboat, along with its crew, was lifted to the deck and swung inboard.

With the lifeboat secured, the men gingerly transferred the body from the boat to the deck of the steamer. McDowell fleetingly wondered why his sea-hardened crew was handling an obviously dead body with such respect. He emptied his coffee cup in one last swig and headed down the ladder to where the crew was gathering.

The small knot of men were still gathered around the body as McDowell came down the last ladder leading to the main deck.

The old Chief Boatswain's mate looked up as he heard his captain's feet hit the metal deck just forward of where the men now stood. Jon

McDowell could see the confusion in his chief's eyes. *What now?* he wondered, as he made his way aft.

The old chief was the first to speak as the men moved out and away from the body. He looked at his captain and said, "You believe in miracles, don't you cap'n?"

McDowell moved into the knot of sailors, his amazement now total.

The man lay on the deck, head raised, eyes staring about in wonder at the men who had just pulled him from the freezing waters of the Canadian bay. Beneath the oilskins, just at the neckline, McDowell could make out the dark cloth of a uniform. Without hesitation, the *Mary Glen* captain knelt beside the man and gently unfastened the oilskins. The black cloth was in harsh juxtaposition to the lighter oilskins. The two runes on the right collar tab leapt out at McDowell: the markings of the SS!

McDowell stood, his mouth moving; no words came.

Michael Shaw spoke first in English, the words coming from deep within, despite the exhaustion and pain. "Captain, you are the best sight I've seen today."

McDowell's mind flashed back to November and the last man who had been pulled from the sea wearing the same uniform. What he was seeing before his eyes was not possible, but he had been at sea too long and had been a Christian for decades. He was beginning to expect miracles.

*   *   *

The crew on board the *James Ballard* cheered as they searched the area for survivors. They found none, but there was no doubt as to what they had just done: the *James Ballard* had just sunk its first German U-boat. The only thing that stopped it from being a complete victory was the launch of the rocket it had been carrying. The young captain wondered what was about to happen.

* * *

"Weather moving in fast, captain," the quartermaster of the *Mary Glen* called out to Jon McDowell.

McDowell moved from the flying bridge back into the wheelhouse and gazed out the window. He'd never seen such clouds in all his life. They had formed-up behind the *Mary Glen* and the *James Ballard* as they had moved due south. It was as if mountains of storm clouds had formed over New York City. McDowell had never seen anything like it.

* * *

The V-5 entered the building cloud mass that covered New York City. The rocket's control gyros were blind, recognizing only the job they had been programmed to accomplish.

That job did not include coping with the internal winds of a building thunderstorm.

The first wind shear struck the rocket just before apogee, upsetting the number one directional gyro. The second sheet of wind hit it as it turned toward the East River.

The gyros fought the directional pressures of the winds, their motors whining as the rocket was forced off course.

A single lightning strike hit the V-5 just as it nosed over, its course altered by the savage winds of the storm. The lightning raised the internal temperature of the rocket fuel to combustion levels.

The cylindrical form of the V-5 plunged into the East River just as the alcohol exploded. The largest portion of the rocket recovered was a tubing maze pulled from the river by two boys playing near the shore the next day. They made a basketball rim from the tubing.

EPILOGUE

As the British lieutenant colonel entered the office, a hint of sadness evident on his lined face, Winston Churchill tapped the last remaining ashes of his cigar into the ashtray and crushed it out. The lieutenant colonel carried the file marked "restricted distribution" that Churchill had requested less than thirty minutes earlier.

"Your call is ready, Mr. Prime Minister," the lieutenant colonel informed Churchill.

"Thank you, Colonel. That will be all." Churchill waited until the soldier was gone and the door secure behind him before reaching for the phone. The familiar buzz was there, telling him the conversation was being scrambled. The next sound he heard was the familiar cough coming from thousands of miles away. Even through the copper wires, the British prime minister could hear the pain. He waited until the coughing had subsided, then began. "I have seen the report. Is it true? Is it over?"

Roosevelt's voice came back, stronger than Churchill expected, the strength coming from a reserve of determination. "It's true. Unlike you, we escaped the nightmare. I can only thank God for his providence in this case."

"I concur. God has been watching over this entire sequence of events. There is no other way to explain it."

The president hesitated. "You are right, of course. But when I think of this situation, I wonder . . ."

"About Coventry? Why was God not watching over us in that situation?"

"You are as astute as ever, Winston."

"And you are as perspicuous as ever."

Roosevelt chuckled. "Perhaps. But it does make one wonder, does it not?"

"About God? About His motives? I don't think so," Churchill said. "It makes me wonder more about man."

"You are being fatuous, my friend."

"Not at all. We, you and I, believe in an all-powerful God. We ascribe to Him certain characteristics. We accept certain premises. Among those is the premise that a wise and intelligent God chose to allow us less-than-perfect mortals the power of choice. Free will."

"I agree. What's your point? What does it have to do with this current situation?"

"We can say that God came to your aid in your time of need. I believe that to be true. From all the reports I've read, there is no other way to explain the sudden appearance of the storm that knocked the rocket from the sky. By the same token, we can say He did not come to the aid of England when she needed Him."

"Coventry." This time it was a statement, not a question.

"Coventry," Churchill agreed, then continued. "We accept the gift of free will. Each person has that within himself. If we accept the premise of free will, we must, in turn, accept the consequences of that will as well. We cannot attribute the state of mankind to God, who gave us the ability to fashion either heaven or hell on this earth."

There was a pause on the end of the line. "You're saying that just because God chooses to exercise His will concerning certain situations, that we can't shirk responsibility for those times He chooses not to intervene?"

"Exactly. We can't have it both ways. It's like the child who gets angry when another child, who does not deserve it, receives a gift and he receives nothing. We want free will, but when things go wrong, we scream and cry to God and ask why. The why should be obvious."

"I suspect your theology would not make you popular among some of your peers."

Churchill laughed, his voice crackling over the transatlantic phone lines. "It would frighten me if it did."

"But you did not call to discuss theology," Roosevelt continued.

"No. I did not. The report says Michael Shaw survived."

"Only you British could say alive with such aplomb. Heavens man! He was blown into the Atlantic! He should be dead."

"What happened?"

"According to the debriefing, which is, by the way, still going on, a brand new DDE spotted the U-boat, opened fire, and hit it with two shells. The boat exploded. It went down with all hands. The explosion threw him into the ocean."

"He should be dead."

"Exactly. He was wearing oilskins. The best the doctors can determine is that they acted as sufficient insulation and protection. He was also wearing an SS winter tunic beneath the skins."

"Wool."

"You are to be commended for your knowledge of insulating materials," Roosevelt joked. "Yes, wool. One of the only fibers that maintains its insulation quality even when wet. He was picked up in minutes, by the ferry the destroyer was escorting. Still, he suffered exposure. Face, hands, toes. Nothing permanent. He may have phantom pains when the weather changes, but he will live."

"The mission? Was it as we thought?"

"It was *exactly* as we thought. The Germans have developed a rocket. According to Shaw, there are three versions. Our designations are the V-1, V-2, and V-5. The V-5 was the rocket they attempted to launch from the submarine. And there was more to it than just a rocket launch."

"How so?" Churchill asked.

"The warhead material came from the Ruhr. From . . . Leverkusen." Roosevelt ceased, letting the significance sink in.

"Chemical or biological?"

"Chemical. They call it sarin. Actually the chemical was a more potent form of the chemical. One-fiftieth of a gram anywhere on the skin will kill in minutes."

"That is disgusting. What about the chemical now?"

"It's at the bottom of the East River. Fortunately it is water soluble. It was diluted by the water. It will pose no major problems."

"It is hard for me to believe that Admiral Dönitz allowed such an action to take place. He's a tough warrior, but this doesn't sound like him."

"Dönitz put the original machinery in motion. Seems he figured he needed to tie up as many of our ships as he could. Between our ships and your development of the ASDIC, the war in the Atlantic has changed. He was only trying to even out the playing field." The President of the United States paused, a dry cough insinuating itself into the conversation. "But even Dönitz realized that such an attack on America could have far-reaching consequences. He ordered the project canceled."

"We deduced as much. We have the Ultra signal where he tried to recall the submarines involved."

"He tried. By that time the SS had already taken over the project. It was the SS—Himmler to be exact—who came up with the chemical warhead idea."

"It's criminal," Churchill added.

"Yes, it is that. But we are dealing with forces beyond those we have come to know."

"Now *you* are talking theology."

"Perhaps. Maybe theology is the only way we will ever be able to explain what is happening in this world."

Churchill leafed through the secret report folder in front of him as he listened. "I am truly glad that it has turned out for the best. There is no way we can predict how history will judge us in these matters."

"Such judgments, made by revisionist historians, sometimes have a tendency to ignore immediate contexts. It is better that it will not come to that. The bottom line is, of course, the Kriegsmarine is not aware that England has a Schlüssel M, the German Navy version of the Enigma. You will be able to continue monitoring U-boat movements for a while longer. Long enough for the United States to move the matériel necessary for an invasion of the continent."

Churchill sighed. "That is the ultimate victory, of course. Would the lives of thousands have been worth it? To England or the U.S.?"

"I don't know," Roosevelt replied sadly. "We may never know. That is what I mean about immediate context. Even we, no more than a few weeks removed from that context, cannot properly evaluate our actions. It would be foolish to expect better treatment in the future."

"But we know we had to play out this charade, just as I did at Coventry. We couldn't let the Germans know we have now acquired the German Navy's version of the Enigma machine."

"From our point of view, we did the correct thing. We cannot compromise the machine. The information we are receiving from it is too valuable."

"Can we really say that if we had attempted to stop the rocket U-boat, the German Navy would have deduced that England possesses the Enigma?"

"Again, we may never know. We can thank God for His intervention in this, though."

"Yes. The Ultra network is still operating. We are receiving information almost every minute."

"Good. I do not like deceiving our citizens. With any luck at all, this will end the SS intervention in the Navy's war effort."

"I don't think so," the prime minister said. "I already have messages on my desk about some other things the SS is involved in. We have not heard the last of them."

"I fear you are right, Winston. At least we can be forgiven this one deception. I think history will treat kindly the motives under which we operated."

"I hope so, my friend. Take care of yourself. I believe we will see each other later this year on that beautiful resort island."

Roosevelt laughed. "I've never heard Malta described quite that way. But yes, we will meet at Malta."

"Are you going to tell Shaw that he was used?"

"I think he already knows that. I don't think it makes much difference to him. He is a man possessed. He is already talking of returning to Germany and working within the SS structure to bring it down. He is determined."

"I would describe it as driven."

"And you would be right. Whatever it is that's driving him now, it must be used to our advantage."

"You sound as if you might already have selected another 'project' for him."

"Not yet. There are possibilities. After he has recuperated."

Winston Churchill fixed his gaze on the report in front of him. The words leaped from the page. They had been intercepted in a message only days earlier. The subject matter dealt with a topic so sensitive that he hesitated to share it. He quickly reviewed the text and decided. Maybe this Michael Shaw would be the one to send.

"I have a report in front of me," Churchill began. "It concerns a scientist from Norway and a project named for one of your islands."

The answer, when it came, was whispered. "What man? What project?"

Churchill cleared his throat. He reached for another cigar, jammed it into his mouth and left it unlit. "The man you will know from the context. The project is, according to this report, named for your famous New York Island. Is that enough information?"

The reply was again whispered. "It is enough. Thank you for sharing that. God be with you, Winston. Let us pray that we never have to formulate such a deception again." Roosevelt replaced the receiver and leaned back in his wheelchair. He reached for a cigarette, loaded it into a long holder, and lit it. He coughed with the first breath, then moved from behind his desk.

He had been lucky. The American people would never know how close they had come to having the obscenity of war touch them in their living rooms. Had the V-5 been successful, people would have died. And he, Franklin Delano Roosevelt, had sanctioned that risk to conceal England's possession of the Germans' code machine. Churchill had done the same in Coventry, and people had died. It was the part of the presidency he struggled with the most. Decisions—his decisions—killed people. Sometimes it was the enemy. But sometimes not. Would it have been worth it? Was he right to think in terms of the currency of human life? Sacrifice a little here to save a lot somewhere else? Did anyone have that right?

Roosevelt sucked on the stem of his cigarette holder and held the smoke in his lungs. It calmed his ragged nerves, but only for the time being, he knew.

Now Churchill had made an obtuse remark about another project. A project *named for your famous New York Island!* It could only mean one thing.

The president touched a button on the underneath side of his desk, and the door to the Oval Office opened.

"Yes sir," the aide said, coming through the door.

"Harry, get me the file on the Manhattan Project. I think we may have a problem." Roosevelt stubbed out the cigarette in the ashtray and wondered. Maybe Michael Shaw could be useful one more time.

This time the mission would be all the more important. Rather than dealing with a chemical weapon, he would be dealing with a weapon that could kill millions.

"God," Roosevelt prayed, *"when will it end?"*

march 6, 1943
missisquoi bay, ontario

Michael Shaw sat in silence, his gaze carefully scanning the interior of the cabin. It had taken several weeks before he'd finally been released from Bethesda Naval Hospital following the explosion of the U-135 and made his way back to the cabin in the Canadian woods. The most difficult part had been the endless hours and days of debriefing, Shaw trying to recall details, his interrogators probing the darkest corners of his mind.

March snow was beginning to fall outside the cabin window. At first, he'd not been sure why he needed to return, but now that he was here it all became clear.

This would be his last journey to the cabin. He would sell the property; he no longer needed it. He would remember it fondly. For a short period, it had been his sanctuary, his refuge. He knew now that he'd used it as a place of recrimination. But there should have been no recrimination, no self-inflicted isolation. He had been wrong.

And the dreams had stopped. Since the U-boat explosion and the destruction of the V-5 rocket, there had been no dreams.

He was still lonely. He missed Barbara, his mother, his father. But he could live with that now. He understood—not completely, but more than before—the workings of a benevolent God. No, not just God, but *his* God. *Barbara's* God. His parents' too.

Shaw rose from the cold chair and walked out of the cabin, abandoning it forever. He didn't look back as he made his way down the trail toward Phillipsburg.

If you enjoyed this book and would like to contact the author, you may do so at the address below:

John F. Bayer
P.O. Box 640552
El Paso, TX 79904
or
JohnFBayer@aol.com